Caine's Cover-up

A Tony Carson Mystery

Peter James Faux M.D.

Caine's Cover-up

Copyright @ 2024

by Peter James Faux

to Mary T, my wife

A special thanks to Talin Vartanian for her advice and editing.

Chapter 1

Tony Carson opened his eyes on a Wednesday morning, it was not yet 7 am and if he hurried, he could get in an hour of fishing and be at the police station on time. Jumping out of bed, he slipped on track pants, a sweat hoodie, and runners; no time for a shave although he did run a comb through his hair. Downstairs, he shot through his kitchen and adjoining woodshed and out the back door of his farmhouse. While it was mid-October, he was met by the balmy breeze of an Indian summer that had hijacked the fall, grounded robins, and frozen autumn colors. A weak yellow glow flickered on the eastern horizon as if the sun was undecided whether to rise or not. In his Malibu, he turned on the headlights, backed down his lane to the side road and once on Raymond's Road, a four- lane highway, he floored the gas pedal.

Parking in the doctors' section of the Osprey Mental Hospital's parking lot, a stone's throw from the Osprey River, Tony opened his trunk and grabbed his Winston rod and favorite carrot lure. On the riverbank, he inhaled refreshing and invigorating country air and looking upstream, spotted flies hovering over an eddy in the dark blue waters. His gut thrilled at the thought of a rainbow trout dinner. But looking downstream, police habit to cover the perimeter, he spotted a suspicious, white blur on a sand bar in the middle of the river, just out from the newly constructed weir.

Curiosity got the better of him. With rod and reel in hand, he walked down to a majestic willow tree in line with the sand bar, and peered out through a screen of thin, silver leaves. He looked twice to be sure he was not seeing things. Beached on the sand bar was the motionless upper half of a naked, female body. She was dead. Around the sand bar were black fins and snouts of carp, aquatic vultures; they were closing in on her. Tony yelled and swore at the carp for all the good it did as the fins and snouts closed in on the sand bar. They weren't there to pay their respects.

Dropping rod and reel, he slipped off his hoodie and pants, and plunged into the river, only to let out a shrill gasp. The water was damn cold, nothing like the air. After a couple of vigorous strokes he was at the sand bar, and while the black fins had dispersed, they were fast regrouping and he sensed, this time they meant business.

The dead woman had long, grey hair; two wide-open brown eyes were frozen in defiance; a jaw that was a black-and-blue bruise, and a bloated and discolored neck. A blood-stained twisted piece of cloth was embedded in it. She'd been strangled. On her right wrist was a plastic wristband: "Miss Arabelle Sirene: Ward B,

2

Room 203." He was stunned. She was a patient from the Osprey Mental Hospital.

Quickly, he scanned her body: no cuts, no blood on or under any of her fingernails, no rings, no needle marks, no old scars, and no tattoos. She had smokers' wrinkles, her teeth were tobacco-stained, and her palms were stained with what looked like red clay. There were red clay flats up-river, but they were no where near to the hospital.

Then he noticed that the black fins were almost within reach, no reverence for the dead. He pounded and splashed water at them but they inched closer. No way were they going to mutilate a dead person. Diving straight down, he jack-knifed up and pummeled them for all he was worth at scaly, whitish bellies, he. It must have worked for when he surfaced, all he saw was a scattering of dark scales, a curdling of yellow bile but not a single carp.

He was going to head for the shoreline until he saw that the carp were one step ahead of him and lying in wait for him, there. Checking down river to the newly constructed weir, he saw no carp. On the other side of the weir, the river ran for 50 feet before it cascaded over High Falls. All he had to do was dock her body on the weir, retrieve his clothing, notify security, and call the coroner. In a small way, he was excited about his first murder since being made detective and couldn't wait to begin his virgin investigation.

As he eased her body off the sand bar and aimed it at the weir, he noted that the soles of her feet were also red-stained. For sure, she had been at the red clay flats. The sun had risen and while he was no longer chilled, he couldn't wait to get her docked and dressed. As they were moving downriver, he kept looking behind him to make sure they were not being followed, and they weren't. The necktie-noose must have loosened as the ends fluttered in the current. With care, he extricated it and cast it high in the air. Sailing to the shoreline, it snagged on a jutting rock. He made a mental note of where it had run aground.

When he was almost at the weir, he heard the din of High Falls and was so thankful that the weir was there. But as he began to reverse her body so that her head didn't slam into the weir's cement, her toes nose-dived, he lost hold of her hips and her body disappeared below the surface with a gurgling sound. Then he too was pulled underwater, closed his mouth, stopped breathing and was slammed hard into cement. His right hip jammed up against her ice-cold flesh. She was impaled in a round portal, low down on the side of the weir, her legs straddling a single, vertical steel bar.

Straining against what felt like a g-force undercurrent that flowed through the portal, Tony planted one foot above and the other below the portal and grabbed her by the armpits. He pulled for all he was worth but she never budged; she might as well have been welded into the bar. His breath was spent and he clawed his way back up the cement wall to the surface. Hanging on to the edge of the weir for dear life, he gulped and gasped for air. But as he looked down and saw a slow-moving black murkiness that was slithering along the river bottom toward her, he just knew she was not out of danger. What the hell was it?

Taking a deep breath, he let go of the weir and his body descended as if in a vacuum tube. This time, his feet landed on the river bottom and dislodged a cloud of black silt. He grabbed both sides of her waist and yanked but again, nothing. Over his shoulder he saw that the black, wiggling, heaving, jerking mass was getting closer. His numbed, bruised fingers groped on the edges of the portal for a release. Only he lost his footing and staggered but he never lost his footing. Lungs were on fire; fingers felt like dead sticks; eyes were bleared. Yet he continued to feel for a latch and finding it, pulled on it and the bar snapped outwards.

His body shot through the portal as if fired out of a cannon into a pitch-black void. Hands and feet felt cuffed and an oily noose tightened around his neck. His skin burned and stung as if on fire. Suddenly his feet touched down and he stopped moving. Still, he couldn't see a thing.

Wrenching his hands apart, he tore at what was binding his ankles, kicked hard, and hit the river's surface. What bliss to see blue sky and feel a warm summer breeze on his burning skin. But he wasn't breathing. He was gasping for air. Tearing at a tough, scaly, oily band around his neck, he felt a life-saving whoosh of air hit his lungs. Swimming to the side, he sat down in a foot of water only to feel and see a single black, oily, wart-covered eel slither across his chest. His body stiffened and froze. To his horror, he was sitting in a pool of wriggling, squirming eels.

His gut heaved and he almost vomited. In an insane fury, he grabbed, tore, and beat down on his arms, chest, abdomen, thighs, and feet. Soon, although not soon enough to suit him, he was sitting in an abattoir of dead eels. Jumping to his feet, he breathed a sigh of relief until he felt an eel wiggling down the inside of his right thigh, too close for comfort. He grabbed at it, missed, checked and was relieved to see that he was alright.

Then he heard the roar of High Falls. Where was Arabelle Sirene? An ice-cold shiver ran down his spine. Scanning the river, he raced along the shoreline to the very brink of the falls and when he didn't see her, he gazed down at the glistening rocks, the churning rapids, the whirlpool's dark concentric circles and the river beyond. No sign of her, anywhere. She had to be at the bottom of the whirlpool.

What cop loses a murdered corpse to Davey Jones' Locker. No body, no case to investigate and no killer to catch. He felt as wretched as when he had stood on the shore of a frozen Lake Ontario in the late spring of that year, and looked out at a black hole in the ice. His parents' car had skidded on black ice, gone through the guard rail and the ice of Lake Ontario. Neither their bodies or even their car were ever recovered. Feeling depressed, there was no other word to describe how he felt, he returned and found his clothes. His skin was on fire and there was a leaden weight on his shoulders and in his shoes. Before, he'd thought he couldn't feel any lower than when he'd lost his parents. How mistaken he'd been.

Chapter 2

Back in his farmhouse, Tony rushed upstairs and tore off his track suit. In the mirror, he saw that he was covered in welts, stinging and burning welts. When he jumped into the shower, he felt a blast of ice-cold water and quickly exited. The hot water tank was on the blink. Throwing on a bathrobe, he tore out of his house, crossed the side road, sprinted through a sliver of forest to the large, turtle-shaped rock that overlooked a pond in the wetlands. Dropping the robe, he plunged into warm water from the hot springs on the pond's bottom. Surfacing for a few seconds, he dove and came up again, over and over again, like a junkie on crack. Like magic, he felt relief and no longer felt or saw a single welt.

After he climbed back onto the turtle rock, he dried himself with the terry-cloth bathrobe, tied it around his waist, sat down on the rock's edge to catch his breath. What a morning and he had yet to make it to the office. Everything that could have gone wrong, had gone wrong. Trying to distract from the guilt, he gazed at the pond's crystal blue surface and the sun-dappled, maple leaves in full autumn color. They certainly were having a good morning. But when he spotted, along the bottom of the pond, grey-white, rotten tree trunks the guilt came screaming back and he got to his feet and headed home, with a heavy heart.

At home, he put on his blue-serge uniform, slipped on his underarm holster-harness and Glock, downed a bowl of Wheaties, and sat down at the baby grand Bechstein piano in his living room. Placing his fingers on the keys, he was reminded of Miss Beverly, his old music teacher. She had shown him the "Berlin" stamp on the lid's underside and had told him that it was a valuable piano. When his father had arrived at Palermo, Sicily, he pick up his adopted son, he was surprised to find that the Bechstein piano on the dock was to accompany 'Antonio.' Music was in his blood and Miss Beverly had told him that he was her most gifted student. All he had to do was to hear the song once, and he could play it by ear

Giving full reign to his fingers, out came "America" by Neil Diamond, a favorite of his mother's. Warm tears welled up in his eyes as he remembered her telling him that he was the best son she could have ever had, and for him not to be so hard on himself. She knew him so well. His father, a sergeant on the Metro Toronto police force had been equally supportive, if not in so many words. As he finished the song, he wiped his eyes. How he missed them. His father's partner, Sergeant Ronny Mansfield, was in charge of the search for them but, to date, had come up empty. No way was history going to be repeated, if he could help it. Even though she was a complete stranger, he felt responsible. On the spot, Tony vowed that he would look for Sirene. While

9

that made him feel better, he had no idea how he was going to do it.

Chapter 3

Even though he was going to be late for work, not by much though, Tony headed back to the parking lot of the Osprey Mental Hospital. This time, it was chockablock full of the Caddies and Lincolns of Toronto consultants who visited the hospital every weekday morning. After circling twice, he found a spot and parked. Quickly, he walked down to the river's shoreline, passed the willow tree and its fluttering veil of silver-leaved streamers, and spotted the blood-stained piece of cloth on the neck of a jagged rock. Picking it up, he was surprised that it was an old T-shirt with a faded 'XXL' Eaton's label on the inside of the neck, and an equally faded 'Make Love not War' logo on the back. It had to be the killer's. But why would a killer use an old T-shirt to strangle someone? And who wore T-shirts in the late fall?

After he placed it in the evidence bag and deposited it in the trunk of his car, he sprinted up the steps of the administrative building and down the hallway to the office of Dr. Aaron Ramsay, the chief psychiatrist. Tony had been called enough times to the hospital to settle a dispute as to whether it was a suicide or a homicide, that they were on a first name basis. When he opened Aaron's door, both his secretaries looked up at him. They could have been twins in

11

matching beige sweaters and navy-blue skirts and with their brown hair pulled back in buns. One only wore large, brown-rimmed glasses, and that was how he told them apart. In one voice, they told him that Dr. Ramsay was on break.

In the cafeteria on the top floor, Tony grabbed a coffee and headed to the doctors' section, a step above the rest of the room. It had a breath-taking panoramic view of the Osprey River and the surrounding countryside. Dr. Ramsay sat alone in the far corner with three empty coffee mugs and an ash-tray full of butts for company. His Trinidadian complexion, thick black hair and dark-brown eyes were upstaged by his gleaming white teeth. He could have been a poster boy for Crest. He was wearing, when wasn't he, a tan-coloured summer suit, an Italian blue dress shirt and a multi-colored Calypso tie. As Tony sat down, Aaron flashed a warm, welcoming smile.

"Just the man I wanted to see, but what's on your mind? You look troubled, Tony."

In a low voice, no need to broadcast what had happened, Tony got right to his faux pas,

"This morning, I found one of your patients, an Arabelle Sirene, on the sand bar just out from the weir. She'd been strangled with a T-shirt. As I was docking

12

her body on the weir, an undercurrent sucked her down and wedged her in the weir's portal. But when I managed to release her, she went over High Falls. I'm sure that she's at the bottom of the whirlpool."

Aaron wiped the smile off his lips, and his face became a shadow. He spoke in a deep voice,

"You say her name was Arabelle Sirene. You must have read it from her armband. Sometimes they trade them; that's all they have in here to barter. Describe her."

"She had long grey hair and had red clay stains on her feet and hands..."

He held up his hand, pulled out a Henri Winterman's Slim Panetela from a silver case, lit it with a silver lighter, and took a couple of puffs. With it in the corner of his mouth, he spoke with resignation in his voice,

"That's Sirene, alright. Strangled you say? Unbelievable. If it wasn't for that damn portal, I'm sure you'd never lost her. Damn Green Peace. They insisted for the sake of the bloody carp. How I hate them, the vultures. Have you notified security?"

"Not yet."

"Good. Don't and neither will I. They'll report it to the Ontario Provincial Police who'll descend like bees and set off all the paranoids in here."

"Okay then, I was going to ask but, is it all right if I head up the investigation?"

After looking around, he leaned closer, took out the panetela cigar, placed it with care in the ashtray and spoke in a soft voice,

"I thought you'd never ask. I know you'll be discreet and not set off the paranoids, and more importantly, that it'll never make its way into The Gazette. Publicity always goes against us. And now, let me tell you about Miss Arabelle Sirene. She is, was, a lifer, spent most of her adult life here. The police brought her in a homeless Jane Doe with no ID; she was agitated, ranting and delusional that her daughter was missing when she was childless. The old chief diagnosed paranoid schizophrenia and threw the works at her: wet packs, insulin coma treatments, shock therapy and Largactil. With treatment, she announced that she was Arabelle Sirene but remained delusional that she had a daughter. The police never found any other Sirenes in the Golden Horseshoe, and she's never had a single visitor. So sad. Why anyone would want to kill her is beyond me. Must have been random."

He picked up the smoldering panetella, leaned back and puffed away while Tony sipped on his lukewarm coffee. A random killing left him feeling he was in Plato's cave. What chance did he have of finding her killer? About as much as finding her body. But Tony while discouraged was not finished and began his investigation when he said,

"She had clay stains on her hands and feet. There are red clay flats, up-river. Is it possible that she could have been there?"

Aaron sighed and flicked the ash of the panetella on the floor.

"A sore point with my peers. When I arrived, I unlocked the backwards, and haven't lost a single patient, until now. Tony, this is no prison, this is home for the lifers. Sirene was free to go wherever she wanted to go. Good luck in finding her killer. Anything you need, just ask. And now for what cost me a night's sleep. When you showed up, I thought it was because Judge Lispway had sent you. He told me he would. Well, did he?"

That took Tony aback. Judge Lispway never called him. What gave? "No, he didn't but then, Aaron, I haven't made it to the office this morning."

Aaron stubbed out the slender cigar, again leaned closer even though again, there was no one within earshot. Tony had never seen the psychiatrist looking as troubled as he did then.

"I use her as a sex surrogate. I ran it by the College and it's all above board. The paperwork is daunting but she's so good as what she does that it makes it all worthwhile. Well, she went missing yesterday evening. No word, just up and vanished. I called the police and got Brock Cook; he told me that his hands were tied for 48 hours. She had told me that a Judge Lispway used to visit her, and I called him. Well, he took me seriously, told me that I was not over-reacting, and he'd assign you to investigate."

"Aaron, I'm not a mind reader. What's her name and where does she live?"

He didn't like the sounds of it, not one bit. Lispway knew that missing persons was not his department. Why else would he assign him if not because he suspected foul play?

"Her name is Miss Fanny Maple. She's an escort who operates out of her apartment in the Glendale apartment building, unit 302. Cook knew her although she has no record."

"I'll drop by on my way to the office and see what's what? I won't get back to you until I know the lay of the land."

Chapter 4

The Glendale apartment building was the cornerstone of Pinolta's war-time housing development (single family, prefabricated homes). Surprisingly, even though dated, the neighbourhood hadn't gone downhill except for the Glendale. Tony parked out front and noticed a solitary, dingy red Ford Escort in the parking lot across the street. Just as he was entering, he spotted a black BMW 6 Series coupe parked up the street, had to be a visitor.

The foyer's floor was muddy, dusty and littered with junk mail and the occasional autumn leaf. When he smelled stewed cabbage, his gut recoiled; cabbage was on his blacklist. He was not impressed when he saw that apartment number 302 was beside Fanny Maple's name, and less so when he saw that the lock on the inner glass door was busted. So much for security. The super, identified only by the initials L. L., was in apartment 105 and to get there, he had to pass apartment 102, ground zero for cabbage. Even though he held his breath, his gut flinched but did not vomit. At apartment 105, he breathed in the smell of stale beer, and pounded hard on the door, a television was blaring on the fight channel, and waited.

When the door opened, he was surprised to see Lefty Lowland, an ex-boxer who had gone the distance with the world's heavyweight champ, only to lose on points. Lefty was a good six feet with a bald, bullet-shaped head, a pounded-flat face and a punched-in-nose. Long, muscular arms were crossed over the front of a Joe's Gym T-shirt. He was wearing jockey shorts and no shoes and looked none-too-pleased to be disturbed. Even though they'd met several times at Joe's Gym, Lefty didn't recognize him, but then rumor had it that Lefty was as punch-drunk as he was beer drunk. When Tony flashed his badge, Lefty shrugged his shoulders.

"I'm here to investigate a missing Miss Fanny Maple in 302. What can you tell me?"

"Nutting. She's a bad penny and they always turn up. A dago in a suit was snooping around here last night, probably her pimp. Ask him."

"Is that her Escort in the parking lot?"

"Yeah. Her backseat office if you get my drift. Look, I'm busy. You know her apartment number, it's not locked."

Lefty slammed the door in his face, and Tony trudged upstairs, fuming mad. How he hated it when someone slammed a door in his face. He'd have loved to have slammed a cell door in Lefty's face. The door to apartment 302 was ajar. Typical for the building. Tony slipped into a dark hallway with a glimmer of light peeking around a partly opened door at the far end. His standard-issue leather boots squeaked on the hardwood, no rug to muffle the sound. At the end of the hallway, he was startled to hear a woman sobbing.

"Fanny, Fanny, where, where are you. What, what did they do to you? Why, why didn't you call Pet, Mabel or I…"

Tony felt coldness snaking down his spine. If one of her friends didn't know where she was then, Maple truly was missing and given her profession, it wasn't looking good. Pushing open the door with the toe of his boot, he stepped into an oversized bedroom. Sunlight was streaming in from a large plate-glass window on the outside wall. To his left was a king-size bed and on it, a fire-engine-red bedspread and on it, a woman. She sat on the edge of the bed, hunched over with her head in her hands and long blonde hair shrouding her face. She was wearing a blue knit dress, pulled up high over muscled thighs. On the floor beside her was a designer gym bag. He cleared his throat and spoke,

"I'm Detective Carson of the Pinolta Police Force. I'm investigating the disappearance of a Miss Maple. Who are you and what are you doing here?"

Her face shot up; she was startled. There was fear in her blue eyes but not in her voice.

"Hot Dog, you're too late? She's not here. I told her not to waste her hard-earned money on the likes of you. Where were you when she needed you?"

Tony was caught off-guard. Who the hell was Hot Dog? Sounded like a cop on the take.

"I'm not Hot Dog, never was and never will be. Like I said, I'm Detective Tony Carson. Does Hot Dog have a name? I'd like to report him."

"Oh, I'm so sorry, so sorry. I apologise, Detective Carson. Unfortunately she never knew his name and never described him. You say you're looking for her but I thought you had to wait 48 hours before looking."

"We make exceptions. About your name, that's your call. I'd like you to answer a few questions. I gather you are a good friend and I know next to nothing about Fanny Maple."

The glare in her eyes softened but didn't evaporate. She wasn't letting down her guard all the way. As she got to her feet to face him, he saw that was a tall, Hollywood '10:' face and body. If he'd seen her on the street, he'd have looked at least twice. Then she sighed,

"I'd do anything to help, she was a dear friend. We met most every morning. I used to call her an ass-to-the-grindstone lady, she'd laugh, it was our inside joke. I'll tell you straight-up; she was robbed. She kept all her money under the bed in large envelopes; one for each year. She was paid only in 20s and 50s. I told her to get a safety deposit box but she never did. There's not a red cent left. Her two suitcases are here and they're empty. No missing shoes or clothes that I could see, and she never took a holiday. When I came in here, the drapes were closed and I opened them, she never closed them; she was claustrophobic. I never touched anything else except to check under the bed."

Tony looked around; nothing was out-of-place, nothing was overturned, no signs of a struggle. Besides the bed, there was an end table with a lamp on it but nothing else. The walls were bare. "I could use a picture of her."

"Oh my God."

She spun around and reached out to the end table only to stop dead. Then, her outstretched arms dropped like stones, and her eyes and voice registered panic,

"Our picture was in her jewelry box. She made me put it there. I never wanted her to snap it, but she insisted. What could I say when she told me that it made her feel like a person, knowing it was there. Apparently, she never really looked at it. But if my husband ever sees it…I don't want to think of what he'd do. It's suggestive if you have a dirty mind. It's missing but why would anyone take it? There was nothing in it but my picture and what looked like a rag. And as for anything else missing… Oh my God, the Persian rug in the hallway is not there. I was always after her to have it cleaned, but she never did."

When he heard that a hallway rug was missing, he had a sinking feeling that he wasn't about to share. Instead, he asked,

"Okay, can you describe her? I need something to go on."

"She is mid-thirties, five foot four, blonde hair, brown eyes, a looker. She wears a petite-size dress, and a size-five boot. I'm so worried. Detective Carson, will I ever see her again?"

Tears were in her eyes. Damnit, he thought. She was no fool but why throw cold water on hope. It was all she had.

"I don't know. But I will look for her, I promise. Before I go, I'd like to look under her bed."

As she stood aside, he flipped up the bedspread and there was a drawer that ran the length of the bottom of the bed. Pulling it open, he spotted several large envelopes that had never been opened. Like she said, no cash. He closed the drawer and pulled back the bedspread. She had wiped dry her eyes and was touching up her make-up.

"My name is Linda Stonemill. If I can be of any more help, just ask. My number is in the phone book. My husband never knew we were friends. He'd never approve."

Chapter 5

Tony finally arrived at Pinolta's police headquarters on the second floor of the Louis Craig estate home at the corner of King and Victoria. It was a three-storey Gothic mansion with turrets, leaded glass and stone gargoyles. On Craig's, a rural newspaper baron, death, it had been bought by the town of Pinolta as their city hall. The jail was Craig's oversized garage.

At the sign-in desk for the police sat Camelia Hussdon, a Romanian white slave who had been rescued by Florence Coldwell, a local do-gooder and her Salvation Army brigade. Hussdon was a thin woman, probably in her late 20s, with wispy, dirty blonde hair that was always in disarray. Her beige dress, Tony was sure that she owned only one, had seen one too many washes. When Tony approached, she had a "don't-step-closer" look in her eyes and without a word, he'd never heard her speak even though Coldwell had said that she was fluent in English, and thrust the book at him. He handed her the Eaton T-shirt to be sent to the lab, and signed in while she handed him a written reminder from Nigel Gold of their meeting that morning.

Gold was a clock watcher and Tony knew it was best not be late. He bolted up the stairs and down the hall to the end door. After he rapped three times, the insiders' calling card, he entered Gold's corner office, the largest on the floor, with bay windows facing out on to King Street and Victoria Avenue. The office with space to spare had a large rosewood desk, a leather high-back desk chair with arms and an assortment of armless chairs in front of the desk, a gas fireplace, and a rosewood shelving unit. On each wall was an identical Westclox in a rosewood frame. Tony had never known anyone to have four clocks, all telling the same time. Everything rosewood had been hand-crafted by Nigel's father, Abraham Gold, the previous police chief. Nepotism was alive and well in Pinolta.

Gold remained seated when Tony entered the room, but then, he never rose to greet him. Gold had expressionless eyes, close-cropped brown hair, thin colorless lips, and a physique that was short on muscle. It was hard to believe he was the son of Abraham Gold, a mammoth of a man. While Gold wore the same blue serge uniform as everyone else on the force, his alone sported gold epaulets. Gold was flushed, not a good sign.

"Have a seat, Carson. I've just got off the phone from that old fart, Judge Lispway. He asked me to assign you to the case of a missing whore, a Fanny Maple. I told him that Brock Cook in vice could oversee it, but he insisted that I assign it to you."

26

No way was Tony going to tell him that he was already on the case. If Lispway hadn't assigned him, he'd have had to have conducted his search, undercover. Not the first time he had gone behind Nigel's back. Nigel was seething mad that Lispway had pulled rank and blurted out,

"I tell you Carson, the old fart has gone senile. Next, he announced that he's opened our only cold case. Why Abraham made it a cold case is beyond me? He should have canned it. And worse, he's assigned you to that case. He's lost it, I tell you. I can't wait until the senile old fart retires and I'm rid of him for good. He's been nothing but a pain in the ass."

Tony saw all too well that his boss's feathers were ruffled and he was in a foul mood. He had to bite his tongue for he thought the world of Judge Lispway. To voice his opinion would have been a waste of words for Gold although a relatively young man was an old man when it came to changing his mind. And Tony also knew that soon Gold would be onto another topic and sure enough, he picked up a framed photo on his desk and thrust it at him. As he stood up and reached out, Gold thrust out his chest and flushed with ego, pontificated,

"I helped raise funds down at the Port Malvern Marina for the Coast Guard to purchase a bathyscaphe.

When Brock Cook saw it, he was blown away. It can dive over 200 feet, go where a diver wouldn't dare, and can retrieve objects up to 200 pounds. Coast Guard asked me to choose its maiden voyage. I asked Brock but he didn't know. What about you, Carson? Do you think that Mansfield could use it to search for your parents?"

The colour photo was of Gold and three other men, all in suits and ties, grouped behind an erect, blue torpedo that towered over them. On the ground, beside a stand that suspended the prop off the ground, was a black suitcase, most likely the command center. It had to be the bathyscaphe and it had to be remote-controlled. Tony had never seen one before but didn't see how it could help Mansfield.

"Mansfield told me he'd hired scuba divers three times and no luck. Between you and me, I get the feeling he's closed the search although he's yet to tell me."

"Too bad. This thing can go where divers can't."

Out of the blue, Tony heard his earworm playing Paul J. Smith's "Captain Nemo's Theme" from the movie, "20,000 Leagues Under the Sea." And before he knew it, Arabelle Sirene popped into his head. He had purposely not brought her up for he knew that Gold would say that he'd get around to retrieving her body.

His political way of saying he wasn't going to raise a finger to find her. Crazies were on Gold's do-nothing list. And not only did she pop into Tony's head but also a devious plan. Careful, not to rush his words, he spoke,

"Nigel, you won't believe this, but this morning when I was fishing, I spotted a blonde-haired woman going over High Falls. I raced down and saw her body disappear into the whirlpool. I checked, and the hospital has no missing patients. Do you happen to know if the missing Fanny Maple is or was a blonde?"

Nigel scowled and said,

"I have no idea… Just a minute. Yes, I did hear Brock say she was a blonde bombshell. He's looking for her or told me he was. He's so onto things. Most would have waited 48 hours but not my Brock. So, a blonde corpse is in the whirlpool. Has to be her. I'll tell him."

Tony saw he had taken the bait, now to reel him in and make him think that it was his idea. That was so important if he wanted Gold to act. With innocence in his voice, Tony continued, "I doubt your bathyscaphe could plumb the depths of a whirlpool?"

"Of course it could. No sweat. Child's play. Just a minute. Why not? I've just had a brainwave. I'll call Coast Guard."

"Why would you call Coast Guard?"

"Tony, sometimes you are slow on the uptake. I'm going to have the bathyscaphe get the body of the whore out of the whirlpool. As this is murder, I want you there. I'll tell Brock to stop looking and that you are now in charge."

Chapter 6

Tony Carson parked in the Elm Street lot, across from the courthouse, and walked by Judge Lispway's red Charger with the white trim, a Dukes of Hazard spin-off. The old boy was rumored to have a heavy foot. When Tony crossed the blue-rose slate floor of the crowded courthouse foyer, he waved at Betty, the white-haired matron on the reception desk who gave him a thumbs-up. Opening the painted-white door adjacent to the main courtroom, he walked down a darkened corridor whose outside glass wall was curtained by elm trees. At the end of the hallway, he rapped on a painted-black door and immediately heard a muffled voice.

"Is that you, Tony Carson?"

"Yes, Your Honor."

The door released with a click that had more punch than the judge's voice. Judge Samuel Lispway's office was a glass fishbowl in a forest of more elms. Unlike Gold, he was standing behind his diminutive oak desk to greet him. Lispway, a small man looked like he had shrunk from the last time that Tony had met with him. His scarlet robe with the expensive silk facings hung on him. While his thinning snow-white hair aged him, his brown eyes still had the brightness of youth.

He sat down with an arthritic sigh, and motioned for Tony to have a seat. For a Supreme Court justice, his quarters were sparsely furnished with a wooden desk and chair, two armless chairs and an armoire. On the desk was a day planner, ash tray and Bible. He fished out a Lucky Strike from his top drawer, lit it and inhaled deeply.

"I appreciate you coming on such short notice, Detective Carson. Did Gold tell you that I wanted you to head the search for the missing Fanny Maple?"

"Yes, he did. I didn't tell Nigel, but Dr. Aaron Ramsay, who if I'm not mistaken had called you last night, already had asked me. I've dropped by her apartment. Her life savings are missing as is the hallway rug. There was no sign of a struggle. Her suitcases and clothes look to be all there. I hate to tell you but it doesn't look good especially with the missing rug."

Lispway stubbed out the Lucky Strike, even though he had just started to smoke it. He sighed and grimaced. His lower lip quivered when he spoke,

"Why, why kill her? I don't get it. Rob her and leave it at that. She got off lucky years ago when she was almost beaten to death in a brothel in Hamilton. I warned her that there's no second time in her business. I can tell you now that she was in witness protection.

Only Abraham Gold and I knew. When I heard last night she was missing, I called Hamilton where she had been beaten, years ago. I talked to who had put her into protection, and he was sure that who had tried to kill her, finished the job. But now that I hear she was robbed, I'm not so sure. Either way, I feel responsible as she was on my watch. Abraham Gold is off on his world trip, bucket list."

Tony was stunned. Who would have thought that Fanny Maple was in witness protection? It didn't sound like Brock Cook or even Nigel Gold, knew. And he doubted that Dr. Ramsay knew. So, Hamilton thought the original killer had returned? But how could he have known who she was? Hopefully, they had changed more than her name.

"I see now why Nigel told me that you wanted me to look for her."

"Yes, yes, I asked for you. I hated to ask you for I'm sure you have a lot on your plate, but I trust you and know you will not tell anyone what I just told you. And you're good and finding her is not going to be easy. Hamilton already sent me a VHS tape she made when she was in the hospital. Have a look at it. You never know. Betty has it, and will give it to you on your way out."

Great, thought Tony, at least with Sirene he knew there was a body out there, with Maple he didn't even have that to go on. All he had was Linda Stonemill's verbal. He wondered how it would size up against who he saw on the VHS tape. But, unlike Sirene, he had a motive or did he? If it wasn't a robbery that went south, and there was no evidence of a struggle, then he was back in Plato's cave, blindfolded and with his hands tied behind his back. Lispway picked up the Bible, leafed through it to a passage that he read silently, and then looked up at Tony with concern in his eyes.

"Did Chief Gold tell you I've opened the cold case from the distant past, and if he did, did he give you the low-down?"

"Yes, he told me that you wanted me assigned to a cold case but nothing else. I don't have to tell you that he was not happy."

Lispway chuckled, although all too briefly.

"Okay then, I'll tell you all I know. 20 years ago, Abraham Gold told me that he had found child pornography in Jonathan Spratt's locker, he was the gym teacher at Thackeray's High, and sacked him on the spot. Never gave the poor bloke a chance to defend himself. The next day, Spratt returned to the school and was found shot in the showers. Abraham was sure it was suicide, and to keep it and the child porn out of the papers, he iced the case. Last night I awoke in a sweat, my heart was pounding, and the name 'Jonathan Spratt' was flashing in neon lights in my mind. And with it was the nagging doubt, 'suppose he was innocent?' I tend to feel guilty that I've slipped up at the best of times. I jumped out of bed and came down to the office. No one was here. The sun hadn't risen."

He wiped his brow with a handkerchief. Tony was surprized to hear that he too felt guilty. He'd never thought of a judge having doubts. Then Lispway pulled out two elongated brass keys from his top drawer that he placed beside the Bible. With a louder groan, he got to his feet, walked over to his armoire, lifted out an old mahogany chest, and brought it over to his desk. Quite breathless, he inserted the keys, popped the lid, pulled his chair around and sat down. Turning to Tony, he explained what he was doing,

"This is a trust box that two nuns brought over from Toulouse to Quebec City in the 1700s. Trust meant each nun had her own key. Abraham Gold stored his only cold case in it. I'll show you what I found inside, I'd never opened it before, and then you tell me what you think."

Lispway handed Tony a neatly clipped, but faded column from The Gazette. "Jonathan Spratt collapsed and died today of a massive stroke at Thackeray's High School. The board at Thackeray's wants to thank Mr. Spratt for his many years of loyal and dedicated service. His remains will be cremated at the town's expense."

"Abraham told The Gazette what to print. On cover-up, there was none, better."

Then, Lispway produced two, 8-by-10, black-and-white photos, and handed them to Tony. Both were rear shots of young, naked boys taking a shower on Fujifilm paper.

"They are what Abraham found in Spratt's locker. Spratt denied that he even owned a camera. You see now why I had doubts. Who said they weren't planted."

He then opened a dirty-white envelope, extracted a slug, and passed it to him.

Tony recognized it immediately, and replied,

"It's from a Colt."

"Right you are. At the time, the only Colts in town belonged to Abraham Gold and Benjamin Robins. They had enlisted in the Korean war. Abraham told me that Spratt must have lifted the Colt from the trophy case in the back of Robins' hardware store on his way to school, and shot himself with it. Abraham returned the gun to Benjamin Robins. You might check to see if it's still there."

With a theatrical flourish, he produced another 8-by-10, black-and-white photo, handed it to Tony, and while he stubbed out his cigarette in the ash tray, he never took his eyes off Tony. A fully clothed, fat Chinese man was lying on his back in a pool of blood. There was a small blood stain in the middle of his chest. A Colt pistol lay on the floor, just outside his right hand. It had no blood stains on it. Two fingertips of his right hand were blood-stained, and above them, was a bloody "/\" marking on the floor. Tony took his time before he spoke,

"If Spratt shot himself, why is there not more blood splattering on his chest, on the gun and on his right hand? As for the marking in blood on the floor, why shoot himself and then try and tell us something? My money is on he was shot and, he knew the shooter."

"Brilliant, Tony. Now, tell me, what do you make of the marking on the floor?"

"My first thought and I'm going with my first thought is that Spratt was trying to make an 'A' when he died."

"Mine too. And in my books, 'A' stands for the Amigos, the name of the group that Nigel formed in high school. I didn't tell you but Nigel was a student there when Spratt was shot, as were his friends. My take on it was that Abraham was again on cover-up, this time for his son or one of his son's friends. I want you to investigate the Amigos for the murder of Jonathan Spratt. And don't worry about repercussions. I'll call Nigel and tell him it's all my idea, which it is."

Chapter 7

Tony parked in front of The Gazette on King Street, just down from Mabel's Diner. When he opened his car door, his stomach picked up the aromatic trail of eggs, Canadian bacon and home-fries, and was none too happy when he headed toward the unappetizing Gazette. It was a dirty white stucco, two-storey building whose windows were almost opaque with grime. Inside, Tony spotted Judy Fontaine sitting behind a waist-high counter. She had short black hair, dark eyes set in a perpetual glare, and wore a long-sleeved mechanic's coveralls with a black arm band. Who would have thought she was as strong as she was, but he had seen her throw a punch and kickbox at Joe's Gym. She ran the presses when she was not on the desk. What couldn't she do? As much as he was impressed, he'd never voiced his opinion as he sensed she'd take it the wrong way and he needed her to be a little receptive.

It was quiet inside; the presses out back were on break. When he placed the faded news article about Spratt on the counter, she glanced at it and then smirked as if to say, 'why are you wasting my time?' In a voice that was as snippy and sharp as one of her shears, she said,

"Yep, that's ours. Retired that press ten years ago. I can tell from the 'S.' Didn't know this Spratt fellow, before my time. Well, what can I do for you, officer?"

As often as they had met at The Gazette and at Joe's, she always addressed him as 'officer,' even though she knew his name. He'd never called her 'Judy.'

"If Grant is in, I'd like to discuss it with him, if you don't mind."

She pressed a button and within record time, Cornelius Grant stepped out of his office, it was just down the hall. He was a badly stooped six-footer with long, sandy hair in a ponytail. He always wore a seen-better-days Harris Tweed jacket with leather patches on the elbows, along with black jeans and cowboy boots. His large spade-like hands and square jaw came from a long line of Dutch lumberjacks. He bellowed even though the presses were quiet,

"What do you want, Judy?"

"The officer here has an obit for a John Spratt. He wants you to see it."

"John Spratt, you say. Let me see it."

Grant bypassed Tony without as much as a nod and went straight for the article. As he scanned it with the searching look of a customs officer, he smiled, and then turned to Tony who he had to have seen, all along. In a loud voice, they were next to each other, he said,

"Never thought I'd see the day. Pop thought for sure that hell would freeze over before any cop came asking about Spratt. Who sent you? I'll be a monkey's uncle if it was Nigel Gold. No way would he dare go against his old man."

Tony hated to have to answer to Grant like he was a puppet but he had no choice, and it sounded like he knew a thing or two as why else would he have recalled Spratt so quickly.

"Judge Lispway just opened Spratt's cold case, and ordered me to investigate. You're my first stop."

"Detective, you tell His Honour that he has the wisdom of Solomon; being a Jew, he should like that. I visit pop at Peaceful Meadows every Tuesday, today, and will tell him the unexpected but good news. Come into my office, and I'll spill a can of worms."

Grant spun around and marched back into his office, the man didn't know how to walk, and Tony followed. Was Grant really going to open up or was he just going to shoot the breeze? He strode to the end of an elongated, narrow room, and stood behind a standing desk that had a glass vase with paper-white Narcissus on it. Tony sat down in the middle of three chairs grouped in front of the desk. On the right wall was a large bulletin board covered with newspaper clippings, while on the left wall was a blank blackboard with a piece of chalk on the lip. Grant picked up a pipe from his desk, and took a long puff. Tony smelled Flying Dutchman tobacco, his least favorite brand. Grant wheezed, stuck his face into the white Narcissus, and inhaled deeply. After a couple of gulps of air, he surfaced with a smile.

"Works every time. My doc told me I had asthma and gave me two inhalers. My naturopath told me to buy some Narcissus. I'm asthma free and still smoking. Okay, down to business. No ride is free in life. If you want to hear what I know and it's plenty, it'll cost you."

"How much?"

"My readership has an insatiable appetite for sex and mayhem, and I hate to disappoint them. A Miss Fanny Maple is missing, and I want first rights on her story. No going to the Telegram. Well, do we have a deal?"

As Tony had never called the Telegram, he had no problem with Grant's request.

"I'm sure His Honour will agree. You can't tell Nigel who slipped you the story."

"You have my word, Detective, and why should I break it? Nigel never calls me and I have always returned the favor. Now, anything to whet my readers' appetite regarding Maple?"

Everyone knew that Grant had a mole in city hall. How else did he know of Maple's disappearance? And as he had to know about the bathyscaphe, Tony had no choice but to tell him otherwise he'd fail the test and be shown the door.

"An eyewitness saw Miss Maple's body go over High Falls and end up in the whirlpool. We're sure she was murdered. Gold is renting a bathyscaphe to see if he can fish her out."

Grant placed down his pipe, turned a ghastly color and looked visibly shaken.

"Poor Miss Maple is dead. I was expecting it, but hearing that she's dead, is unsettling to say the least. I never met her, but I hear she was well known and even more, well received, if you get my drift. Why would anyone kill such a lovely woman? And as for renting a bathyscaphe, good luck. They say that whirlpool is bottomless."

He laughed with a cynic's curl on his lips. Then, he shocked Tony when he walked around his desk, sat down in a chair next to him, slipped off his Harris Tweed, rolled up the sleeves of his white shirt, leaned closer and spoke like they were confidants.

"I was out back having a smoke when I saw a cop car tearing up King Street, no siren and no lights flashing. I jumped into pop's jalopy and followed them to Thackeray's. Saw Abraham Gold and a lackey race into the school. When I walked in, no one was in the main hallway, and I thought at first it was a false alarm until I heard Gold's voice coming from downstairs. I sneaked down, peeked around a corner, and got the fright of my life. Spratt was lying on the floor in a pool of blood. I'd never seen a dead man before, I almost puked."

Tony couldn't believe his luck. Grant had been an eyewitness to the police investigation.

"Gold bent over Spratt, sniffed like a dog, swore and told the lackey to turn off the shower. He then said that the water from the shower had washed away all the powder burns. The lackey didn't question him, no one ever did. But there was no water anywhere near Spratt. Then Gold pointed to a gun that was near to Spratt, and said it was suicide. The lackey pointed to a large, bloodied shoeprint on the floor, near the stairs to the rich kids' rooms, and Gold said that it was from his size 14 shoe. But he'd never been anywhere near it. Shit, I'm late. Meet me in a couple of hours at Mabel's, and I'll tell you more. Finally I get to give my opinion. I feel like a real detective. Whoever wears a size 14 shoe was there and if it wasn't suicide, neither pop nor I thought that it was, then I'd say that size 14 is a prime suspect."

Chapter 8

After Nigel Gold got off the phone from Judge Lispway announcing that he was going ahead with the cold case, he checked that the windows were shut, and then cursed out loud. And to add salt to the wound, the old fart had said that his Amigos were prime suspects in a murder investigation. So much for Spratt having snuffed himself. And why hadn't Abraham burned the records? He must have known it was murder and not suicide. Nigel felt doomed. Abraham was on a world trip and was not to be disturbed. But that was why Lispway had acted. Nigel hadn't followed the bit about a bloody mark on the floor. As far as he was concerned, the old fart was Don Quixote fighting windmills. It'd never stand up in court. He'd tell his Amigos it was a tempest in a teapot, but to pay it lip service. How embarrassing to have to call them and admit that his hands were tied. When was the old fart going to retire or better still, kick the bucket?

He'd call Waverly Stonemill at his brickyard and ask him to contact Carl Robins. He'd heard that Carl was in the poor house, and didn't want to be hit up for a loan. While he'd call Herb Liefson at his garage, he'd leave it up to him to relay the message to Reggie Moorehouse. They hadn't talked in years, and he tried to avoid queers. They gave him the shivers.

Frustrated, ashamed, and angry was how he felt, and Nigel knew he needed a break or he was going to give himself a headache. Getting to his feet, he walked over to the Victoria Street window, checked that the coast was clear, opened it and extracted a Virginia Slim from the marigold bed. There was nothing more calming that sucking on a Slim, his mother's favorite cigarette. But after a couple of puffs, he re-opened the window and mashed the cigarette into the bed of marigolds. It wasn't working. He needed a distraction and fast.

Leaving his office, he walked down the hall and, without rapping, opened Brock Cook's door and entered his spacious office, second only to his own. Light from the two bay windows on Victoria Avenue highlighted the Kierstead prints of stone mills and farmhouses that covered his walls. Nigel dabbled in oil painting and envied Kierstead, an Ontario Provincial Police officer who'd made it as a painter. Brock Cook, who'd been sitting behind his desk, jumped to his feet when he saw Nigel, and flashed a warm, welcoming smile.

Brock was a tall, well-built, handsome man with gelled blond hair. Nigel could never decide if it was dyed or not. Every time he saw it, he was reminded of the Brylcreem commercial, 'A Little Dab'll Do Ya.'

"Hi boss, what can I do for you? You don't look so good. Want me to get you a Coke?"

47

"Brock, Carson saw the missing Maple woman go over High Falls this morning and end up in the whirlpool. I've ordered a bathyscaphe and Coast Guard will deliver it."

Brock blushed, which he always did when he was caught off-guard. With color in his cheeks, Brock was even more handsome. Nigel felt his heart race.

"Really, I'll have to call off my major search. I was just about to ask for permission to requisition a pack of Metro Police dogs."

"Brock, you're always so efficient. I wish I had more men like you. And now for what's bugging the hell out of me. Judge Lispway went over my head and ordered that Carson be assigned to the case. Sure, I'd have assigned him but I hate like hell in being told to do it."

"Can he do that? Aren't you the police chief?"

"Sad to say Brock, but yes, he can. He would never have dared to have gone over Abraham's head, but he walks all over me like I'm a doormat."

"Boss, give him hell and he'll respect you. I'm surprized your old man didn't teach you that, but then, he wasn't much of a father, was he?"

Nigel felt a cold lump in his throat, hadn't felt it in years. No, Abraham had not been a good father. How could he forget, he must have been aged ten, when Abraham took him aside, and told him that he was a wimp, a Namby-Pamby. He'd cried himself to sleep for months, and he'd never forgotten his father's words. How could he when it was the only time that his father had said anything about him. Then Brock said,

"Talking about Miss Maple, your dad told me she was off limits and never to step foot in the Glendale Building. Do you think he was shagging her?"

Nigel could have crawled under a rock. Hadn't his mother gone on and on that Abraham was screwing half the women in Pinolta. No wonder she drank as much as she did. He shrugged his shoulders. No way did he want to go there.

"Boss, to change the topic, I've had my eyes on one of your Amigos, a Carl Robins. I'm sure he's peddling booze and drugs and I need your permission to investigate him."

"Brock, I have no sacred cows. No man is above the law. You have my permission."

Chapter 9

Carl Robins sat in a shabby and uncomfortable wooden chair behind a fire-sale desk, looked around at his bare office and moaned. The Repo boys had taken his solid oak desk and chairs, his first edition prints and his Dinky Toy truck collection. His ten, leased Volvo reefers were still in the yard but they were on borrowed time. When he heard a car on the gravel outside, he got to his feet, none too fast, barely opened the door of his corrugated metal office building, and peeked outside. If it was a bill collector, he'd hide out back. When he spotted a gleaming red Cadillac that was parking next to his 1960 Ford 150, rust bucket, he breathed a sigh of relief. It was Waverly Stonemill's. Who else could afford a brand-new Caddy?

Carl slicked down his thinning hair, walked outside, and flashed his Marlboro Man smile, the same as on his overhead sign. Waverly was short, fat, and spilling out of the grey-pinstripe three-piece that he always wore and thought was trimming. What really bugged Carl was that Waverly had a full head of black hair and he was losing his. Waverly waddled up to him, cleared his throat, and spoke without looking him in the eyes. But when did he ever look at him?

"Jack, my mechanic called this a.m. He was here yesterday, got inside the cargo compartment of one of your Volvos, but couldn't remove the cooling unit. He said it weighed a ton. Sorry Carl, but I can't use your reefers to lug my bricks. Gas isn't cheap since those Saudis took over."

Shit, Carl thought, he was up shit creek. Swallowing his pride or what was left of it that had not been repossessed, he threw a Hail Mary pass.

"Waverly, any chance you could float me a few thousand? As soon as Florida's orange crop recovers from the frost, I'm back in business. You know me, I'm good for it."

Waverly remained stone-faced; a sour pus if ever there was one.

"Carl, the tin boys have me on the ropes. Bricks are out and aluminum siding is in. They've made a hostile bid to buy me out. I've had to drain my bank account to fight them."

Carl saw that Waverly was hopeless and mumbled a curse. Who else was there? Nigel had been taken to the cleaners by his ex-wife who'd run off with the pilot. Herb Liefson was just a car mechanic and barely making it. He hadn't talked to Reggie Moorehouse in years. And he was too proud to ask his wife, Petula, who had taken over the failing hardware business and turned it around. Tightening his fists, he regretted not having kept up with boxing for if he had, he'd be the heavyweight champ. Waverly mopped his brow with a silk monogrammed handkerchief and muttered,

"More bad news. If it rains, it pours. Nigel called me. They've opened the cold case on Spratt. You know, the gym teacher at Thackeray's. Well, he didn't die of a stroke. He was murdered. And Judge Lispway named us, the Amigos, as prime suspects. Nigel tells me there's nothing he can do to abort the investigation. Do you recall Spratt?"

Carl nodded. How could he forget the pederast? His old man had accused him of shooting Spratt with their Colt, and had given him the licking of his life. When he read the 'stroke' article in The Gazette, he'd thought Abraham was doing his old man a favor and letting him off the hook. Damn judge, he thought, why hadn't he let sleeping dogs lie?

"The judge is sending a Detective Carson to question us. Do you know him?"

"Yeah, I've seen him several times at Joe's Gym. He's fast on his feet but I'm faster. Why are you sweating it? Don't you have an alibi? I have one."

The fat man was sweating up a storm. Enough sweat to have gone through a box of handkerchiefs. He opened his mouth, shut it, looked around, leaned closer, looked at him in the eyes and whispered,

"I can't say where I was. If it gets out, well, it's not getting out. Where were you? Any chance that I could have been with you? I'll send Jack back, I promise."

Suddenly Carl was feeling great. Hadn't felt that great in years. Like he was the heavyweight champ and the Marlboro Man all wrapped in one. What a rush to know he had Waverly just where he wanted him, in his back pocket.

"Waverly, on the day Spratt was murdered, I was on a dig at the Indian burial site just outside Midland, and didn't get home until late. Didn't I see you on the same dig? And so unfortunate for the likes of Carson but there are no school records."

Just like that, the fat man stopped sweating and smiled, actually smiled. Then he turned and almost skipped back to his Caddy that he gunned and burned rubber as he drove off the lot. Carl looked up at his mug shot on the overhead sign and grinned for the first time in what felt like years. But his moment in the sun was short-lived as a dingy, beat-up purple school bus pulled into his lot. Cursing out loud, how many times had he told the bloody fool never to come around in broad daylight, he bolted out to Raymond's Road. Looking up and down, he didn't see a cop car, but he was still fuming mad when he returned.

Leaning against the bus, Reverend Jake Mulgrave was smoking a joint. He was a flabby six-footer with dark brown eyes that could spot a sucker a mile away, a winning smile that never left his lips, and a warm, southern drawl that he had learned in an Oral Roberts crash course. His off-the-rack black suit, collarless dirty-white shirt, and runners were all a front to appear poor and one of them. He had a smirk on his face as he spoke,

"Carl, stop worrying. My guardian angel sent me a new-fangled, Fuzz-buster. I passed three speed traps on my way here and not one ticket. But what's this I hear? You're in Gethsemane and yet, you still have ten reefers."

"They won't be here in the morning, Jake. The repo boys haven't left me a pot to piss in."

"The Pharisees, they'll get their comeuppance in the next world. I'd loan you a few thousand Carl, truly I would, but I can't jeopardise my tax exemption status."

Carl inhaled deeply on Jake's second-hand smoke, and was too proud to ask for a drag.

"Jake, I've run out of dime bags. You couldn't loan me a bale of your finest, could you? I'll pay you back. You know I don't welch on loans."

"Sorry Carl, the Lord doesn't do credit. He got fleeced once by those Pharisees and never again. I am a man of the Lord and follow in His ways."

What bullshit thought Carl. Mulgrave took the biggest drag of the day, and exhaled with a guttural, 'Aaaaah.' Hearing the crunch of gravel, Carl turned and saw a white van, with something about turkeys painted on its side. It pulled into his lot, and out stepped a tall, lanky man with red hair and in blood-stained whites. As he sauntered toward them, Carl clenched his Rocky Marciano fists. He was sick and tired of dough-heads getting lost, and treating him like an information centre. When he heard a Newfie drawl, he almost threw a punch. Those damn Newfies were always getting lost, the dimwits.

"I need cold, gobs of it. Got ten tousand turkeys and can't sell for too weeks. Taught Thanksgiving was tis week. I see ice on wheels. I count ten. I have cash.'"

"You got ten thousand turkeys. Do I care? Go home to the Rock, and lasso an iceberg."

But Jake stepped in between him and the farmer who smelled of turkey shit, and threw an arm around him like he was his long-lost son.

"Bro, did I hear you have ten thousand birds in need of ice until Thanksgiving that is two whole weeks away? And did I hear you say you'd pay for refrigeration for those darlings in cash? Bro, I'm an ordained minister of the Lord, and don't often talk about such worldly matters as money. But how much are you willing to pay to ice those ten thousand birds?"

The turkey farmer ran his hand through his red hair, like he was waking up his brain.

Chapter 10

When Tony stepped out of The Gazette, his gut tugged in the direction of Mabel's, but he headed to Robins' Hardware. In its two large plate-glass windows were a clutter of tools, paint cans, wallpaper rolls, lawnmowers, and wheelbarrows. He was in luck for between the rolls of wallpaper and the paint cans, he spotted an 'OPEN' sign. Not having been inside the store since his teens, Tony was dismayed that all that remained of the old days were the two narrow aisles. Now, the shelves were neatly stocked; the oak floor was swept and polished; and behind the cash-out counter at the back, where grumpy, old man Robins in his American naval uniform had sat, was a woman in a white shirt and a plain black skirt. She had auburn hair to her shoulders, deep-set brown eyes and an impish nose. Her voice was as warm as her smile.

"Can I help you officer? I'm Petula Robins."

She had to be Carl's wife. He'd heard that she'd taken over the store when Carl's father, Benjamin, had died of alcoholism, and Carl had jumped ship to truck oranges from Florida. The hardware store had been on the verge of bankruptcy but she had turned it around and opened a successful, tool-rental division. Never having seen her, Tony had pictured her as a hard-nosed, won't-give-an-inch alpha woman. Was he wrong?

"Pleased to meet you, Mrs. Robins. I'm Detective Tony Carson and, don't worry, I'm not here on official business. Was in the neighborhood and thought I'd drop in. Hate to say it, but I haven't been in your store since I was a teenager. You've certainly have picked up the place."

"Well thank you, Detective Carson, I work hard at it."

Then he noticed that Robins' Colt trophy case from the Korean War was not on the back wall, behind her. Looking around and not seeing it, he spoke and when he did, he tried hard to keep the disappointment out of his voice. "Mrs. Robins, wasn't Benjamin's Colt on the wall behind where you're sitting?"

She grimaced and sighed. He heard the ring of frustration in her voice.

"Yes, it was there. When Benjamin passed, I wanted to get rid of it. We have a young son, but Carl insisted we keep it. I hated to sit here with it behind me. It gave me the creeps. Carl reassured me it was not loaded but tit made no difference. One day, Carl was showing off with the Colt like he was the second coming of Wyatt Earp didn't he fire a shot into my new mahogany counter. It was loaded. I took the Colt and said either adieu Colt or adieu Carl. He knew he had got off lightly, and handed me the Colt."

Tony realized that she had an alpha side and also that the Colt was history, most disheartening about the Colt. He'd have to take Lispway's word that it was the murder weapon.

"Well, I'll be leaving. Sorry to have troubled you, Mrs. Robins. You see, I'm giving a lecture on the Colt pistol, and wanted to show the class what one looked like."

"Just a minute, I still have it. I didn't know how to dispose of it. Would you do me a favor and take it off my hands? I have it in a locked drawer and what a relief it will be to know it's not in the store. I made Carl dig out the slug he'd fired into my counter, it's loose in the case. I also made him pay me for a new counter which I've ordered but which, has yet to come."

Chapter 11

Tony jumped into his car, headed over to police headquarters, parked, and shot past Camelia on the front desk and upstairs to his office. He never looked sideways at his saltwater fish tank, plunked down in his desk chair, cleared a space for the loose slug from the Colt case, and got out the slug that had killed Spratt. With a magnifying glass, he compared the two slugs. They were a match. It was true then that Robins' Colt was the murder weapon. But if it was true that Spratt had lifted it from the case on his way to school, and if he hadn't shot himself with it, then somehow the shooter had relieved Spratt of it, shot Spratt and then planted it on Spratt to make it look like suicide. And if Grant hadn't steered him wrong, then the shooter wore a size 14 shoe.

No sooner had Tony put away the slugs and the trophy case, than he heard a rapping at his door. Swearing under his breath, when was Camelia Hussdon ever going to screen people, he yelled,

"Come in."

He almost fell off his chair when in walked Waverly Stonemill. Although they'd never formally met, Tony had seen enough pictures of him in The

Gazette to recognize him. The initials "W. S." on his white shirt's collar told Tony that he was right. Up close, Tony saw bushy eyebrows, pinpoint flat eyes, a bulbous nose, and a triple chin. He was much fatter than in the newspaper photos. His three-piece suit was bulging at the seams. Without being too obvious, he glanced at Stonemill's shoes, no more than a size eight. Not looking at Tony, Stonemill spoke in a loud voice,

"Detective Carson, you should have a name plate on your door. If my good friend Nigel hadn't described you, I've had to ask your name, young man."

"What can I do for you, Mr. Stonemill?"

Tony sensed that he was being talked down to with the "young man" bit, and tried to ignore it. Stonemill was Pinolta's success story. He had taken his father's brick company that was collecting more dust than fees, and turned it into a national enterprise. He had every right to throw around his weight, if Pinolta had royalty, Stonemill would be king. But still, Tony was irked for Pinolta had no royalty, and so-what if Stonemill was nouveau riche.

"Nigel shocked me when he told me I'm a suspect in Spratt's death. I was outraged that I would be suspected. I'm here to have my name removed from the list of suspects. I'm giving you my word that I have an alibi, and I expect that will suffice."

Tony felt a surge of anger. No way was he going to be ordered around in a murder investigation. For a brief second, he had an ounce of empathy for Gold although what he had to put up with from Lispway was nothing compared to what Stonemill was trying to get away with.

"Take a seat, Mr. Stonemill."

"I prefer to stand. This won't take long."

"How long it takes, I'll decide. Take a seat, Mr. Stonemill, and let's hear the alibi."

Stonemill's eyes narrowed, teeth gritted, but then shoulders shrugged as if to say, 'No big deal.' While he sat down, his shoes were poised on the floor to spring. For the first time, Stonemill's eyes zeroed in on Tony, and glared at him.

"On the day that Spratt died, I was on a field trip with Carl Robins. We were digging at an Indian site in Midland for Indian relics. I didn't get home until late."

Tony doubted there were school records that he could check. He had to accept their alibi even though he didn't trust anything that Carl Robins had to say. Almost at once, Stonemill was on his feet and about to leave. Tony thought 'why not,' and said,

"Well, thank you Mr. Stonemill for saving me a trip. I'll have your name removed from the list of suspects. But, before you go, I'm also investigating the disappearance of a Fanny Maple. She resides in the Glendale Building, and went missing on Monday, late afternoon to early evening. Where were you, yesterday afternoon and evening? You are under no obligation to answer, purely voluntary, Mr. Stonemill."

Stonemill sneered at Tony and in a 'gotcha' voice, replied,

"Detective, I'll have you know that I've never set foot in the Glendale Building. They didn't use my father's bricks, and I don't trust that it'll collapse some day like the house of cards that it is. As for where I was on Monday afternoon, I attended Bruce Liefson's inauguration into the Amigos at his family's home on Dairy Street. Nigel Gold and Carl Robins were there and can vouch for me. Reginald Moorehouse was a no-show else he too could vouch for me. Afterwards, I went home, had a bite to eat, and then attended an important board meeting. They too can vouch for me. And now, I'm leaving."

Chapter 12

Reginald Moorehouse parked his blue Porsche in the lot of the Osprey Mental Hospital, slowly got out, looked around nervously to make sure no one had seen him, and walked slowly up the front steps and down the deserted hallway to Dr. Ramsay's office. He was not feeling well. Usually, he bounded up the steps and down the hallway. Besides a splitting headache, his heart was pounding and he was short of breath. Last night, he'd tossed and turned and felt like he hadn't slept, a wink. Opening the door to Dr. Ramsay's office, he couldn't even manage a smile when the two secretaries looked up at him. He always smiled. And he was too distracted to even look at them. Most unlike him. At the inner door, he rapped but when he went to speak, his throat was so dry that all he could do was to whisper.

"Dr. Ramsay, it's me, Mr. Moorehouse."

"Come in."

He was sure that the doctor sounded abrupt. While Reginald always felt he was a nuisance in the busy man's schedule, that day he felt he was pariah. But as soon as he had stepped inside the office, he checked out Dr. Ramsay to see if he should turn and exit. Actually, he wondered why he'd shown up for his session. Why didn't he just once, take the easy way out? But he couldn't believe his eyes, Dr. Ramsay was behaving as though nothing was wrong. His dark eyes were smiling warmly at him. No way was he glaring at him. He couldn't recall his mother's eyes smiling at him. Remaining seated as always behind his desk by the far wall, the doctor pointed to a chair under his diplomas from Port of Spain, Trinidad. Reginald preferred it to the chair by the portrait of a young Queen Elizabeth.

"Mr. Moorehouse, you don't look so hot. Your voice sounds like your throat is bone-dry. I'll get you a glass of water."

Dr. Ramsay pulled out a plastic water bottle from a drawer, poured a hefty amount into a paper cup, walked around his desk and extended it to him. When he took a drink, he was surprised how refreshing it felt on his throat. As he returned the cup, Dr. Ramsay, who was standing over him, took it with one hand but his other hand felt the top of Reginald's head. But when he did, Reginald felt a sharp lancing pain that brought tears to his eyes.

"Mr. Moorehouse, what happened? You have a sizable lump on your head and your blond hair is matted with dried blood. Did you fall? Any concussion?"

"I was at Miss Maple's when the lights went out. I woke up on the floor with a headache from hell. Yes, I fell but I swear I blacked-out before I fell. And yes, I must have had a concussion. I was out for hours. Tylenol did nothing for it. I hardly slept all night."

Then he saw alarm and concern in the doctor's eyes.

"You blacked-out at Miss Maple's? Tell me all about it but first, I'm tossing the cup in the basket. And start at the beginning, I want to hear everything that happened."

After he'd discarded the cup, he pulled up a chair and sat down beside him. Never, had he done that before. Up close, Reginald realized how handsome the doctor was but then he'd never seen anyone in real life before from Trinidad. He'd seen Harry Bellefonte on the screen and for the first time, was sure there was a resemblance. Sweat was trickling down the sides of his face, and his breathing was raspy. As much as he had dreaded talking about yesterday, he knew he had to and what better person than to his doctor. If anyone could make sense of it, he could.

"When I met Miss Maple, she told me to call her Fanny but I couldn't. I asked if I could close the drapes, I felt I was on Main Street, I know that no one could see us, but she told me that she was claustrophobic. That made me feel better, knowing she had a fear too, and I then told her I had a phobia for looking at nude women. She had long blonde hair, was quite pretty; had kind eyes and was wearing a bright red robe with a cloth belt that hung too loosely to suit me. She handed me a matching red robe and told me to change, but I couldn't change. Not in front of her or anywhere near her. She took back the robe and shocked me when she asked, out of the blue, if I'd ever seen my mother naked. My mind went blank, and my eyes closed. She said that she could see that I was frightened, and when I wasn't frightened to open my eyes but I need not tell her anything. When I opened them, she said that she knew I had a phobia for naked women and to help me, she was going to make herself less feminine. And jus t like that, she pulled off her wig. I was stunned. Her head was covered with black stubble. But I must say that I had no trouble looking at her. Then she asked me to close my eyes and relax and when I was ready, I was to open them. No sooner had I closed them than I heard her scream but when I went to open my eyes, everything went black."

All the time that Reginald had been talking, he'd been looking at Dr. Ramsay. When he finished talking, the doctor's eyes were exploding with concern and alarm, especially at the end. He returned to his chair, sat down, pulled out a silver cigarette case from a desk drawer, lit a thin cigar and took a couple of puffs before he spoke,

"She screamed and then you blacked-out. You know what I think, Mr. Moorehouse. Someone came up behind you or you would have seen them, she saw this person and screamed as he clobbered you on the head. She's as tough as nails and doesn't scare easily. I wonder if she recognized who it was. Mr. Moorehouse, I don't like the sounds of this, not one bit. Okay, tell me what happened when you came to?"

"When I opened my eyes, my head was throbbing in pain. I never thought I had been hit on the head but it makes sense. The room was pitch-black. The drapes were drawn. I looked around and when I didn't see her, I called out her name but got no response. Then I was feeling scared. It was like I was in a haunted house. I crawled to the front door and again, called her name. Nothing. How I drove home, I have no idea. My maid, Pearcum, had waited for me and had dinner in the microwave, but I had no appetite. I downed three Tylenols, went to bed but couldn't sleep."

Dr. Ramsay placed down the cigar and leaned forward on his desk. "What I'm going to tell you is going to spook you but I have no choice. Miss Maple is missing and the police are looking for her. You may very well be the last person to see her, alive."

Reginald felt terror-stricken. His heart wasn't beating, it was fluttering. It was as if the bottom of his world had dropped away and he was in a dizzying free-fall. He grabbed the chair arms or he would have fallen to the floor. He moaned and muttered,

"I swear, I never touched her. I didn't. I can't look at naked women. How could I touch one and let me tell you, she was half naked in that robe. I'm no Frankenstein or am I?"

Dr. Ramsay jumped out of his chair, whipped around and grabbed Reginald by the shoulders. Looking him straight in the eyes, he almost shouted,

"I told you that there was someone else there who scared her and who knocked you out. If anyone harmed her, it was whoever was in the room and not you. Mr. Moorehouse, you did not harm her. Get that through your guilt-ridden head. And whatever you do, don't go to the police, they'll never believe you. I believe you but Mr. Moorehouse, for once, you have to believe in yourself. You are no killer. No Frankenstein. Come back, tomorrow."

Chapter 13

After Tony parked behind Grant's Ambassador, he quickly walked down to Mabel's. Just as he stepped inside, Mabel shot past him with a tray of chips and steaming coffee. He jumped aside, felt the swishing of her long, blonde hair, and watched her weave her way between wooden tables and rose-colored paper tablecloths. The place was packed and was noisier than the courthouse's foyer. On the walls were photos of Betty Crocker cake mixes, Andy Warhol soup cans, and McCain's potatoes.

Tony spotted an arm in a patched Harris Tweed waving at him, and he followed the aroma of Flying Dutchman tobacco to Grant's table. No sooner had he sat down than a steaming cup of coffee and a plate of fries landed in front of him. Looking up were two smiling, hazel eyes and a luscious body; Mabel was a heart throb. But she was a woman on the 'go' and disappeared as fast as she had appeared.

He turned to Grant who was filling in the daily crossword with a fountain pen, obviously not expecting to ever make a mistake. On his plate were a few fries and beside it, two empty Pepsi cans. When he put down his pen, he looked up and without as much as a 'hello,' spoke,

"Detective, now for the second installment. The day after the shooting, I slipped back down into the showers. They were as clean as a whistle and reeked of Javex. I saw the janitor Bert and offered him a pack of cigs if he had any juicy news. He grabbed the pack, led me out of the showers, down a corridor, and through a door I'd never noticed before into a sliver of a closet. There was a phone on the side wall and Bert told me that was where he called his bookie. Then he pointed, this will rock your socks, to the far wall and there was a peephole that Bert said looked into the showers. Under it was a ledge with crushed Coke cans on it. Under the ledge, on the floor, was a moldy towel with the initials 'J. S.' on it. Jonathan Spratt. No doubt in my mind. So, he was a pervert. Probably had taken photos from the peephole. Abraham was right in sacking him. Boy, did I have a scoop but, pop refused to print it. Said we didn't know for sure but I sure did."

Tony could see that Grant's mind was closed shut and there was no sense in arguing the point. If he hadn't listen to his father, he wasn't about to listen to him. Instead, he asked,

"Grant, do you happen to know whether Abraham Gold knew about the closet?"

"Funny, you should ask. I asked Bert that very question. He told me that when Abraham found the porn

71

pictures in Spratt's locker, he asked Bert if he knew from where they'd been taken. It was then that Bert showed Gold the closet. Well, I'm off, another meeting. Do you mind getting the tab?"

Tony nibbled on the fries but had lost his appetite. Pushed aside the plate of fries, got up and went over to the cash register to pay only to see Mabel behind the counter; she was never on cash. But what really stunned him was when she trashed his bill, and said,

"He's a slippery one. I'm sure he removed the button on his jacket's sleeve to look poor. But you got off lightly, usually he has more to eat. Detective Carson, did I hear you talking with Grant about Mr. Spratt, the gym teacher at Thackeray's?"

Caught off guard, he had no recourse but to nod. She leaned closer, her blonde hair brushed against the side of his face, and whispered,

"Mr. Spratt was a dear friend of mine. He lived upstairs in the Glendale where we lived. He got me into cheerleading in high school. I owe him so much. Did he really die of a stroke? He was so against smoking although he liked his Coke but he told me that he never had more than one can a day."

What luck. Mabel knew Spratt. And from what she had just told him, it didn't sound like she would buy

Grant's story. Or was he getting a way ahead of himself. Regardless, she knew the man and for that reason alone, Tony had no reservations in opening up to her.

"No, he didn't die of a stroke. The article in The Gazette was a cover-up. Mabel, brace yourself. Judge Lispway just opened his cold case and is questioning if Mr. Spratt was murdered. He's assigned me to look for his killer."

She blanched and leaned even closer. His heart took off like a runaway horse although surprisingly, he didn't feel like he was in the saddle. But then as enticing as Mabel was, he'd never felt as gung-ho as his heart was at that moment.

"Drop by after four, if you're not too busy. I live upstairs. I have something he gave me that I've kept all these years. It might help you, who knows? And when I have you, Linda Stonemill was just in and told me that you're looking for Fanny. She and Linda were regulars in here. I won't put you on the spot and ask for any details of your search, but you should talk to Florence Coldwell and see what she knows. I often saw her and Fanny, deep in conversation, in here and sometimes on the street."

Chapter 14

Back in his office, Tony immediately opened the top of his saltwater tank, and sprinkled a handful of flakes onto the surface. The steel-grey trigger ate first, followed by the peppermint-spined lion and finally the blue-finned queen. Sitting down, he glanced at his police college graduation certificate, an autographed color print of 'Kojak,' and then the mound of paper on his desk. Where to start? But before he moved as much as a finger, he heard a rapping at his door. Dammit, who was it this time? And when was Hussdon going to announce visitors?

"Come in."

In stepped a slip of a man, no taller than Tony, with neatly combed brown hair, twitching brown eyes behind over-sized eyeglasses, and trembling hands. Stylishly dressed in a sports jacket, dress shirt and slacks, he walked at a snail's pace and spoke even slower,

"When I signed in, she never looked at me but just pointed upstairs. Are you Detective Carson?"

Tony sat back in his chair, laced his hands behind his head, and wiped all expression off his face. "Yes, I am Detective Carson. What can I do for you?"

After a loud clearing of his throat, his visitor spoke in a squeaky voice. "I'm never this nervous but the missus told me to tell you. I had an appointment last night at five o'clock with Miss Maple, was in the bushes checking to make sure I had enough cash, when I saw a man leaving the Glendale Building. He was carrying a large, bulky rug on his right shoulder. After he rounded the corner, I heard a car start up. I went up to her apartment and her door was open, it's never open. I peeked in and left."

Tony sat up straight at his desk. Shit, he thought. Was Maple in that rolled-up rug? And if she was, for sure she was dead. Less likely that she had been drugged and rolled.

"Who are you? What's your name?"

"My name is Carl Honeywell. I live in Pinolta, and I work in men's clothing for The Bay. I know what you are going to ask if I can describe the man with the rug. But I only saw his back and it was dark. The streetlights weren't on and I wasn't wearing my glasses. He was wearing a cap, windbreaker and pants. I never saw his face. He was tall and must have been strong for the rug was bulky and he wasn't bent over."

Tony saw sweat on Honeywell's forehead and his voice was soft and hesitant. Not witness stand material but good enough for him. "Mr. Honeywell, okay, you didn't see him clearly but did you see the rug clearly? Could you identify it in a line-up although we don't have line-ups for them?"

"Oh, it was a cheap Persian knock-off rug, not a genuine one. They sell rugs like it at The Bay next to my department and sometimes, I help out although I've never sold one. I didn't tell you but when I peeked into her apartment, I noticed the hallway rug was missing. I often thought she should have had a genuine Persian. They are so much better."

Damnit, he thought. That clinched it. Both Honeywell and Stonemill had noticed that her hallway rug was missing. Maple was dead. And her next stop was anyone's guess.

"Thank you for coming, Mr. Honeywell. You've been a big help. As I may need to contact you in the future, make sure your name, address and phone number are in the registry."

Mr. Honeywell left but at the door, stopped and turned around. "Detective, I'm going to keep an eye on the Glendale Building at night. You never know."

Chapter 15

No sooner had Mr. Honeywell exited, than Dr. Ken Neckroff, the coroner, walked into Tony's office, unannounced. What else was new? He should have an office on the ground floor before one ever got to the sign-in desk. Ken was a beanpole of a man at six-foot plus, blue eyes and parchment-white skin. After his older brother had died of a melanoma, he had avoided the sun and never sported a tan. In his black civies, he looked thinner than he already was. Without as much as a 'how do you do,' he tossed the Eaton's T-shirt at him.

"Tony, another of your puzzles. There are three blood stains on it. Two are fresh, within 24 hours, and one is as old as the hills. There are two bleeders. Each with their own fresh stain and one of them the owner of the old, not so fresh stain. How old you ask and ask you will? Well, as old as the T-shirt. I'm going out on a limb and will say at least two decades old. But what really is a stunner is that there are no bodies in the morgue. What gives?"

Shit, he thought, nothing made sense. How did the blood stains of two separate people get on the T-shirt? One of them had to be Arabelle Sirene. Ramsay hadn't reported any other missing patients. Who could the other be? A blood stain was not much of a lead. Was he dealing with a serial killer? But why us an old T-shirt? Again, nothing made sense. Okay, he wasn't giving up but where to start? Why not the red clay flats and see what was there. As far as telling Ken about Sirene, they were on a first name basis and he had no reservation.

"Ken, I found the T-shirt this morning around the neck of a dead female patient by the name of Arabelle Sirene. She was beached on a sand bar in the Osprey River. Don't ask how she managed to but she went over High Falls and, I'm sure, is at the bottom of the whirlpool. I got Gold to order a bathyscaphe to drag up her body on the lie that she was the missing Miss Maple. Again, don't ask me for the details."

Ken smirked and then laughed and said,

"Your secret is safe with me. I never told you but my brother who died of the melanoma was schizophrenic. He'd go on long, solitary walks to be alone with his voices and the walks cost him his life. Life is a bitch. By the way, I know what a bathyscaphe is, and good luck with fishing in a whirlpool. If you ever do find her, I'd like to be there and hear how you're going to explain it to Gold."

Chapter 16

As soon as Ken left, Tony got out his print kit and headed to his car. After he parked in the Osprey Hospital's lot for the third time that day, a record he didn't want to repeat, he got the print kit out of his trunk and headed up-river, past the eddy with flies still hovering above it. It was another glorious Indian summer day: azure sky, cobalt-blue river, technicolor in the leaves and a warm breeze.

He passed several signs flagging the Bruce Trail, Canada's longest and oldest hiking trail. Soon, the riverbank on his side dwindled seamlessly into the shoreline, while on the opposite side there was a good six feet of nettles, burdocks and clumps of yellow-flowered nut grass. Tony whistled an old Huck Finn tune as he walked, and soon spotted patches of rose-coloured weeds on the other side, a good sign he was on the perimeter of the red clay flats.

Around a sharp bend, he came upon rapids: surging black water, frothing white caps, and the crashing sound of waves against rocks. If Sirene's body been dumped above them, he was not yet at the red clay flats, it was a miracle that she had made it through them in one piece. After another corner, and the river was a slow-moving, soundless current. The day's heat was starting to get to him, sweat was dripping off his forehead. He shed and carried his jacket. Then he spotted a rusted metal bridge in the distance that spanned the river to a stretch of the red clay flats. He knew they had to be on the other side and had wondered how she had gotten over to them. Mystery solved. He would have to see if that was where she had been garroted?

The bridge was more rust than metal and its floorboards were worn thin and loose. He stopped and explored his options but the only one he had was to cross on the bridge. Sirene had crossed it and she had weighed a lot less than he did. But would it take his weight, the unanswered question? Nothing to do but go for it. Taking a deep breath, he then shot across two-third's of the bridge, leaped, and landed on both feet in a cloud of red clay dust. He had made it and was he in luck for quite close to where he had landed, were a set of small footprints that led to a crumbling, cement boat ramp. It had more cracks than Humpty Dumpty.

Following the footprints, he came to the boat ramp: a mishmash of shoe prints, rose-coloured lichen, yellowing crabgrass, black skid marks, and coyote tracks. They ended on the bottom of the ramp in a crimson swirl. Had it been made by her feet twirling around and around, touching down too infrequently to sustain life? If so, that was where Sirene had been strangled, a met her Waterloo, her killer. That meant that her killer had been on the boat ramp. Why hadn't she avoided him like the plague? What was he doing there? No way was he waiting for her. It was too late in the year to launch a boat.

In the mid-day sun, the ramp was a skillet. Fanning his face with his hands, Tony plodded up to the top edge of the ramp where a narrow two-lane road from the east came to a dead end. It had car and boat trailer tracks with the odd boot print, but nothing jumped out at him. Sweating more, a combination of heat and frustration, he threaded his way down the other side of the ramp to the bottom without a single scratch from the over-hanging wild roses.

The grey, sleek body of an osprey with tucked-in wings splashed down in front of him, and then rocketed out of the river, a good ten yards down from where it had landed. There was a large piece of grey cloth in its beak. Rising in the air, the osprey must have felt as frustrated as he was for it let go of the flapping piece of cloth, realizing that it was no fish. Tony watched the cloth hang glide down and surface on the river before it snagged on an overhanging bush. He jumped off of the boat ramp onto the riverbank, and raced across red clay deadpan to it. When he picked it up, he saw "Province of Ontario" stamped on the piece of cloth with ragged edges.

81

It must have come from the top that Arabelle Sirene was wearing although there were no sleeves. When he'd found her, she had been naked. Until that moment, he had not thought of what had happened to her to lose her clothing but when he did, his blood curdled. The cold-blooded son-of-a bitch had torn off her clothing and raped her before, after or during when he'd strangled her. More than ever he had to retrieve her body, and swore that he would catch her killer if it was the last thing he did. He was fuming mad, so mad, the sweat on his flushed face evaporated. Into the evidence inner pocket in his jacket went the piece of clothing.

Walking back to the boat ramp, he tight roped along its edge on his way back to the bridge when he came to a jarring stop. How could he have missed it but he had? A bare footprint, too long and too large to be Sirene's, was framed in a bed of lichen. It looked as fresh as Sirene's prints. No sooner had he thought it, could it be Miss Maple's, than he dismissed it. Hadn't Linda Stonemill told him that Maple wore a size 5 boot. The footprint was too long to be a fit. He felt coldness snake down his back. There was another body in the river. What good it would do was not on his mind when he took a print of the bare foot impression and placed it in the evidence pocket alongside the cloth.

Chapter 17

No sooner had Tony hit the southern town limits, than he saw a white clapboard bungalow with a blue '69 Ford Mustang convertible parked out front. For years, he'd had his mind set that someday he'd own a Mustang convertible. If he ever won the lottery, that's what he'd buy before he even cashed in his ticket. Beside the house, was a grove of lindens around an imposing granite statue of Dr. Norman Bethune. As soon as he saw the statue, he knew it had to be Florence Coldwell's house. She had nursed in China with Dr. Norman Bethune and later, served in Mao's army. On returning home, she had joined the Salvation Army and hadn't her brigade rescued Hussdon who manned their front desk. There was no end to the stories about Coldwell the likes of Paul Bunyan. As he was driving past her home, ogling the Mustang, he recalled that Mabel had told him that Coldwell had known Maple, and he parked in front of the Mustang, careful not to bump into it.

At the front door, he rapped and almost simultaneously, the door opened and there stood none other than Florence Coldwell. He'd met her several times and knew her by sight but had never talked directly with her. She was a tall, heavy-set woman whose large hands were lightly powdered in flour. Although she was wearing a brown, silk Chinese-looking top and matching pants with open-toed sandals and had served in China, she was not Chinese. She was as white as he was. He always found that interesting although no one else remarked on it. When he saw tears in her eyes, he had second thoughts but she spoke before he could turn and leave,

"Detective Carson, is there a problem? I'm sure this is not a social visit. Has something happened to Camelia?"

"No, nothing has happened. I just wanted to know if you knew anything about Miss Fanny Maple who's gone missing. But I see that I caught you at a bad time. I'll come back later, it's not urgent."

"No, no, you won't. Come in, I insist. And call me Florence, I'm only major when I'm on duty. I've had my cry. Linda Stonemill just told me about poor Fanny and didn't hold out much hope for her. I don't promise I can help but I'm not sending you away, empty-handed. If nothing else, I just baked some bread and would love it if you would have a piece. I hate always eating on my own."

Coldwell led him into a small living room that was crammed with a sofa, La-Z-Boy, reading lamp, and a pine table with an old, leather-bound Bible on it. On the walls were black-and-whites of Chinese temples, rice paddies, soldiers in Red Army Uniforms, and a young girl and Chinese boy, arm-in-arm. A glass case with a Browning .32 pistol caught Tony's interest and, when he stepped closer, she said,

"It's a Chinese knock-off, with an eight-inch barrel and sights tailor-made for Chinese eyes. I smuggled it through Canadian Customs, but don't you tell anyone."

She pointed to the sofa and when he sat down, she began, "Detective Carson, about Fanny, I haven't much to report. She was as close-mouthed as they come. What I can tell you was she was a bundle of secrets with the Great Wall around them. Gave up trying to get inside and just listened to myself talking. I'll get you a cup of tea and a piece of bread, fresh out of the oven. I hope you're not one of those who's sworn off white bread. They make me sick."

What she had said about secrets jogged his mind that he had the VHS tape that Maple had made in his trunk. For sure, he was going to have to play it. As Coldwell marched out of the room, he wondered if she ever just walked. About calling her Florence, he hadn't taken up her invitation. Curiosity drew Tony back to the photo of a tall, gangly young girl in a summer dress with her arm around a short, fat Chinese boy in a T-shirt and shorts. The girl had to be Florence and the boy, a friend.

When he heard her voice behind him, he was caught off-guard and jumped.

"That's me and my brother, Johnnie. I was adopted into a Chinese home. Here, have a bite and I'll tell you all about myself. Unlike Fanny, I work hard at being an open book. Secrets are shackles, I always say."

Florence placed down the jam sandwiches and cups of tea on the pine table on the table, beside the Bible, and beckoned for him to serve himself while she continued.

"My biological parents died in a car crash when I was ten. No relatives and was I fortunate to be adopted by Chinese parents. They loved me, like their own. Shortly after I arrived, my new mother gave birth to my brother, she'd been childless until then. And shortly after that, my new father was killed in an industrial accident. No such thing as workman's safety for the Chinese in those days. God, what they endured and without a word of complaint. Johnnie was a fat kid and I looked out for him as he was often bullied. Kids can be savage, don't kid yourself. I was so proud when he was hired as a gym teacher. Yes he was fat but was he flexible and strong. I still can't believe and am so sad that he died of a stroke at school."

When he heard that Johnnie had died of a stroke, Tony felt his neck hairs tingle. Was Johnnie Coldwell one and the same as Johnathan Spratt, a fat Chinaman? But how could that be? They didn't have the same surname. With nothing to lose, he asked,

"Your brother wasn't Jonathan Spratt, was he?"

Coldwell looked at him in amazement. "Yes, Johnnie Spratt was my brother. I know what you're thinking. How can that be if my name is Coldwell. But it was Spratt. In China, I was married to a Canadian surgeon, Coldwell, not Bethune. A week later, he was killed. But Tony, how did you know my brother?"

Christ, he thought, she was Spratt's sister. How to tell her that her brother had not died of a stroke? After he gulped, his throat was desert dry, he began and this time, he called her Florence. "Your brother didn't die of a stroke. Florence, your brother was found shot in the showers at school. Abraham Gold, the police chief, thought your brother had taken his life and the school didn't want it getting out…"

"But that's preposterous. Johnnie would never have done that. He was a Christian."

"You're right, he didn't take his life. This morning, Judge Lispway determined your brother had been murdered and asked me to look for his killer."

She abruptly sat down on the sofa, picked up a wooden sandalwood fan, thrashed the air over her head, and with tears streaming down her flushed cheeks, screamed,

"Who would shoot Johnnie? He wouldn't hurt a fly. He was a God-fearing man who lived by the Bible. I questioned that he'd died of a stroke but never thought he'd been murdered." Still thrashing the air, she opened the Bible with her other hand, and handed him a note. "Johnnie sent me his Bible when I was in China, just before he died. This note was in it. Read it and I'll decipher it for you."

"Flo, good news. I've met a young woman, Mary, and we are getting along just fine. I feel so happy when I'm with her. At school, Peter is on his last term and will graduate. I will miss him. He has no father and has always looked up to me. But I have bad news. There is an evil person at school, Cain. He's taking pictures of naked kids and I'm sure is doing worse things. I am gathering evidence and plan to expose him."

Tony could have cheered. Grant was dead wrong. Spratt was no pervert. No way, he was a whistleblower. Was Lispway ever right in opening the cold case? A man's reputation was in the balance, and didn't some say that one's reputation was as sacred as life itself. Tony was on the fence in that regard. Quickly, he looked at her, and she cleared her throat and spoke,

"My brother had trouble recalling surnames. He renamed everyone after someone in the Bible. That name he always remembered. I was the Angel Gabriel. Mary, his girlfriend, I assume was the blessed Virgin Mary. Peter, the apostle, was his pupil and from the sounds of it, a protégé. As for Cain, no better name for a killer."

Chapter 18

Outside of Coldwell's, the clouds were being whipped into a grey sludge by a gale-force winds. The Indian summer had been wiped clean from the sky's slate. Fall had started with a vengeance and was fast making up for lost time. No sooner was he inside his car, than rain and sleet slammed against his windshield. With his wipers at full blast, he could barely see past the Malibu's hood. And then just like that, the rain dropped to a gentle pitter-patter on his windshield. Wisps of warm air from his heater chipped away at the chill that had knifed through his car. At least it worked, unlike the water heater at home.

Before he knew it, he was in the Dogpatch section of King Street populated by 'For Rent' and 'For Sale' signs, padlocks, graffiti, boarded-up windows, and nailed-shut doors. When he spotted Joe's Poolhall and Gym, he parked out front. While the poolhall was at street level, the gym was down a set of stone stairs, imported from a quarry in Italy near where Joe had been born. Built pre-World War I, its bricks and stones had turned a grimy grey, and its sign had more mold than lettering. But it had outlasted Vic Tanny's Gym.

As Tony got out of his car, he spotted Carl Robins' Ford pick-up on the street. And just like that, he switched from working out to questioning Robins. For all the good that it would do for he already knew what his alibi was going to be. Slowly, he walked down the stone steps that were wet and slippery. The gym was short on light but then there were no windows and the fluorescents were flickering. Along the sides were heavy bags, speed bags, and rope-ladders. In the middle, was a raised professional boxing ring and behind it were the locker rooms and the showers. At that time of day, it was crowded with men in white shorts and T-shirts while the two boxers in the ring wore red shorts and black T-shirts.

Joe, the owner, was pacing in front of the ring, yelling orders, and puffing with frustration on a cigar. He was a short stub of a man with a balding head, gorilla arms and stove-pipe legs. Tony had never seen him wearing anything but a navy blue, un-pressed suit, and a T-shirt with his home colors on it: red, white, and green. When Joe saw Tony, he raised his right hand to grab Tony's attention, and mouthed for him not to leave before he spoke with him.

Then Tony heard, "Carson, bet you can't do as well as I'm doing."

Speak of the devil. To his left was Robins who was whacked away at a speed bag with bare fists, no timing and no finesse. He was of average height and except for large, un-co-ordinated hands, had the build of a pencil pusher. His large mouth was as restless as were his squirrel-eyes. Tony couldn't resist. He stood up to the bag, and bare-fisted it with rhythm and finesse, without a single jam. Stepping closer, he machine-gunned it before jumping back. Carl's face never lost its sneer. Looking down at Carl's runners, Tony swore under his breath. They were no more than a size 9, max. How he had wished they were a size 14?

"You got lucky, Carson. I know why you're here. Nigel warned me you're investigating the Chink's case. Well, you're wasting your time. I'm in the clear."

"Carl, I'll decide that. Why don't we go into the locker room for a chat?"

Carl's face slipped into a half-assed smirk, and he muttered out of the corner of his mouth, "Only too willing Detective Carson. Sure, I'll go into the locker room but, like I said, you're wasting your time."

Lockers lined both sides of the narrow room with a long, wooden bench in between. Carl pointed to a locker whose door was wide open, and sneered,

"That's Lefty Lowland's locker. What a washed-up has-been. I went two rounds with him before he hit the canvas. Would you believe it, at noon we had the official weighing-in of Joe's next hot-shot contender, the

East End Kid, and didn't Lefty pay for beer for everyone with a shitload of 50s. He's moving down East, today. Good riddance."

Tony's ears picked up when he heard that Lefty was throwing around 50s. Hadn't Maple been paid in 50s? And wasn't Lefty the super in her building? Was that why Joe wanted to speak with him? Joe was no fool although he couldn't say the same for Carl. In the locker, Tony spotted a lone jade plant on the top shelf. Carl turned to face him, legs apart and hands on hips.

"Carl let's cut to the chase. Your Colt .45 shot Mr. Spratt…"

"I wasn't even at school that day, I was on a dig…"

"Yes, yes, I know all about it. Stonemill already told me."

"Well then, why are you bothering me? The Chink stole it from the trophy case when the damn fool returned to school. And who cares, he was a faggot. I saw him take off his towel in the showers, the queer. He got what he deserved."

When he heard 'Chink,' Tony's blood boiled. He was so close to losing it. But he wanted to hear more about this towel-dropping and said, "Oh yeah, when

Spratt dropped his towel, you weren't in the peephole, closet, were you, Carl? And don't try and weasel out of this one."

Carl's face turned the color of a dirty rag. After he glanced at the door to make sure they were alone, he shifted from foot to foot in a nervous tap dance.

"If I tell you, you can't tell the others. Believe it or not, I was only there once, I swear. You know me, I'm no peeper."

"You have my word, Carl; I'll tell no one. Now, out with it."

Carl sat down on the bench, checked again that they were alone before he spoke in a quivering voice. His bravado wasn't even skin-deep.

"I was in the VIP shower. I know I wasn't allowed there, but the water was hotter and I like a hot shower. I saw there was a brick removed. Always knew the bloody principal was a fairy. So, I peek. No crime in that. I saw the Chink yakking away to Reggie who was taking a shower. Suddenly the Chink yelped and jumped like he'd been stung by a bee, and his towel dropped. Was he hung! I heard, 'Faggot. Dirty faggot,' and in walked Abraham Gold and the principal. Gold screamed at Spratt, 'Pick up your towel, and show me what's in your locker, faggot.' Then he turned to Reggie and spat,

94

'Namby-Pamby, I'd tan your sorry ass if you were my kid.'"

Questions tumbled in Tony's mind, like numbered balls in a bingo machine. "You said Reggie. Are you referring to Reginald Moorehouse?"

"Dummy, everyone knows that. He was the Chink's only friend at school. Two birds of the same feather, if you ask me."

"Any idea who yelled 'faggot?'"

Carl licked his lips and then shrugged his shoulders. "I dunno. The voice was too deep to be the principal's and not deep enough to be Gold's. But hey, lets not forget the Chink was about to come on to Reggie, big time. The bit about jumping was all an act to drop his towel. Why do they always go after the good-looking ones who have no father?"

Tony was not off who had yelled, 'Faggot.' Had to be someone in the other peephole closet. The showers were a peepers' delight. Who knew about the other closet, Carl didn't and Grant hadn't until he was shown it? Two nosey parkers. And he wasn't buying Carl's thinking Spratt's jumping was an act. Too coincidental with the yelling, 'Faggot,' and Gold being in the vicinity. A set-up? Weren't the cans and the towel in the

95

closet also a set-up? Meanwhile, Carl was looking like he could bolt, any minute, and he wasn't finished.

"Carl, where were you on Monday afternoon and evening?"

Without hesitation, Carl rhymed off what sounded like a prepared spiel. "On Monday afternoon, I attended Bruce Liefson's initiation, and after that, I went with Petula to a PTA meeting for our son. Ask Waverly as he was at the initiation and my wife about the PTA meeting. I know you don't believe me. You coppers are all the same. Well, I hate to disappoint you but I'm in the clear. And now I'm leaving. You got nothing on me, Carson."

Carl began to walk away but as he passed Lefty's open locker, he grabbed the jade plant and bolted out the door. The brazen sleaze-ball. Who but a complete idiot steals in front of a cop? And how had the likes of Carl ended up with a gem of a wife? But as the locker room's door slammed shut, it flung open, and in strode Joe. His cigar was spewing black smoke and he snarled out of the corner of his mouth,

"Paisano, did Carl just swipe Lefty's lucky plant?"

"You got it."

"Well, Lefty has no one to blame but himself. He left it behind when he cleaned out his locker, today. How he loved to tell the story of how a Chinaman had given it to him for good luck, and how he'd misplaced it on the eve of the fight with the world heavyweight champion. Or else, he would have won. What bullshit. I know for a fact that Gus, his trainer, gave it to him. When he and his Chinese gal split, she left him with the plant and he wanted nothing to do with it. And Gus was as Chinese as I am. But long story short. I'm worried about Lefty. He was throwing around 50s and I don't have to tell you where he lives."

"Joe, I'm on my way to pay Lefty a visit."

Chapter 19

Outside, it wasn't raining but there was an Arctic chill in the air. Where had the warm, summer breeze gone? Tony buttoned up his damp overcoat, cursing that it wasn't waterproof or windproof. It was a short drive to the Glendale apartment building that stood out like a gargantuan, dark tombstone against the grey sky. The same fliers, dirt and leaves were on the floor of the foyer. This time, the inner door with the busted lock was wide-open. Stepping into the hallway, he smelled cabbage and heard Lefty's TV blaring louder than the last time. Why would a man leaving town, have on his television?

He pulled out and cocked his Glock, inched along the wall until he came to the side of Lefty's door jamb. When he pressed hard with the toe of his right boot against the bottom of the door, it opened. His heart pounded. Peering into the room's semi-darkness, the lone outside window was curtained, he saw that no furniture and no empty beer bottles on the floor had been overturned. Turning off the television with the barrel end of the gun, only magnified the sound of his beating heart that was unnerving.

The inner hallway was darker than the living room. On the right was an open bathroom door and on the left, a closed door. At the end, there was an open doorframe leading into the kitchen. Flattening against the left wall, he turtled toward the closed door, had to be Lefty's bedroom where if Tony was lucky, he was still packing. The squeaking sound of his boots on the parquet flooring was louder than his heartbeat. When he got to the side of the door, he listened but heard no sounds from inside. His right index finger tightened against the cold steel of the trigger and he shouted,

"Lefty, it's Detective Tony Carson. I know you stole Maple's money. Come out with your hands up and the court will go easy on you."

No response; not even a faint echo. "Lefty, I know you're in there. Make it easy on yourself. Come out with your hands up and let's discuss it."

Again, no response. Should he call for back-up? Instead, he grabbed the knob with his left hand, and to his surprise, that door too opened. Without hesitation, he catapulted into the room, gun lowered to chest-high, only to freeze in mid-air.

On the opposite brick wall, a gallery of awards and newspaper articles, was a splatter of bright-red blood, splinters of skull bone, and gobs of brain mush. Sitting up in bed, with his back to the wall, there was no headboard, was Lefty Lowland. All that was left of his head was a boney saucer, suspended between two gaping eye sockets and a right ear. The rest of his head, blood and gore, was on the wall and on his black suit and T-shirt. Tony didn't smell powder burns. He must have been shot from the doorway. The shooter had never given him a chance. In the biggest fight of his life, he never as much as raised his fists. This was no home invasion. This was cold-blooded murder.

Tony mentally traced a line from the middle of where the top of his head should have been to the wall, and spotted a blood-filled circle, the size of a dumdum bullet. If the outside wall was double bricked, he was in luck to retrieve the bullet. Then he looked around the bedroom. All the pulled-open drawers of the bureau were empty. The twin doors of the armoire in the corner were open, and it was as empty as the drawers. Also, he didn't see a single suitcase, anywhere, even under the bed. The killer must have made off with them. When he searched in Lefty's back pockets, he found no wallet. The killer had been thorough.

Back in the living room, Tony put on gloves, picked up the phone, and called the coroner's office to report another murder, to dust for prints and to dig for the bullet in the brick wall. He took one last look around, and left. In the foyer, he closed the inner door, for all the good that it would do. The killer was long gone with the suitcase or suitcases. No one was on the street and there were no cars, about. When he recalled, it had been as deserted when he arrived as when he was leaving. So much for an eyewitness.

Chapter 20

Reginald Moorehouse left school early to avoid a contentious Identification and Placement Review Committee meeting. With his pounding headache, he could not have faced an incensed mother whose son with a significant learning disability was still on the waiting list to receive special assistance. As he got into his Porsche, he noticed his hands were shaking, and immediately worried if anyone had mistaken him for an alcoholic and that he was leaving early for a snort. Ridiculous, he told himself. Why was his mind so cruel although he had to admit that people were just as cruel? Fumbling with the car key, he hit the wrong frequency on his FM radio, and heard Tom Jones belting out "What's New Pussycat?" It was so vulgar and so loud. His head felt that it would explode. And to think that it was his mother's favorite. Quickly he managed to press the 'off' button and to turn on his car that was thankfully, soundless. He headed to the peace and quiet of Peaceful Meadows for his weekly visit at his mother's grave.

After he'd parked and removed his mother's last vial of Chanel No. 5 from the glove compartment, he walked over to her five-foot granite cross, his mother's exact height. When she had died, it had been her wish to replace her husband's and son's gravestone with the cross. All three names were on it. His older brother Adam had drowned in a quarry when Reginald was just seven. He was his mother's favorite but not Reginald's. Adam had tormented him, endlessly. As for his father, he knew next to nothing about him as he had died when Reginald was just a newborn. How he wished that his mother would have talked about him but she hadn't. She said it was too painful although his mother was not the crying type.

Looking around to make sure he was alone, he had seen another car in the lot and there was an overflow lot as well, he silently read the inscription that had not been on the tombstone. "The Lord is my Shepherd and I lay down in Green Pastures." Tears filled his eyes, and trickled down his cheeks. Out loud, he said, "Mother, I love you," and to himself he whispered, "I wish you would just once have said that you loved me."

And then he heard and jumped. "Pardon me, Mr. Moorehouse, did you attend Thackery's High School?"

Reginald froze. Someone was behind him. It had been a woman's voice. Slowly he turned and faced a tallish, plain-looking woman with grey hair. She was dressed in a neatly pressed grey jacket, black shirt and pants. When he saw an old Bible in her right hand, he cringed. He wasn't in the mood to listen to a Jehovah Witness preaching doom and gloom. But she had warm blue eyes and was asking about his high school. No J. W. had ever asked him that and just like him, obedient to a fault, he answered her,

"Yes, I was a student at Thackeray's, many moons ago, and now if you don't mind..."

"Did you know my late brother? He was the gym teacher there. His name was Jonathan Spratt. I have his Bible. I was just visiting our mother's grave."

He felt off-balance, grabbed the cross, and when he did, he dropped the last vial of his mother's perfume. It smashed against the stone cross. Why could it have not landed on the ground? If he'd not been so clumsy, he would not have dropped it. His head throbbed and he felt so wretchedly guilty.

"Oh, you don't look well, Mr. Moorehouse, not at all. Here, I have some water; don't worry, I haven't drunk out of it. I do try to be a good Samaritan."

She produced a yellow thermos from her knapsack, poured a goodly amount of water into its plastic top and handed it to him. As he drank it slowly, he savored its coldness and began to feel less dizzy and collected himself although he never let go of the cross. Who was she really? Spratt had never told him he had a sister. And she wasn't Chinese. Why was she saying that Spratt was her brother? Was she crazy? She had to be and just his luck to be stuck with her in his mother's graveyard. Why had he said that he had been at Thackeray's?

"Oh, I know what you're thinking. How could I be his sister and not be Chinese? I was adopted into the Spratt home when I was a young girl. My name used to be Florence Spratt. I married in China and I'm now Coldwell. You may have heard of me. I make it into the papers, every so often? And I almost forgot, Johnnie called me his Angel Gabriel."

He gasped. Angel Gabriel was his sister. How could he forget? Spratt had talked endlessly of her but he had no idea that the Angel Gabriel was his sister. He called everyone by a biblical made-up name and never said who they really were. Hadn't he said that the Angel was living and working in China. Well, Coldwell had spent time in China and had the statue of Bethune to prove it. So, she wasn't crazy. She really was Spratt's sister. When he returned the cup, she smiled at him with those warm eyes. He could see that she was a nice person. As nice as Spratt had been? Time would tell.

Then he heard, "And did my brother have a biblical name for you? I prefer biblical as opposed to code."

That took him down memory lane, if he already wasn't there. But whenever Spratt had called him it, he's always felt uncomfortable. To be honest, he didn't think that he deserved it. While he'd never told anyone the name that Spratt called him, he figured he could tell his sister. She was asking and suddenly, he didn't want to disappoint her, if the truth be told.

Blushing, he said, "Peter. I always wondered why but I knew that he thought a lot of me although not as much as I thought of him. We had a kinship, you see. They called both of us names that I can't repeat."

She smiled, more warmly than before. When had a woman last smiled at him? "I am so, so fortunate to have met you. I never thought I would ever know who my Johnnie called Peter. You have made my day, well, a little. I was having the worst day of my life until I met you. They say God looks after us, and so He does. You are just as I pictured 'Peter.' A caring, sensitive man. I won't ask you what you do for a living, everyone asks that. It's so trite. I just know like my brother that you care for people. And I now have a question for you. Did my brother ever mention anyone by the name of Cain?"

Reginald thought long and hard, he so wanted to please her, but out of the blue, he began to feel dizzy, light-headed, and held on tightly to the hard granite of the cross that he was still holding. What was happening.

"No and I have to go. Sorry." He walked slowly, ever so slowly, to his car, and never once looked back.

Chapter 21

When Tony signed in at the front desk, Camelia Hussdon looked up at him, and smiled weakly, but nevertheless, a smile. Her first. And when she smiled, she was a different woman, well, a different looking woman. But then there was nothing uglier than tension. He wondered if that meant that she was going to announce visitors, although he had yet to hear her speak. Slowly he walked up the stairs and down the hall to Nigel's office, rapped three times, and entered. Nigel, seated as always behind his desk, glared at Tony and snapped.

"Well, what is it, Carson? I'll tell you straight up, I'm not in the mood for any more bad news."

What was he going to do? Turn around and leave. Nigel had to know, and if he didn't tell him then, he'd be cursing him when he read it in The Gazette. And he had to keep his boss on his good side for there was always the matter of the bathyscaphe that was hanging over his head. "I just came from Lefty Lowland's apartment. He'd been shot and whoever did it, got away with his suitcases and whatever was in them."

That caught Gold's attention, and he sat up, straight in his chair. "Doesn't surprise me. At Joe's, I saw him throwing around 50s like a bigshot. The poor sap doesn't even own a car. I'm sure whatever dough he had, that he threw it away at Joe's. Always played the big shot. He was a so-so boxer who got lucky once and never let anyone forget. Whoever shot him may wish he hadn't when he opens h suitcases and finds nothing but dirty underwear."

Nigel had a habit of jumping on a horse and riding it for all it was worth. Never would he admit the horse was a loser. But as far as Tony thought, it was all for the best. This way he wouldn't connected Lefty to Miss Maple's money or to her murder. Yes, Lefty had robbed her. Of that he was certain. And he was just as certain that he hadn't robbed her. But Gold, if he thought he had robbed her, would for sure jump on he was the killer. And there would be no changing his mind.

"Tell Grant at The Gazette that Lefty Lowland was robbed and murdered, and be sure to tell him I sent you. He's always complaining we tell him nothing. Oh, I've ordered that bathyscaphe. Can't wait to try it out. Coast Guard will deliver it. I want you to be there. Brock is busy on some undercover work."

Chapter 22

Tony parked in front of The Gazette, behind Grant's Ambassador. Even though, it wasn't that late, King Street was almost deserted. The Osprey hospital's parking lot would have been busier. He could see why Petula Robins had opened a rental division. There was no aroma of fries or burgers in the air but then, Mabel's was closing. When he entered The Gazette, chain-smoking Judy Fontaine, behind the beige linoleum counter, eyed him with anything but friendliness. She was wearing a blue visor and matching navy-blue coveralls with long sleeves and the black band on her left upper arm, and actually looked spiffy. But no way was he going to say a word. Judy would always see a dark side to anything he said. The presses out back were on break, and he didn't have to raise his voice,

"Judy, any chance I can see Grant? I have something to report."

"He just returned from his weekly visit to his pop, but I have no idea if he's free. He never tells me his schedule. Wait."

She pressed a button and after no more than a minute, Grant stepped out into the hallway. As soon as he spotted Tony, he shouted and beckoned, "Detective, come in. Just the man I wanted to see."

Grant disappeared back into his office, humming a Wagnerian Opera tune, off-key. While he had a nose for news, he had no ear for music. Tony followed and closed the door behind him. Grant strode up to his standing desk with the Narcissus, picked up his pipe, and puffed out a cloud of Flying Dutchman smoke. No choking, this time. Then he erupted,

"Well, Detective, give me the full report. Was Miss Maple in the whirlpool? Did you manage to fish her out? How was she murdered? My readers need to know."

"Sorry to disappoint you, Grant, but I have nothing to report on Miss Maple other than Gold has ordered a bathyscaphe. Believe it or not, but Gold sent me to give you hot news."

"Really, well let's hear it. I'm all ears. I can't wait and don't disappoint me."

"An hour ago, I found Lefty Lowland in his apartment. He'd been shot, and whoever killed him, made off with his suitcases. Apparently, Lefty was throwing around 50s at Joe's and, while Gold is sure he was penniless, his killer thought otherwise."

Grant's jaw dropped and he let go of his pipe only to catch it before it hit the floor. When he spoke after he'd collected himself, it was in a hushed voice.

"Poor Lefty, the greatest Canadian boxer we ever had. He came so close to winning the world heavy-weight title. You say that he was shot and robbed. Where exactly did you find him? My readers have an insatiable appetite for all the details."

"He was shot while sitting up in bed. He must have known the shooter as he hadn't raised as much as a finger to protect himself."

Crimson with anger, Grant puffed out a storm cloud of smoke, while his fingers drummed out a military marching tune, not off-key this time. "I'm going to write our champ a hell of a send-off. I'll have Lefty putting up a hell of a fight, his best by far, and just as he was about to knock-out the killer, he was shot. His killer had an unfair advantage. I'll even post a reward for his killer's capture. But as police, you can't claim the reward."

Tony was reminded of what his father had told him that under Grant's pop that The Gazette could be depended on to get the facts straight, but the same could not be said for his son who leaned a little too far to suit his father in the direction of the sensational.

Chapter 23

Tony hung a left on Elm Street, turned into the court-house's parking lot, and pulled up next to Judge Lispway's Gran Torino. Inside, Betty on the front desk pointed without a word to the white door, and, as he walked down the glassed-in hallway, he berated himself for not making time to look at the VHS that she had given him. Although, he had been on a timeline with not a minute to spare. Hard to believe what he had accomplished that day. Shadows from the elm trees darkened the hall and before he knew it, he was at the black door, almost ran right into it. When he spoke, he felt his heart pounding and knew he was uptight.

"Judge Lispway, it's Detective Carson. Are you in?"

"Come in, Detective."

It was then he realized that what had happened to Lefty must have rattled him, for he sensed relief when he heard Lispway's voice. This time when he knocked, there was someone home and he was very much alive. Lispway was standing behind his desk, barely visible in the gloom from the elm trees that had pooled around him. His robes were lacklustre, his watery-brown eyes were faded, but his voice was clear.

"Have a seat, Tony. I've had a marathon of a day. There's nothing more tiring than sifting through words for the truth. It's like panning for gold. Lots of sand and not much gold. If I'm not mistaken, from the look on your face, you have something to report on the Jonathan Spratt case. Make my day as they say in the movies."

They both sat down and Saul picked up and resumed smoking the Lucky Strike that had been smoldering in the ash tray beside his Bible.

"I got lucky. Cornelius Grant at The Gazette was there when Abraham Gold arrived on Spratt's crime scene. Gold didn't smell powder burns which had to be there if it had been a self-inflicted gunshot, but claimed the showers had washed them away. According to Grant, Spratt was not that close to the showers to even get wet. Both he and his father were sure that Spratt had been murdered."

"Really, I like the sounds of that. I value Grant's father's opinion. Good to know I hadn't sent you on a wild goose chase especially when I'd named the Amigos as suspects. Did Grant have any other findings of interest?"

"Oh yes, it wasn't in the photo, but there was a size-14 bloody shoeprint to one side, near the stairs into the living quarters. Gold claimed it was his although Grant was sure he'd never been over there. Grant more than insinuated that it was the killer's shoe print. So far, I've ruled out Stonemill and Robins; they have a conjoint alibi and neither wears a size-14 shoe."

"You can rule out Nigel Gold. Abraham used to call him Small Foot."

"That's not all, Grant was shown on the day after the shooting a closet with a voyeur's peephole into the showers. On the floor, was a towel with the initials "J. S." on it. In Grant's mind, there was not a shred of doubt that Spratt was a pederast. Also, he found out that Abraham Gold had also been shown the closet, after he found the incriminating photos in Spratt's locker."

Lispway put down his cigarette. He looked gaunt, frustrated, and sighed, "I don't get it. Grant is an intelligent man. And yet, it never dawns on his that Spratt could have been set-up and the photos and towel, planted. If the closet had a peephole, then the photos of the boys' rear ends could have been taken from there, and going out on a limb, Spratt could have been shot from there. Any luck in locating Robins' Colt?"

"Yes, it's a match for the bullet that killed Spratt. Don't ask for I have no idea how the killer got his hands on it." Tony kept a straight face as he dropped the

bombshell. "Saul, brace yourself. I just found out that
Florence Coldwell is Spratt's adopted sister. And before
he died, he sent her his bible and it she found a note that
she showed me. Good news. He was about to blow the
whistle on an evil one in the school who took dirty
pictures and harmed young girls."

That jolted Lispway and his mouth half-opened
in disbelief. As he went to butt out his cigarette, his
hand shook so much that he dropped it on the floor.
Then he laced his hands behind his head and in his eyes
was a burning vigor.

"Good work Tony. Should show Grant the note.
No, no, his type would say it was a lie. There's a killer
out there Tony, who has gotten away with murder. We'll
have to change that. Tony, I thank God that I chose you
to lead the investigation."

Tony didn't know how to respond. The more he
tried to appear cool, the more he blushed. At that
moment, he thought of his mother who had been so
positive.

"Change of topic, Tony. Any news on Miss
Maple?"

That brought him back to earth with a thud.

"A john saw a man carrying a bulky rug out of the Glendale Building on Monday evening. He identified the rug as Maple's hallway rug. Confirms our suspicions."

Judge Lispway covered his face in his hands, bent over, rested the top of his head on his Bible, and sobbed. Tony had never seen the judge cry before. Was he blaming himself? That made no sense but then how often had Tony berated himself for not driving his parents' car on the day of the accident? After a couple of minutes, Lispway raised his head and wiped his eyes with his sleeve. His voice was an old man's at the end of his journey.

"Tony, I know I shouldn't but I feel so responsible. As soon as Dr. Ramsay called me, I knew she was a goner. Hamilton, who was sure she was dead, was also sure that whoever had almost killed her, had finished the job."

Should he or shouldn't he tell him that Lefty Lowland was dead? Why not. "Judge Lispway, someone murdered, shot, Lefty Lowland, the boxer."

"Really, what is the world coming to?" His face darkened and he said, "Are you telling me because you feel there is a connection to Miss Maple?"

"Indirectly, yes there is a connection. You see, I'm more than suspicious that Lefty, he was the super in Maple's building, had robbed her, and no, he didn't kill her. For one thing, whoever killed Maple had a car, and he had none. Why transport the body if he had killed her? Why not incinerate it or stash it in a freezer? Lefty's mistake is he threw around 50s like confetti just before he was shot and robbed. His killer might have been a professional for he was in and out without a trace."

"Damnit, a home invasion, but you never know. According to Hamilton, anyone who is involved in any way, is not safe. I'll ask Betty at the front desk to phone Miss Coldwell and warn her that her life may be in danger."

Chapter 24

An overcast sky and a cool breeze left no doubt it was fall. Usually Reginald was sad when it was time to bid 'adieu' to summer, but he was too confused to know how he felt as he wrapped his sports jacket tighter around himself on his way to his Porsche. Looking around, Reginald had the uneasy feeling he was not alone, but there were no other cars but his in the lot, although there was an overflow lot. In his Porsche, he turned on the radio and heard a piano concerto by Chopin. While it should have been soothing, it wasn't soothing, but at least it was not jarring like Tom Jones' "Pussycat."

As he drove up to his mansion's portico, copied from the one in "Gone with the Wind," he spotted a black Ford 150 pickup and Herb Liefson in black coveralls, standing beside it. Of all the Amigos, Reginald felt the closest to Herb, even though they had next to nothing in common. The Liefsons came from the other side of the tracks, as his mother used to say. Why had Nigel ever picked him was a mystery, but Reginald was so glad that he had. But as Herb had never visited him before, Reginald wondered what the occasion was. No sooner had he parked behind Herb's Ford and gotten out, than he heard.

"Reginald, I hate to bother you at home, but Nigel told me to warn you."

"What is it?"

"A judge, I never caught his name, has opened Mr. Spratt's cold case. You remember him, I'm sure. Detective Carson is questioning all the Amigos. Nigel told me that we are the prime suspects but not to sweat it as he's sure nothing will come of it. But Nigel also told me it's out of his hands."

Reginald felt faint and plastered his right hand against the side of his Porsche. "What do you mean, we are suspects? Suspects in what? Oh my God, was Mr. Spratt murdered? But The Gazette said he died of a stroke. I blamed myself for not being there."

"Reginald, the story in The Gazette was bogus. He was shot in the shower room at Thackeray's. Nigel told me they have a photo."

Reginald grabbed on to the Porsche's door handle for dear life, to steady himself as he felt so dizzy. Worse than anything he'd felt in the graveyard. What was happening and how were the Amigos involved? Had one of them shot Mr. Spratt in the shower room? How often had he been in the shower room? Then he had a feeling that felt his head was twisting into a pretzel. He shut his eyes, but it didn't go away. He had to know and asked,

"When you found me in the showers, Herb, the day I slipped on soap, the same day that Mr. Spratt had died according to the papers, was Spratt...was he dead?"

Herb walked up to him, grabbed him by the shoulders, and holding him firm, looked him in the eyes and spoke with concern in his voice, much like Dr. Ramsay,

"Reginald, I never wanted to have to tell you, but I see now that I have no choice. Listen to what I have to say, and don't jump to any of your conclusions. I heard a gunshot in the school and when I went down to the showers, I saw Spratt, he was lying on the floor, dead. He'd been shot. You were lying off to one side. I thought at first that you too were dead as you weren't moving. But then I saw your chest move and a squashed bar of soap near you. I figured you had slipped on it and knocked yourself out. I picked you up and took you up to your room."

Reginald felt wretched, no, more than wretched. His head was back spinning. That twisting agony was gone. If he let go of the door handle, he'd be face down on the ground. He'd been there and not known he'd been there. Damnit, why couldn't he recall a thing but then, he hadn't really tried. Then he heard,

"Reginald, you never told me but now is as good a time as any. Do you recall anything? If so, I'd like to hear what it is before you talk to the police."

Yes, he had to do what Herb asked. It was not going to be easy. He closed his eyes and opened his mouth and like Dr. Ramsay had taught him, he thought of nothing but what Herb had asked him to do,

"I was taking a shower after gym. I had left early and I was alone. I was upset over what they were saying about Mr. Spratt who had not been at school. I did not believe he had been selling dirty pictures. Suddenly Mr. Spratt rushed in. He was waving a pistol and a photo and was screaming at me to help him. I was terrified. I backed away, and next, I was spinning in the air and then, stars and darkness."

Reginald opened his eyes. They were filled with tears. Until that moment, he had no recall for meeting Mr. Spratt in the shower room. He had simply thought he was taking a shower when he'd slipped on a bar of soap although he'd found that out from Herb. Why had he backed away? Why had he not been there for his friend? But guns terrified him, they always had. Surprisingly, he was no longer dizzy but was feeling

122

sad, so sad, and moaned like a dog hit by a car. Not again? Had he been the last one to see Mr. Spratt alive just as he'd been the last one according to Dr. Ramsay to see Miss Maple alive?

Herb who was still holding him, said, "You say he was waving a gun and that's all you recall, is that right?"

"I never recalled anything until you asked me. So, when you came, he'd been shot and I was comatose. Was there anyone else there? I'm sure there was no one else there when Mr. Spratt rushed into the showers and saw me."

"No, but there must have been to have shot him. Too bad you were unconscious or... No, of course not, or else he would have shot you too…"

Herb let go of him and when he did, Reginald sat down on the ground. His hand was cramped from hanging on to the door handle. His throat was so dry and yet, he had spoken. Then he saw that Herb too looked troubled. He even blushed and stammered,

"Reginald, I was hoping to take it to the grave. If you had been awake, the killer would have shot you but as you were out cold, I hate to tell you, he planted the gun in your right hand. I removed the gun, wiped it of all prints, kicked it away, picked you up, and exited. I

123

heard footsteps on the stairs. Reginald, you did not shoot him. You are left-handed. Don't ever tell the police what I told you. They will never believe you."

Herb flashed a weak smile of support. Reginald felt numb. He was past feeling anything. Herb's words rang in his ears, over and over. Somehow, he managed to say in a voice so weak that a whisper would have been louder.

"Herb, I can't tell a lie. If I try, I will only make it much worse for myself. I believe you. And if you have to tell the police what really happened, I understand. You are a good friend. Without Mr. Spratt, you are my only friend. I know I can trust you and what you say."

Chapter 25

Reginald surprised himself when he got to his feet and waved as Herb drove away. He walked along the flagstones through the gap in the privet hedge to the grassy embankment. Taking no chances, it could be slippery for the long grass was known to trap raindrops, he slowly made it to the bottom. Looking up at the six large plate-glass windows, custom-crafted in Nova Scotia, on the side of his ballroom, he heard strains of Mozart's final concerto. And then he saw that the ten-foot French door, the only one at the far end of the ballroom, was wide-open. That was how he was hearing Mozart. But Pearcum, his maid, always locked it and turned off the stereo before she left. His heart pounded. Had there been a break-in? There were more and more of them in the area. But would the robbers have left the door, open?

Taking a deep breath, he walked inside, flipped the light switch and closed his eyes. There was always a blinding flash of white light from the ceiling halogens. Opening his eyes, he quickly scanned the teak walls and the bamboo flooring to the teak desk against the far wall, and beside it, the mannequin in the jade-green gown. Nothing was out of place. But he had to check the mannequin to make sure.

But as he got up to the mannequin, he froze when he saw on top of the desk, his mother's red-and-black lacquered jewelry box. It was always in the mannequin's chest-wall safe. Inside it was a look-alike Great Wall jade necklace with priceless, real gems worth more than the house, ten-fold. The room began to spin, and he grabbed onto the edge of the desk. There must have been a break-in and they had no security, no alarm, no camera.

Just a minute. Why was the gown on the mannequin not disturbed. Leaving the back door open had told him that the robbers were not all that careful. He was confused. Letting go of the desk, he reached over and opened the jewelry box, it was empty. Sweat dripped off his forehead. What to do? Call the police? Did he really want the police involved? Not after Herb telling him that the police could be gunning for him. Then he had a refreshing thought. Was it his mother's jewelry box? Possibly, Pearcum had an identical one for they were rather common. And possibly she had forgotten to turn off the stereo and lock the door. Only one way to find out.

Placing down the jewelry box, he gently pulled down on the left shoulder of the mannequin's gown and exposed the safe's silver-and-black dial. With a shaking hand, he dialed the combination, opened the safe and looked inside. When he saw a red-and-black jewel box, he was so relieved. Quickly, he removed and shook it and heard a rattling sound. Opening it, he saw the jade stones and diamonds. His heart thumped with joy. It had all been a false alarm.

Under the necklace was a four-by-six colour photo. He'd never seen it before. Never known it was there. Curiosity got the better of him but when he removed it and looked at it, he saw a blur of reds and whites and his eyes closed shut. For a good minute, he couldn't open them. It was happening, again. Hadn't happened in years. There had to be a naked woman in the photo. That always caused his eyes to shut. But what was a photo of a naked woman doing in his mother's jewelry box? On that score, he'd never know.

With his eyes shut, he was sure that he could have opened them but knew that the coast was not clear, and with a shaking hand, he opened the desk drawer and placed the photo at the very back of the drawer before he closed it. Then and only then, he opened his eyes. His plan was to show it to Dr. Ramsay without looking at it.

He returned the necklace to the jewelry box and locked it back in the safe. After he'd re-arranged the mannequin's gown, he stepped back, but when he did, he slipped and fell. And as he did, his head hit the corner of the desk and everything went black.

Chapter 26

Before Tony came to Mabel's Diner on King, he turned onto a side street, parked, and found the entrance to the alleyway that ran behind Mabel's. It was almost pitch-black, there were no streetlights, and the pavement was uneven; he walked slowly. At her back door, between two dumpsters, he pressed the buzzer and stared into the lens of a security camera. Downtown Pinolta with its druggies and prostitutes was no longer safe at night. After a muffled sound, the steel door, it was not as thick as a bank vault's but was getting up there, opened. By the light of a 40-watt bulb, Tony ascended a narrow set of rickety wooden stairs to the top where there was another door only this time, it was open.

When he stepped through the open door, he was shocked to find himself in an open concept loft that belonged in a magazine. Four large skylights, two on each side of a peaked roof, looked down on pine-paneled walls and a polished oak-plank flooring. On the walls were several, large, colorful prints that highlighted white leather furniture, white cupboards and stainless-steel appliances. A lacquered Chinese divider separated a king-sized bed and on-suite bathroom from the rest of the room.

Mabel stepped out from behind the divider. Her hazel eyes were smiling impishly at him. She was flushed and her long, blonde hair was dripping wet. She must have just stepped out of the shower and thrown on a white, mini summer dress; she was bare-footed. "Didn't expect my pad to look like this, did you, Detective Carson?"

"No, I didn't. I'm speechless, well almost. It's breath-taking. I've never seen anything like it in Pinolta or anywhere."

"Thank you for your kind words. I'm so proud of what I've done to the loft. I wasn't sure if you'd come, but I'm so glad that you did, Detective."

The blush on her face surfed down her neck to the top of her chest. There was no doubt, blush or not, that she was a beautiful woman. His heart was racing but he didn't feel attracted. If he didn't know himself, he might have questioned if he was gay.

"You don't know how long I've waited for someone who cared about poor Mr. Spratt to come along. I've never found the police to be that helpful, but I've often wondered if you were different. I can tell that you care about setting the record straight about Mr. Spratt. Finally, I've found someone to give it to."

Her hazel eyes darkened as she bent down and opened the top drawer of a glass-inlaid table. Taking out an 8"x10," monochrome photo, she handed it to him. Tony saw a young naked girl, had to be under-aged, on her hands and knees on a wet, shining floor, most likely in a shower room. While her long, black hair hung down over the sides of her face, Tony could still see that her eyes were glazed and drugged. A muscled, young man with flying black hair and a fist-thick cock was riding her ass. Tony cringed and squirmed. How degrading, how humiliating, how soul-crushing. Flipping it over, he saw that it too, like the photos of the boys found in Spratt's locker, was printed on Fujifilm paper. Looking up at her, he saw anguish in her face.

"Mabel, who gave you this photo and when?"

"Spratt gave it to me. It was the morning after he'd been sacked. He rapped on our door, handed it to me and, told me to guard it with my life. He was waving a photo and was talking fast, machine-gun fast. But I heard him say, 'I got evidence that'll put Cain away.' When I saw a gun in his other hand, I freaked. He left before I could get out a word. Take it, Tony. I never want to see it, again. I hope and pray it helps you."

Suddenly, Tony's earworm cranked out Cat Stevens' "I'm Gonna Get Me a Gun." This confirmed that Spratt was a whistleblower, and he was the one who had lifted the Colt from Robins' Hardware. When Spratt had arrived at the school, he was armed. Somehow, the killer had got his hands on the Colt. Had Spratt put it down for while he was fat, he was a gym teacher and had to be fit? In the crime photo, it didn't look like he had been in a fight. After he'd shot Spratt at a distance, he'd made off with the photo. Was the hunk in the photo, the killer? Before he could ask, Mabel said,

"I know what you're going to ask, and the bull on Belinda's backside was Sean O'Brien. He was our second-string quarterback. Spratt called him Dropsy. A year later, he was killed in a single-car accident; he was always driving too fast."

Damnit, thought Tony. Another dead end. But if Spratt called him Dropsy then doubtful he was Cain. He asked,

"Mabel, you said the young girl's name was Belinda. Any idea what her surname was, and you wouldn't happen to know what happened to her, would you?"

She grimaced, not a good sign. "Don't ask me what her surname was, the school never tell me. When she didn't turn up at school the next day, I went to the police and they were of no help but then, I didn't have her full name and no one had reported her missing. I

131

even went to the bus terminal and they said two tickets were bought for Winnipeg that day, but couldn't tell me who had bought them. I tried but got nowhere."

"Mabel, I couldn't have done better, myself. Let it go. You tried that's the main thing."

Chapter 27

With photo in hand, not that it was a break-through, Tony was about to leave when Mabel asked, "Would you like to stay for a home-cooked meal. I know you're a bachelor, and I've never met one who can cook worth a darn. I'm Swedish, but our maid was from Mumbai, and she taught me how to make chicken masala. If you have something to do while I'm in the kitchen, go for it. What do you say? And do you mind if I call you 'Tony?' I feel comfortable with you and I can't say that for many men. You are a gentleman."

No way was he turning down a home-cooked meal, especially when the cook was Mabel. About her calling him 'Tony,' why not. Though about him being a gentleman, while that was not always the case, it was with her. Never had he imagined that he and Mabel would be friends. And he was alright that it was friends without benefits.

"I'd love to try your chicken masala. And yes, call me Tony. I'd like that. And I have a VHS tape in my car that I need to review. I'll have a look at it while you're making dinner."

When Mabel went into the kitchen, Tony headed to his car and was back in record time with the tape. On his return, he inhaled the fragrance of basmati rice and the tangy aroma of chili and cinnamon. Mabel, in a white apron, waved at him from her open kitchen, and asked, "Tony, why don't I give you a cooking lesson, before you watch your tape?"

On the back burner was a banged-up pot with basmati rice boiling in it. On the front burner was the largest black wok he'd ever seen, and into it she poured hot oil, diced chilies, cracked cinnamon sticks and a bay leaf. Turning to him, she said with another impish smile,

"Next, I'm adding the good stuff. Green cardamom pods, black pepper, Indian sea salt, sesame, coriander, cumin, and turmeric seeds. More seeds than you have, Tony."

She giggled, then threw in enough chicken breasts and thighs for four people, turned up the burners, and when it was bubbling, tossed in onions. "Go and watch your tape. It will take me some time to add the tomato paste, garlic, cilantro, ginger, masala powder, yogurt, and cream. When I'm finished, I'll bring you a glass of red."

He found the converter between the sofa's cushions, inserted the VHS tape into the player, and turned on the television. But when he pressed "play," the screen remained pitch-black. Just as he stood up to check the player, he heard a chair being dragged across a floor, and a man's gruff voice coming from the blank television screen.

"Fong Ching make it brief. I don't have all day. I'm on duty and should be out on the streets of Hamilton. Oh shit, the bloody lens cap is on."

Suddenly, Tony saw in black-and-white, a teen who was standing in the middle of the screen. Her feet were wide apart, her hands were on her hips, and defiance was in her eyes. Her hair was long and black, her face was badly bruised, and the middle of her neck had a black-and-blue choker. She was dressed in a drab hospital gown. As Tony looked closely at her, he felt blindsided. Fanny Maple was Fong Ching was Chinese? Lispway had never told him and he wondered if even he or Abraham Gold knew she was Chinese? Linda Stonemill had never said she was Chinese when asked to describe her. The only explanation was that Hamilton had given her a make-over when they changed her name. But if no one recognized Maple as being Chinese, Hamilton had to be wrong. No way had whoever tried to kill Fong Ching ever recognized her as Fanny Maple.

"Yeah copper, you want me to chirp like a good little budgie, while you sit on your fat ass? Find the son-of-a-bitch who almost killed me, and you'll be doing something. Look at me; I'm a freak. I look in the mirror, and I don't even know it's me."

"Don't dump on me, Fong Ching. You've been no help. You've given us no description, no name, nothing to help us nail your attacker. Your sisters scattered like the wind, and the names you gave us for them came off a Chinese menu. Fat chance we had of ever finding them."

Tears clouded the defiance in Ching's eyes and her hands dropped to her sides. "How I miss Oil and Dumpling, Egg Noodle, Fortune Cookie, Hot and Sweet, Spring Roll, and Soo Gai. How did I know their names came from a Chinese menu? I've never been in a restaurant in my life. We were family, one big happy family. Did you find Peking Duck, big momma? She saved my ass when I was on the streets. She wouldn't run out on me."

"We did find the body of a woman burnt beyond recognition on the other side of town in a dumpster. Our pathologist couldn't tell us if she was Chinese but he did say that she was fat."

Fong Ching stopped crying and sneered. No one would ever get the drop on Peking Duck. It's not her. As for my sisters blowing town, who wants a one-way ticket to some stinking rice paddy in China?"

"You said you had a Chinese boyfriend. Well, give us a name, a description, anything to help us find him."

"My boyfriend is a blur. Ever been in a coma for a week? Try and see what you recall. All I know was he treated me well. And even if I knew his name, I'd never tell you. I know you coppers, you'd blame him and never look for anyone else."

"Give us a break. We went over the top for you. Our plastic surgeon gave you a freebie on your eyes. No one will ever know you are Chinese. We all chipped in and bought you a wig. Fanny Maple, you are a blonde bombshell. And now Fong Ching, let's hear your sordid story for the record. I don't have all day."

After she wiped her face dry with both sleeves, Ching sat down, smoothed the hospital gown over her knees that were locked together, and began in a quiet voice,

"My mother was born on the West Coast. Her old man worked on the railroad, and her mother came in the post from China. She said they fought like dogs and cats. When the war came, she lied that she was Japanese, and got shipped in a cattle car to a camp in Alberta. She never saw them again, never looked for them nor they for her. My old man was a white guard and that was why

I came out white like him. But if I thought I was better than her, she'd tell me to get lost. She could be a bitch. Only time I heard the word 'love' was on the radio.

"After the war, we lived above a Chinese laundry in Vancouver. She worked day and night on the presses. She smoked dope, all the Chinese did. How else to deaden the pain? But if I took a drag on her cigarette, she'd beat me. I went to school because it was the law, and learned to read and write. The only thing she taught me was to trust no one.

"One day, no warning, my life was like that, we moved to a tent in a swamp: a stinking hellhole with long snakes, fat toads and foul-smelling, sewer water. I walked miles to school, and had to shovel shit into rotting logs after school or I got no rice. I smelled like shit and sat at the back of the classroom. One day, I'll never forget it, I get home from school and there's cars and white people in our swamp. And they're paying money for those stinking mushrooms; they're crazy but hey, who's complaining. We got a trailer with hot water, and I got real soap, and my first pair of jeans. But I always had to wear her shoes. God, did they hurt."

Fong Ching jumped to her feet, threw punches, right and left at the camera, and then, just as suddenly, she slumped back into the chair. Bowing her head, she muttered,

"I get back from school the next day and she's gone. A whitey in a black suit says he owns the place and to vamoose. I run to the cleaners but she's not there. And worse, another Chinese family was living upstairs and, there was no room for me. I went to the cops, but they laughed in my face and told me to get lost."

When Tony heard the policeman's voice, he sounded frustrated. "I'll have you know I checked and your mother was never reported missing. I agree, it was and is a bloody shame how you Chinese were treated, no better than our First Nation people."

Fong Ching looked into the camera lens with a renewed defiance in her eyes.

"I was homeless, and no one gave a damn. I was tempted to torch the god-damned whitey in our trailer, but I had no matches. I slept on park benches, ate garbage, and washed my face in bird baths until one day a big, fat Chinese woman, Peking Duck, found me and took me in. My Chinese sisters wore panties and no bras. They loved to fuss with my hair and bathe me in warm water. I didn't mind, it sure beat the streets. I always wanted sisters and I had a big momma in the bargain. She cooked all our meals, bought and washed our clothes, made the beds, picked the johns, collected the cash, paid the rent and the cops. We had to learn the

"Kama Sutra" and how to be the pictures in it. I learned fast and soon had my own bed."

Just then Mabel sat down on the sofa beside him with tears in her eyes, and Tony pressed 'pause' on the converter. "I hope you don't mind, Tony, I was eavesdropping and peeked around the corner. I know I shouldn't have. That poor, beaten-up, Chinese street urchin."

Uh-oh he thought, the tape was police evidence. Was he in a bind? Hadn't Mabel given him an important piece of evidence? That made her an official police informant. "Mabel, I trust you but I have to insist that you swear never to reveal what you've seen on the tape."

"You have my word, Tony."

"Believe it of not, the street urchin is someone you know. After a near-death beating, the Hamilton police put her into witness protection with a new name and a complete make-over with eye surgery and a blonde wig. Any idea who she became?"

Mabel gasped. "I heard a blonde wig. She sure fooled me. I was sure she had real blonde hair. Unbelievable. I never dreamed that Fanny was Chinese. But what a tragic story. Why, why didn't she get out of lying on her back, why?"

When she sat down beside him, he pressed 'play,' and heard the Hamilton cop say, "One thing I've been meaning to ask you, Ching, is why did you leave the West Coast for Hamilton?"

"Girls from Hong Kong and Taiwan moved in, and they play dirty. Big momma got out a map and saw that Hamilton was on water, had a mountain and, most important, no Chinese."

"You can't believe everything you read. Now listen to me. You're leaving Hamilton for Pinolta, a small town. The chief of police there, Abraham Gold, and Judge Saul Lispway are the only ones who know you're in witness protection. Gold gave me this jewelry box to welcome you to Pinolta. It's a hick town and you'll be safe there. Don't get your hopes up for the jewelry box. There's no jewelry in it. But I put a memento in it to remember what happened to you, but don't look for a long, long time, if ever."

Fong Ching snatched the jewelry box, went to open it but like a good girl, didn't. She smiled as though to say, 'I'm not as dumb as you think. You warn me, I listen, whitey.' The tape ended.

Chapter 28

After Tony had the best chicken marsala dinner he'd ever had, just as he was getting up from the table, he heard on an intercom, "Mabel. It's me, Linda. Waverly is out for the evening. I have to see you. I'm so, so upset over what's happened. I don't hold out any hope for Fanny. And to think, we could have been there."

When he heard that, he knew why he hadn't lusted after Mabel, or even Linda, for that matter. How had his unconscious ever known? Talk about mysteries. He saw Mabel turn beet-red, and knew that she knew what he knew. Without a word, she beckoned for him to follow her and on the other side of the ensuite-bathroom, she opened a door that let to another rickety set of wooden steps. Just before he left, she turned to her and with hazel eyes smiling, she mouthed, "I hope we can still be friends?" He nodded in the affirmation and left.

It was darker outside into the alleyway than when he'd arrived. On the side street, the light from a flickering streetlamp guided him through the night's blackness to his car. Driving home, he took the back streets in Pinolta to mull over what he'd heard on the VHS tape and what he thought of Linda's announcement. He did his best thinking while he was in his car. But on the corner of Victoria and Bethune, quite close to Mabel's, his headlights picked out a man who was standing there and smoking. He was dressed in dark clothing, and Tony almost missed seeing him. His headlights must have spooked him, for he flicked away the cigarette, picked up a large satchel, and took off running down Bethune. Bloody hell. He had to be a burglar.

Tony slammed on his brakes, jumped out of his car, and bolted down Bethune. It was almost as dark as it had been in the alleyway. No streetlights and no house lights didn't help. As hard as he ran, he never as much as caught a glimpse of the burglar. Stopping, he listened and heard next to nothing until he was jolted,

"BANG."

A gunshot and it sounded like it had come from just ahead of where he stood. Who was shooting? The burglar? That made no sense. Drawing his Glock, he cocked it, and slowly walked forward until, all of a sudden, the ground and sidewalk shook as if in an earthquake.

"KERBANG."

An explosion that rocked his eardrums. Ahead and to the left, a spiral of flames gutted the night. Red-hot embers rained down. An insufferably hot and dense smoke enveloped him. He could barely breathe and covering his nose and mouth brought little relief as he gasped and choked. His eyes teared and burned, and he could barely see. He squinted and kept moving although he had no idea of what was ahead until he saw to his left, a blazing inferno. It had to have been a house. Doors, shutters, walls, beams and shingles evaporated into black smoke before his very eyes. Crimson flames rose higher and higher into the night sky. The noise was deafening. No one could have survived. Had to have been a gas explosion.

Quickly he holstered his Glock and walked past it; the heat coming from it was like stepping into a furnace. On the other side of the conflagration, were blackened trees and a tall pillar. His gut knotted. He looked closer through the haze and smoke and sure enough, the pillar was Bethune's statue. Christ, he thought, it was Coldwell's house.

Just then, a collective chant of "Alleluias" almost drowned out the sound of the raging fire. Turning, he saw men and women, in pajamas and robes, marching down the street, carrying pails and buckets of sloshing water. He was about to keep walking, when he heard, "Psst, Detective Carson, can you help me?"

He started, spun around, and spotted the whites of two eyes to one side of Bethune. Whipping out his Glock, he shouted, "Step forward slowly. Hands up."

"I didn't come this far to be shot, Detective Carson. It's me, Florence Coldwell."

Out stepped a tall, blackened woman with singed and smoking curlers on her head. Tony did a double take. It really was Coldwell. He dropped his arm and gun to his side and exclaimed, "Florence, you're alive. But how, how did you survive?"

"I thank God and Betty. She called me and warned me. I camped out for the night by the good doctor. All I have is Johnnie's bible, the clothes on my back and my wits. I thank God that I parked my Mustang at the church. Did you hear a shot?"

"Yes, I did."

"Someone shot at the dummy in my bed. And then my house exploded like it was a tinderbox. I'm sure it was a Molotov Cocktail. I know all too well their sound. Why did Betty warn me? Do you know?"

Damnit, he thought. It had to be who he thought was a burglar when it was Cain. He had come so close, so close to nabbing him.

145

"Florence, I'll explain later. Your life could still be in danger. If he finds out you're alive, he'll try again to silence you. Hide in the bushes down by the corner, and I'll drive by and pick you up. I'll drive you to my house for the night. You can spend the night, there. I know it's irregular, but I don't want it getting out that you are alive."

Chapter 29

Tony awoke with a start, and then realized that he was smelling the aroma of coffee and it was no dream. Someone was in his kitchen. But who? A burglar making himself a cup of coffee? And then last night came flooding back and he knew it had to be Florence. He checked and it was only half six. Who got up that early? Sleep was not in the cards; he got out of bed and ran across the freezing wood floor to the bathroom where he brushed his teeth and combed his hair in cold water. Shaving was having to wait for a new hot water heater. His old one had given up the ghost. After he dressed, he followed the coffee aroma down the stairs to his kitchen.

Florence in his pajamas and robe looked like an adolescent in a growth spurt. He had no idea she was that tall. Was he impressed when he saw rye bread in the toaster, a mushroom and cheese omelette on the cast iron pan, and a bubbling coffee percolator on the stove. The table was set for three with jars of blackberry jam and orange marmalade. Before he could ask who the third person was, she said,

"I've called Reverend Mulgrave and he's on his way. He's a morning bird like me. Lucky for me, his church is just down Raymond's Road. I'm sure that I'll be safe there. In God's hands as they say."

She poured Tony a coffee and, just as he was about to sit down, spoke again, "Tony, I didn't tell you but yesterday, I met Johnnie's 'Peter' in mother's graveyard. He was visiting his mother there. I don't know if you know him but he's Reginald Moorehouse. Oh, I heard a car on your lane. Would you check to see if it's Reverend Mulgrave?"

He was stunned to hear that Reginald Moorehouse was Spratt's 'Peter?' While he didn't like the sounds of Moorehouse knowing she was Spratt's sister, he could tell by the look in her eyes that Moorehouse was the cat's meow. No sense in airing his suspicions. Leaving the kitchen, he walked through the adjoining woodshed and out the back door. A beat-up, purple school bus, spewing thick, grey diesel fumes, was pulling up his laneway. After all the smoke he'd inhaled last night, he could have done without the bus's fumes.

Out stepped a tall, portly man who was dressed in black as though an undertaker. Seeing Tony, he threw up his arms and boomed, in a Mississippi drawl, "Finally, I get to meet the great Detective Carson. I've heard so much about you. My name is Reverend Jacob Mulgrave. My friends call me Jake."

Mulgrave sounded like a used car salesman. His type was a turn-off for Tony but knowing Coldwell thought the world of him, he was cordial. "I hope what you heard about me is all good, Reverend Mulgrave. Miss Coldwell is inside."

He shook Tony's hand, too profusely to suit Tony, and followed him into the kitchen. As soon as he saw Florence, he threw up his arms and thundered, "Alleluia, God be praised. A miracle. My prayers have been answered. Alleluia."

Florence embraced Mulgrave or Mulgrave embraced her, either way it was mutual. With a smile a mile long, he turned to Tony and said, "Detective Carson, I have a camp at Eden Acres. I'll take her, there. She'll be as snug as a bug in our humble but holy abode. We have relics from the Holy Land, the most in all of Canada. Do I see and smell breakfast?"

Chapter 30

Even though Tony had put on an overcoat and gloves, when he stepped outside of his farmhouse, he was shivering. His clothing was no match for an Arctic wind. Coldwell, Mulgrave, and the purple school bus were gone. When he turned on his car's heater, he felt a whisp of warm air; wonders never ceased. Driving along Raymond's Road toward Pinolta, he spotted a black BMW coming his way, doing at least 80 m.p.h. in a 50 m.p.h. zone While he didn't see the driver as it zoomed past, he knew it had to be Linda Stonemill.

Braking and flooring the gas pedal, he threw the Malibu's steering wheel full circle, and burned rubber in a professional one-eighty. The Malibu rocked from side to side but shot forward, and soon was gaining on the BMW. When he had its licence plate in his crosshairs, he confirmed that it was Stonemill's and sounded the siren and flashed his lights. But it was a good mile before the BMW slowed down and parked off the road.

He pulled in behind, cut the siren and the flashing lights, and got out. As the driver's window lowered, he saw blonde hair, flushed cheeks, and an unhinged intensity in her eyes. If it was not for the pale-blue knot dress, he might have doubted it was Linda Stonemill. Was she drunk, or high on drugs, or manic?

Without looking at him, she reached into a large Gucci purse, pulled out and thrust her driver's licence at him and spoke in a high-pitched voice that would have made it in an off-Broadway show.

"Officer, I was speeding. I admit it. Here's my licence. I'm Linda Stonemill, and my husband is Waverly Stonemill. I was on my way to a family emergency…"

"Linda Stonemill, we met at Maple's apartment, yesterday. You were a big help. I'm not going to ticket you, don't worry. What's this family emergency?"

She started, looked at him, and for a moment he was sure she had no idea who he was, then she went pale and muttered, "Oh, it's you, Detective Carson? You know, when I heard your siren and looked at the speedometer, I couldn't believe how fast I was going. I should never have gotten into my car. I should have gone for a long walk. I'm so stressed. But thank you for not ticketing me."

He could see that she was deeply troubled, and was going to leave it at that when she returned her licence to her purse, and fished out a cheap, red-and-black, jewelry box that she almost thrust in his face, although she never let go of it.

"Detective Carson, I went for a chat with Reggie. Waverly is not the talking type. Got quite a shock when the back door was open. Didn't have to rap. A bigger shock when I saw him lying on the floor, holding his head, and moaning. Thought for sure he was in a drunken stupor. But he denied it and he never lies. The only man I know. And I didn't smell alcohol. He'd slipped and hit his head on the desk. There was a bruise on the side of his head. Then I screamed. I saw Fanny's jewelry box on his desk. He'd killed her and had out photo..."

Just then a transport thundered past, she started and dropped the jewel case. Picking it up, she clasped it to her bosom as if it was a child. When another diesel rumbled by, too close for comfort, her dress did a Marilyn Monroe, he said, "Linda, we're in the line of fire. I'll find a safer place. Follow me and bring the jewelry box. But be careful when you get out of the car."

No need to tell her to bring the jewelry box, she was bonded to it. After checking that there were no oncoming trucks, he hugged the side of Linda's BMW until he cleared it. With the crunching of her high heels behind him, he threaded his way through a patchwork of golden-rods, nameless weeds and prickly, wild roses, and descended a grassy bank to the edge of a slow-moving creek. There was no sound of traffic or the smell of diesel fumes. When she had pulled up beside him, she continued,

"He said he had no idea what I was talking about. He said the jewelry box belonged to his maid; said they were a dime-a-dozen at Kresge's. I wasn't listening. I looked at him and had the chilling thought that I didn't know him. I always thought he was meek and mild. Waverly says he's gay and has no backbone, as if the two are connected. I panicked. I thought if he killed Fanny, he could kill me. I bolted. I just knew I had to get away, far away."

She burst out crying and when she brushed at the tears with her sleeves, he took the jewelry case from her. Turning it over and opening it, he saw that it was empty and had no distinguishing marks. Having just seen a similar one in the VHS tape, he cold see where she was coming from. But Moorehouse had a point. They were run-of-the-mill. Putting it up to his nose, he got a whiff of old wood, nothing else. She must have seen him for she said,

"I didn't smell Fanny's perfume in it. Have I been a fool? How brutal I was screaming at him. If I'm wrong, I just lost a good friend."

"Linda, it's impossible to tell if it's Maple's. Why don't you return it, and then, I'll pay Mr.

153

Moorehouse a visit. It's long overdue. What do you say?"

"You might miss him. He's going to our cottage in Algonquin Park. If he's not home, go there. If you park on Highway 35 and take the loggers' trail, you'll come to it. I'm feeling better, all ready. Again, thank you Detective Carson."

Chapter 31

On his way to see Judge Lispway, Tony made a pit-stop at Joe's Poolhall and Gym on King. Parking just down the street, he saw workers in grey overalls and jackets lugging counters and cupboards into the shop next door. The "For Rent" had been replaced by a spanking new sign, "Tim Hortons Donuts."

Slowly Tony walked down the stone steps, still wet with rainwater, to the gym. Inside, he heard ropes slapping the floor, gloves pounding bags, and men grunting and panting. Joe was not by the centre ring. He walked into his office; the door was open. Joe's head topped a mound of paper on his desk; his eyes were dialed onto Tony. Before he got out a word, Joe said,

"Paisano, you could have told me. Grant was just in and showed me a special edition copy, hot off the press. The headline was 'Champ is Gunned Down.' Grant sure laid it on thick about the great boxer we just lost. Reported it was a home invasion that had gone off the rails. Did you tell him that? Even offered a reward for information leading to an arrest."

Tony's gut knotted. He hated being one-upped. While he smelled cigar smoke, he saw that Joe wasn't smoking. Grant's news that Lefty was dead had put him in a tailspin. Closing the door, Tony gritted his teeth and said to a grim-faced Joe,

"Dammit, I wanted to tell you. I found him just after I left here. About the home invasion, that was Gold's idea and Grant bought it. I know what you are thinking that Lefty killed and robbed Maple and was killed and robbed in return. Well, take my word for what it's worth, Lefty robbed but didn't kill her. That's between the two of us. Not even Nigel knows."

Joe's face brightened on the spot, and he reached into a pile of paper and came up with a half-smoked cigar that he relit. After a couple of puffs, he spoke with relief in his voice,

"Thanks, Paisano, I needed to hear that Lefty was no killer. As for robbing a dead woman who had no relatives; we all make mistakes. Grant proposed that we have a memorial corner for Lefty but I told him that Lefty had already sold all his stuff, years ago. Grant then said he'd heard at the launch that Lefty had a lucky jade plant, a gift from a Chinaman, and was it around? I told him it was missing. Didn't tell him that there was no Chinaman but there was Gus, his trainer, a white man last time I saw him, and that Robins has it."

Just a minute, talk about a Chinaman giving away something precious. Hadn't he wondered if Spratt had given the hard evidence that was going to put away Cain for good, it certainly wasn't the photo he had given Mabel, to someone before he arrived at Mabel's? Who better than a heavy-weight boxer who lived in the same building. Out of the blue, Tony's earworm played Adolph Deutsch's theme music from "The Maltese Falcon." He didn't have to be Sam Spade to know what his earworm was getting at. Spratt had given Lefty the incriminating evidence. Why hadn't he thought of it before? And that Cain had tried to silence Coldwell told Tony that the incriminating evidence was still out there.

Tony then had a depressing thought. Did whoever robbed and murdered Lefty have it in one of Lefty's suitcases? What were the chances of ever catching him? It would take the entire Metro police force a month of Sundays to go through the Yellow Pages of Pinolta. Dejected, he looked up at Joe whose forehead was knitted, must have been thinking as thinking was a real effort. Then Joe's face glowed like the ash at the end of his cigar, and he said,

"I know what Grant can put in his corner. Years ago, Lefty had been house-cleaning, hard to believe, and gave me a lucky ornament that he said a Chinaman had given him. Never said who the Chinaman was. But I'm sure, said it was a lucky piece. I'll look for it."

Tony's heart leaped. Was he getting a break? Finally. Or was it another dead end. But no way was he dismissing it and said, "Gus, when you find it, call me. I want to see it."

Chapter 32

When Tony turned onto Elm Street, a cloudburst landed on his windshield. His wipers went under the steady wash of rain. The canopy of stately elms gave him seconds of relief, and then back again, into the teeth of the storm. When Tony spotted a whitish blur ahead and to his right, he slowed down. Standing on the curb was Betty, drenched and waving frantically. Braking, he jumped out of his car and running up to her, saw fear dripping off her face.

"Judge Lispway…"

Not waiting to hear the rest, he sprinted up the steps, through the entrance, across the empty slate floor and yanked open the white door. The hallway was in semi-darkness but he could see that the judge's door at the end was ajar. Breathless, he barged inside. Judge Samuel Lispway was face-down on his desk, slumped over in his chair. Hands hung motionless at his sides. Checking his neck, Tony felt cold flesh and no pulse. Two rosebuds, the size of quarters, were high up and on each side of his neck.

No obvious cuts, abrasions or bruising on Lispway's fingers and hands. Slowly, he scanned the room; nothing was out of place or disturbed. The nuns' chest was on the bottom shelf of the armoire, it was closed. Carefully, he lifted up Lispway's head. It was resting on his bible, open to the Old Testament passage about Cain and Abel in the Book of Genesis. As he closed his lifeless eyes, Tony felt a surge of anger in his gut. Sure, it looked like a heart attack. How he hated that expression: he died peacefully. But that's what they'd say. Tony felt like a voice in the wilderness. All he had to go on were the two rosebuds. If they were thumb imprints that had shorted the old man's vagus nerves, it wouldn't have taken much, Lispway was murdered. A suspicion that he was keeping to himself.

With tears in his eyes, Tony closed and removed the bible, and ever-so-gently lowered Lispway's head to the desk. In the wastepaper basket beside the desk, Tony noticed a folded-up copy of The Gazette. Picking it up, he saw three small, handwritten circles on the front page. One was centered on the "missing local businesswoman" article, another on the "East End Kid's gala" article, and the third one was on "Bruce Liefson's inauguration" article. The circles were in Lispway's shaky handwriting. Had to be a clue. No music this time to give him a hint and then, he heard Betty's hesitant voice.

"Is he dead?"

"Yes, he's dead, Betty. Do me a favour? Get a camera, and take pictures of the rose-colored spots on

160

his neck before they fade. And then call Dr. Neckroff and his son."

Chapter 33

When Reginald Moorehouse entered Dr. Ramsay's office, the two female assistants raised their heads, smiled but said nothing. They were too used to seeing him to notice that he hadn't washed and had slept in his clothes. He had a splitting headache, worse than yesterday's. At Dr. Ramsay's inner office door, he cleared his parched-dry throat and rapped. At once, he heard Dr. Ramsay's voice or what he thought was his voice, and then worried that he hadn't heard it and should he rap again. Enough of this, he said to himself, opening the door, he entered.

Dr. Ramsay, who was seated behind his desk in the far corner of the room, gave him a fright when he jumped up to his feet. Reginald thought for sure that he shouldn't have entered, was turning around when he heard.

"Mr. Moorehouse, are you alright? Have a seat. You look pale. Do you still have a headache? Didn't you take anything for it? Do you want a Tylenol?"

"Dr. Ramsay, you won't believe it but last evening I slipped and hit my head on the corner of my desk. I was out cold until this morning, and woke up with another headache. Then I heard Linda Stonemill asking if I was drunk and then screaming that I had killed Miss Maple and what had I done with their picture?"

"Whoah, Mr. Moorehouse." Dr. Ramsay got him a Tylenol and a paper cup of water. Quickly, he swallowed the pill, then, slowly sipped on the water until his throat no longer felt that it had spent the night in a desert. His head still felt as though he'd been bushwacked. But no sooner did he feel collected, than Dr. Ramsay continued,

"Linda Stonemill rings a bell. She's a friend or should I say, was a friend? I can see why she thought you were drunk if she found you on the floor where you'd slept all night. But tell me, why'd she think you killed Maple?"

This part was confusing and he still couldn't make sense of it unless... That had to be it. His head almost exploded. What if she was right? Turn and run. Not this time. Dr. Ramsay was a friend in court or, he always had been. He had to tell someone. He had to get it out before he incinerated with it inside him. Dr. Ramsay had taught him that and he spoke,

"There was a jewelry box on my desk when I got home yesterday. At first I thought it was mother's but it was in the safe. Then I thought it was my maid's. When Linda screamed at me and stormed out with it, I thought

163

she had flipped. She was always high-strung. But now I realize she thought it was Miss Maple's. phoned Pearcum and it's not hers."

"I've seen Maple's jewelry box. Once, I accidentally opened the side table's drawer and it was there. She almost had a bird and made me close it. The jewelry box is red-and-black, plastic if I'm not mistaken. Was that the same as the one on your desk?"

"Yes, but I've seen them at Kresge's. If you ask me, they're a-dime-a-dozen. They are tacky, no other word for them. And I told mother, so. One of the few times that I voiced my opinion. She said it had been a gift from a dear friend and she would always treasure it. What I'm getting at, Dr. Ramsay, is that there's no way of telling one from another. And I know it was empty for I'd looked. "

"Okay, you've made your point. But this Linda Stonemill was not operating on logic, from the sounds of it. I knew Maple had women friends. How close, I was not about to ask. Stonemill must have been one of them. That's why she was so emotional. Do you know if she's a married woman?"

"Yes, she's married to Waverly Stonemill. His brick company's billboard is at the town's entrance. He's the local boy who's been a national success. I don't think she and he are that close. Why else would she have to come to me for a chinwag?"

"And you said that she was going on about a photo. The plot thickens. I know that you are worrying that she has gone to the police. Well, get that out of your mind. I have a feeling that she cannot afford for the police or anyone else to ever see it. "

That was a relief but the rest wasn't. "Dr. Ramsay, the way you are talking, I can't help but think that the jewelry box was Miss Maple's."

Dr. Ramsay returned to his desk, sat down, pulled out a Panatela, lit it with his silver lighter, and leaned forward. Reginald felt Ramsay's eyes piercing through him. His head felt worse, if that was possible. The Tylenol had done nothing.

"Mr. Moorehouse, let's suppose that it was Maple's jewelry box on your desk and see where that leads us. I'm not saying that Stonemill was right, but we need to consider all possibilities. And we know what she doesn't and you must never forget it. You didn't harm Miss Maple. If it was Maple's jewelry box, then the only way it could have gotten onto your desk was if Maple's killer planted it. Mr. Moorehouse, there may be a killer out there who has it in for you. If anything else turns up, call me at once, and remember, Mr. Moorehouse, you are no killer. You did not kill Maple."

Chapter 34

Nigel Gold didn't even notice what Miss Hussdon was wearing as he strode past her with the morning's Globe and Mail under his right arm. Nigel had slept in and he never slept in, but then he had tossed and turned until 6 am. Sitting at his desk, he re-read with the same disbelief the article devoted to Florence Coldwell. He had no idea that Toronto even knew who she was, let alone that they held her in such high regard. Her life's highlights were laid out on the front page for all of Canada to see: nursing with Dr. Norman Bethune, serving in Mao's Chinese army, freeing white slaves in Toronto, and receiving the Order of Canada.

It was hard for Nigel to admit that Florence Coldwell had been everything that his mother had not been. Coldwell had left her footprint on the world while his mother had never gotten out of her pajamas. But Coldwell hadn't been married to the likes of Abraham and if she had been, then she too would have been driven to drink. How often had Nigel pleaded with his mother to get dressed and leave Abraham?

When Nigel's wife had run off with a pilot, his mother was the one who had embraced him and let him cry on her shoulder. Abraham had called him a cuckold. When his mother lay dying at home of liver failure, she'd asked him to make her look pretty in the coffin. He'd found a mauve dress and she'd truly looked regal in the casket, a queen at the very end. How he missed her? She alone understood and accepted him, and had been there for him, every step of the way.

Nigel felt that he needed a smoke, got to his feet, opened the window onto Victoria, only to see someone on the street. As he slammed shut the window, the phone rang. Mahoney from Coast Guard was on his way to the whirlpool with the bathyscaphe, and could Nigel meet him at the Port Malvern Marina. He could have jumped and cheered. Finally, his big day when he would show them that he deserved to be chief of police on his own merit and that he hadn't been promoted on Abraham's coattails. On his way out, he told Hussdon to notify Carson.

Chapter 35

A dismal gloom blanketed the packed parking lot of the Osprey Mental Hospital, but luck was with Tony. He found an empty parking spot in the far corner, nearest the river. After he parked his Malibu, he walked quickly down to the willow tree where he gazed out at the sandbar. It was barely holding its own against the buffeting waves. He shouted, "I'm coming for you Arabelle Sirene. I'm bringing you home."

As he crossed the weir, Tony looked down and couldn't see a single eel. Too bad if he'd endangered the species. On the opposite bank, he picked up a path that ran through weeds and thistles. When he heard the roar of High Falls getting louder, he slowed down, and soon, not soon enough to suit him, he spotted the platform that led down 350 pine steps to the Osprey River. The same height from the St. Lawrence River to the Plains of Abraham where Canada's future had been decided.

From the top, Tony had a panoramic view of High Falls, a short stretch of surging rapids, and a gigantic whirlpool of swirling black waves and white foam. While High Falls was no Niagara Falls, the whirlpool was without equal in Ontario. Below the maelstrom, the Osprey River was a quiet current that meandered all the way to Lake Ontario.

At the bottom of the steps was an expanse of flat, wet, black rock in line with the whirlpool. On its far edge, stood Nigel in his blue uniform and waders. His gold epaulets were smudged in the gloom. Beside him was a stocky man with close-cropped brown hair. On the back of his black windbreaker was 'COAST GUARD' in white lettering. Unlike Nigel, he wore jeans and dirty white runners. Alongside them, was a beached hydrofoil. Waves splashed relentlessly against its tail and prop which were out of the water, but it never moved.

Tony had sensitive ears, classical music ears, and covered them to muffle the thundering of High Falls and the roar of the rapids. He watched as Nigel and the coast guard lifted an oversized Caribbean-blue torpedo, the bathyscaphe, from the hydrofoil, and carried it to the edge of the rocky expanse. Slowly, they lowered its nose into the river. At that point, Tony descended the steps, two at a time, not wanting to miss the show.

Walking slowly toward them, the rocky plateau was slippier than the steps, he saw that the bathyscaphe had an oversized tail with a rotary prop, four fins on each side, and an elongated snout with side, clear-glass windows. Nigel must have heard him, for he turned, waved and shouted, even though they were only a few feet apart. The coast guard ignored him and sat cross-legged in front of an oversized suitcase that had a

170

spoked wheel, a split-screen monitor and a cockpit of buttons, gauges, dials and switches.

"Tony, you made it, about time. Mahoney here doesn't like to wait. No sweat in navigating it up-river, a minefield of sandbars and rocks. Well, isn't Blue magnificent?"

Mahoney glanced briefly at Tony with expressionless eyes, then turning back to the suitcase, he flipped a switch. High Falls appeared on the right split-screen, clouds on the left; both were in crystal-clear black-and-white. Then Mahoney and Nigel launched the bathyscaphe into the fast-moving water. Immediately, Mahoney plunked down in front of the open suitcase, pushed a couple of buttons, and spoke in a monotone,

"Let's go Blue."

Propeller churned, clouds of thick grey smoke mushroomed from its tail, and its snout mounted and humped ring after ring of the whirlpool. An endless stream of water droplets and bubbles cascaded across both split screens.

"Ground zero. Lights. Action." When Mahoney swung hard on the wheel, his poker-face leaked emotion for a fleeting second. Blue disappeared from the surface and, both screens went blank. "Bitch, go for it."

Tony was aghast when he saw on both screens razor-sharp, protruding spikes of rock on the sides of the rocky maw, interspersed with an open graveyard of skulls, rib cages, pelvises, long and short bones. No wonder they said that the whirlpool never gave up its dead. Mahoney struggled to steady Blue against the current while Gold, who had lost most of his colour, pointed to the right screen. There, a fleshless human skull with long strands of white hair had a stony spike protruding from its right eye socket.

"You think that's her?"

Mahoney pulled up hard on the wheel, and spoke this time with emotion in his voice. "It's not her. And I hate to tell you Gold, but I just hit bottom. Your gal is a no-show."

Gold had a temper tantrum. "Damn it. What a costly waste. Damn, damn..."

Mahoney locked the wheel, got to his feet and stretched. But Tony's eyes never left the split-screens. He was sure there was an ever-so-slight undulation on the bottom of the vortex. When did stone move? Without a word, Tony sat down on the rocky shelf, grabbed the wheel, and released it.

"What the fuck, are you daft, man? That's solid rock. The bitch's not there. Game over."

172

But Tony shouted, "That's not solid rock. I saw it move. I'm sure she's down there, and I'm going for it."

Mahoney went to grab the wheel, but Nigel stepped in and blocked him. For once, Nigel had taken his side, and Tony was most grateful.

Then he heard, "Tony, make it good. Mess up, and it's your neck in the noose."

Tony tightened his grip on the wheel. The pull of the whirlpool's current made child's play of the undercurrent by the weir. With infinite care, it seemed to take forever, he slowly, ever so slowly, turned the wheel and began to invert Blue. His hands and arms were taunt, as they braced against a g-force current that got stronger the more he got into the turn. Hot, burning sweat stung his eyes. His breath was raspy, his heart felt like it was coming through his chest wall, and his hands burned as if pulling on a bow string. Twice he almost lost control and heard Mahoney snarl,

"You're crazy. There's a twenty-thousand deductible on Blue. Give it back to me."

At the mention of money, Gold changed his mind and said, "Tony, give him the wheel."

Gold's face was ashen, while Mahoney's dripped with sarcasm. Tony's hands were about to give out. No way could he keep going. Why, why had he ever taken the wheel? But he'd made a promise to a dead woman. Just as Mahoney went to grab the wheel, Gold had stepped aside, Tony finished inverting Blue and threw her into reverse.

Mahoney screamed, "What the fuck?"

Nigel slipped on the rocky ledge, would have taken a bath, if Mahoney hadn't grabbed him. As Tony rammed down Blue's spinning rotor prop, he had a horrible sinking feeling. What if he was wrong? Time, breath, and heart froze. Then grey blood, slivers of wiggling white guts, and black gobs hit and smeared across both split screens. A kaleidoscope of horror.

Mahoney's eyes bulged, and he let go of Nigel whose knees buckled, but he didn't topple into the drink. Tony let out one long sigh of relief. Slowly this time, he raised and lowered Blue's prop up and down, up and down, and with triumph in his voice, announced, "Eels and more eels, boys. There was a nest of them on the bottom. That's what I saw move."

When the screens cleared, Tony held the wheel motionless and there, on the whirlpool's rocky bottom, was the naked body of a woman. Her hair was dreadlocked with dead eels. Her face and body were disfigured with black streaks, flayed eel skins. She was a Medusa look-alike from a freak show.

Gold lamented, "Those bloody eels. We will we ever know how Maple was murdered?" When Tony didn't see the hospital wristband, he smiled and breathed a long sigh of relief. He had made good on his promise to a mentally ill woman, and Gold was none the wiser.

Chapter 36

Tony gladly handed over the controls to Mahoney who like a true professional, scooped Arabelle Sirene's body into a net, and guided Blue with her passenger home in record time. After he docked Blue beside the hydrofoil, Mahoney reeled in the netted Sirene. And then he and Tony carried her body to the hydrofoil where, at Tony's insistence, they laid it out with reverence. After all three men lifted Blue onto the hydrofoil, and Tony called the coroner's office on Mahoney's remote phone to pick up the body at the Port Malvern Marina.

Mahoney lit a hand-rolled cigarette, sat back in a deck chair, and leisurely smoked it. Although Nigel was dying to join him, Tony took him by the arm, and walked him out of range of Mahoney's hearing. The white noise from the falls and rapids finally came in handy. Then Tony faced Nigel, who was itching to leave, and said,

"I have good and bad news, Nigel. The bad news is that I just came from Judge Lispway's where I found him face down on his desk, dead."

Gold grimaced and then sounded off, "How many times did I tell the old fool that cigarettes were going to be the death of him? Sure, he was a pain in the ass, but he was a damn fair judge. I bought him a gold Timex watch for his golden years. I'll give it to his son."

Then Nigel threw out his chest and proclaimed in his official voice, "Regarding the Spratt case, in deference to Lispway's memory, I'm not icing it. But continue your investigation only after you've closed the Maple case. And now, what's the good news?"

"Before I get to that, I have a confession. I promised Grant to tell him when we found Maple. Between you and me, I hate to tell him before we have her killer. You know how critical he can be. Any chance we could keep finding Maple under wraps until the case is solved?"

Nigel smirked and then grinned, "Absolutely, when I see Dr. Neckroff at the marina, I'll tell him we found a Jane Doe. And I'll inform the mayor's office of the same. I'm sure Grant has a mole, there. What a bastard he's turning out to be. Sure, cop-bashing sells papers, but his old man wouldn't have printed a word against us. So, what's the good news?"

Tony could hardly believe that Nigel had listened to him, and had come up with the name 'Jane Doe' on his own. As for calling Ken, there was no need. Tony replied,

"Thank you for everything, Nigel. The good news will make your day. Florence Coldwell is alive and well. She wasn't home in bed when her house was torched. I have her in a safe house. And I prefer you tell no one until I catch who tried to kill her."

Nigel staggered backwards, but there was no danger of his falling into the river, he was nowhere near the edge. His eyes bulged, and it was some time before he managed to speak,

"When I read that her house had been torched, I was sure that she'd been smoking in bed. You say someone tried to murder her, must be a Russian slave trafficker she put out of business. Thank God, she's alive. Where would Pinolta be without our Florence Coldwell? I thought the world of that woman, and was bereft, yes, bereft, when I read that she was dead."

Chapter 37

Just as Tony arrived back in the Osprey Hospital's parking lot, he heard his name being called by one of Dr. Ramsay's secretaries. The one with the thick-rimmed glasses was standing on the front stone steps, waving at him and shivering, but then she didn't have on an overcoat. A frigid wind was whipping leaves and anything not rooted into the air with tornado-force. When he waved back at her, she shouted for him to wait and disappeared inside.

In no time, Dr. Aaron Ramsay appeared. Dressed in a summer suit, he was impervious to the cold, he beckoned for Tony to follow him. Walking down to the infamous willow tree, Ramsay slipped under the low-lying branches and shimmying leaves. He was not smiling and his white teeth were as grey as the gloom. When Tony stood beside him, he spoke,

"I hope you don't mind meeting me here, but I need privacy when I tell you what I have to say. I found this in Arabelle Sirene's room." Aaron handed Tony a graphic novel by Jean Ache: "Arabelle: *La Dernière Sirene.*"

Leafing through it, Tony saw pages of coloured pictures with French captions. But what caught his attention was a hand-written inscription on the inside cover: "À ma Belinda, joyeux 14eme anniversaire. Ne grandissez pas trop vite. Tante Judy." Tony could not believe his eyes. He had taken French in university and read, "To my Belinda, happy 14th birthday. Don't grow up too fast. Aunt Judy."

How many Belindas were there in Pinolta? The 14-year-old Belinda in the inscription had to be the Belinda in the sex photo that Mabel had given him. Was she then Belinda Sirene and her mother was Arabelle Sirene whom he'd just found in the whirlpool? But Arabelle Sirene was childless. Confused, he turned to a scowling Aaron who threw up his hands in frustration.

"Tony, I apologize profusely for never checking in her room until now. Arabelle Sirene was a name borrowed from the graphic novel in her room. She must have been so addled after the insulin comas that she didn't know 'up' from 'down.' While I have no idea what her name was, I know now that she had a daughter. She was no more delusional than you or me. We were sold a bill of goods that she was childless. She probably told us as much but she spoke only French and no one was bilingual."

Tony's gut knotted. It was getting to be a painful habit. "Aaron, I don't think the police were in on it. Someone got the police to have the mother admitted while he had his not-so-sweet way with her daughter,

180

Belinda. Aaron, I was going to tell you that we just retrieved the body of Arabelle Sirene. I can't go into it, but she's in the morgue as Jane Doe. I'll let you know when you can claim the body."

Aaron caught Tony off guard when he reached over, put his arm around him, and said, "Atta boy Tony, you did it. I knew how important it was that you resurrected the dead from the depth of Hades. Now, you must stop beating yourself up for what happened to your parents. You're not responsible. Plain and simple. Let it go. Guilt is fuelling your flashbacks. I hate to ask but any ideas as to why Sirene was killed?"

Not only had he heard Aaron's words of encouragement, but he was touched by them. Hadn't realized how guilty he had been feeling. To repay him, the least he could do was give him an update. "Sirene was strangled on a boat ramp in the clay flats. She must have come upon a killer dumping off the body of another victim. I was sure it was Maple until I found a footprint. It was too long to be Maple's. He used the same T-shirt on both of them."

Aaron took his arm away from Tony's shoulders, and as he did, concern crept into his eyes. "You said that the footprint was too large to be Maple's. Yes, she wore a size 5 boot. But have you seen her slippers? They are a size 8. He feet were bound when she was small. It's an

old Chinese custom. She felt unbalanced in a size 8
boot. What do you think now, Tony?"

His heart leaped. Then it had to be Maple's
footprint. She too was somewhere in the river.
Hopefully, before the falls and not in them. Then Tony
had an 'aha' moment and felt cold ice snaking down his
back. He felt he had been dropped into a kaleidoscope of
feelings, none good, and the way he looked must have
alarmed Aaron who said,

"Tony, I thought I'd lost you. Do you mind
telling me where you were? It's therapeutic, I can assure
you."

"I believe you Aaron. I just realized that the T-
shirt used to strangle Maple and Sirene came from
Maple's jewelry box. An eyewitness said she saw an old
rag in the box. It had been placed in the jewelry box by
the Hamilton police after a near-death beating as a
warning. Who else would have used it on Maple if not
the man who had almost killed her with it in Hamilton?
But what I don't get is why kill her in the first place, and
how did her killer ever realize that Fanny Maple was
one and the same as Fong Ching?"

Chapter 38

Just after Tony passed the billboard for Stonemill's national brick company that was nothing less than an empire, he spotted Liefson's Garage. Pulling into a narrow sliver of a parking lot, he parked along a wire fence among cars that had been stripped of their hoods, engines, carburetors, radiators, and anything else that wasn't welded to the frame. As he walked by the four closed bay doors, he heard voices, but when he was inside, he didn't see anyone. There was not even a car on one of the hoists, but there was a transistor radio on a bench that was set on an all-day talk channel.

Peeping around the corner into Liefson's office, the door was slightly ajar, Tony saw Herb Liefson chatting away to Matt. Liefson was sitting with his boots up on his desk while Matt, a white-haired, chain-smoking old codger who was the courtesy driver, was standing against the far wall. Liefson was a black-haired, tall man with broad shoulders. He'd been Thackeray's star quarterback and still looked the part. Unlike Matt, he didn't smoke and his long-sleeved coveralls were stained with oil and grease. Matt's were spotless.

When Tony looked twice at Liefson's construction shoes, the ones with steel-toes, his heart raced. They were at least a size 14. Was he Caine? But Liefson was known far and wide as an honest mechanic when there weren't many of them around. He'd come from the other side of the tracks, and worked hard for everything he had, which wasn't much. Unlike the other Amigos, he hadn't been born with a silver spoon. And yet he was an Amigo and he wore a size 14 shoe.

"Detective, Matt here will give you a lift back. What do you need, an oil change?"

"Actually Mr. Liefson, I'm here to ask you a few questions. Didn't Chief Gold give you a heads up that I'd be dropping by?"

Liefson looked startled, took his boots off the desk and sat up in his chair. Matt flattened against the wall, and stubbed out his cigarette with his boot.

"Yes, he did, Detective Carson. I thought he was joking until my twin-sister, Petula, told me that you'd taken Carl's Colt. I never thought that it would be so soon."

When he heard that Petula Robins, Carl's wife, was Liefson's twin, Tony was taken aback. There was no family resemblance. Matt slithered along the wall and left. Liefson stood up and said, "I'll get you a chair although it'll be a tight fit. One of us should be comfortable."

184

When Liefson returned with a chair, Tony found himself sitting in a browbeating position but had no choice. Liefson cleared his throat and began, "I don't want to sound belligerent, but I'd like to know why, after all these years, is Judge Lispway looking into Spratt's death. He had no relatives, and his mother is long dead."

Liefson sounded defensive and weren't defensive people always hiding something? Tony thought best not to be confrontational and responded, "Judge Lispway found new evidence to suggest that Spratt had been murdered. And Judge Lispway wanted Spratt to have his day in court as to whether he was a pervert or not."

"If it counts, I never thought he was a pederast. Am I allowed to ask what this new evidence is?"

"Abraham Gold had taken a photo of the crime scene. Lispway, who'd never seen it before, saw something in it that concerned him enough to re-open the case."

Liefson raised his eyebrows and then blindsided Tony, "Am I allowed to read what Police Chief Abraham Gold wrote down after he interviewed me? He never asked me to sign it, and I never got to see what he'd written."

185

It was news to Tony that Abraham Gold had interviewed anyone, let alone Herb Liefson. "I have no notes from Abraham Gold who, as you know, is on a world trip and is not available. Why don't you tell me what you told Abraham Gold? By the way Mr. Liefson, I know you were at the crime scene. You left your size-14 shoeprint."

Liefson grimaced, and Tony could almost hear him saying to himself, how could he have been that sloppy? After he shifted in his chair, he spoke in a low voice,

"So, that's how Gold knew I was there. Okay, I'll tell you what I told him. A few days after the shooting, Gold dragged me out of school and marched me into the woods. It was bloody dark and cold, there. I always thought Gold favoured me, that I could do no wrong, but that day, I could see that he was pissed at me. He grabbed me by the shoulders and yelled, 'Why did you take the gun out of Spratt's hand? When he shot himself, he was doing us a favor. Were you trying to cover-up for the likes of him? I should book you.'

"I was shocked. He thought I'd taken the gun out of Spratt's hand, but I hadn't. I never touched the gun. I knew enough not to contradict him, so, I played along. I said, 'I thought Spratt would have dropped the gun after he shot himself. And I moved it.' It must have worked

186

for he patted me on the back and said it happens to the best of us. On the way home, he treated me to a Big Mac. Never did that even when I won the big football game."

Tony thought fast. Why had Abraham Gold thought that Liefson had removed the gun from Spratt? How had he known the gun was in Spratt's hand? As for it being Liefson, Gold must have known that he, alone, wore a size 14 shoe. Someone had to have told him. The same person who told him of the shooting for he'd gotten there in record time. The shooter? Who else than Cain? And wasn't there a phone in the peep-hole closet? But how'd Cain gotten the gun off of Spratt? He looked at Liefson, and while he was lying about the gun not being in Spratt's hand, he sure looked convincing. Tony decided to keep Liefson talking and see what came out on the wash. "Mr. Liefson, why don't you tell me everything that happened, beginning with why you went down to the shower room in the first place?"

Liefson hesitated, and then spoke slowly. "I had a spare and was alone in the hallway when I heard a gunshot. It came from downstairs. No one else must have heard it for no one came out of the classrooms. I thought of telling the principal but thought first, I should check. I slowly walked downstairs and peeped around the corner. A shower was going full blast but not near to where Mr. Spratt was lying motionless, in a pool of blood. I just knew he was dead. I'd never seen a dead person before. I felt nauseated and almost vomited."

"Okay Mr. Liefson, what did you do after you saw that Spratt was dead?"

"I stepped closer and saw a bullet hole in his chest. The gun was near him. I never touched it, I swear. I didn't know what to think. I felt sorry for him. What if he wasn't a pervert? I heard the police siren, went upstairs and just missed Abaraham Gold."

But Liefson's footprint was nowhere near the main stairs. Again, he was lying and this time, he didn't look as convincing. He was squirming and he hadn't been when he first talked. "What did you think of the bloody marking that Spratt had made on the floor?"

Liefson looked surprised and said, "Are you trying to trick me? There was no marking on the floor. I would have noticed."

"Mr. Liefson, I can show you the photo of the crime scene with a marking in blood that Mr. Spratt made on the floor with his blood-stained fingers."

He looked bewildered and muttered, "I'm not lying. I tell you there was no marking in blood. And his fingers were not blood stained."

"Okay, but you are lying about returning by the main stairs. Your bloody footprint is nowhere near it. You left by the stairs to the student quarters. Come clean, Mr. Liefson or I'll book you?"

Just then Tony heard his earworm playing Anton Karas' zither music in the movie, "The Third Man." Christ, he thought, was there someone else in the shower room? But that made no sense or did it? The shower had been running. He'd heard that from Grant and Liefson. No way had Spratt been taking a shower. Was it Cain? Had Spratt confronted Cain, but Cain had gotten the best of him and shot him. But Spratt had not been shot, close-up. And Spratt and Cain only made two. Tony felt he'd hit a brick wall. Going out on a limb, he yelled at Liefson,

"I know you're lying Liefson. The gun was not beside Spratt. You left by the student quarters. And there was someone else in those showers. Tell me who Mr. Liefson or I'll book you as an accessory to murder."

Liefson lost all colour as though he was going to fall to the floor in a dead faint, but he didn't. After a good minute, still with next to no colour in his face, he spoke, "Reginald Moorehouse was lying on the floor near the back stairs. He was not moving. I thought he was dead but I saw that he was breathing. I tapped him. No response. Then I saw a squished bar of soap. He

189

must have stepped on it, flipped and knocked himself out when he hit the floor. I knew if he was found there that he'd be charged with murder. And no way had he murdered Spratt. I picked up the bar of soap and Reginald, and took him up to his room. You are right. I exited by the back stairs. I should have told you and I apologize. I was protecting a friend."

Moorehouse kept turning up like a bad penny. But wasn't Moorehouse best buds with Spratt and wouldn't have Spratt wanted him on his side? Spratt saw him alone, in the showers and approached. The burning question was when had Moorehouse stepped on the soap? He had to ask, "Liefson, what did Moorehouse tell you happened?"

"Spratt came into the showers waving a gun. He got frightened and that was when he stepped on the soap. He had no idea that Spratt had been shot. Until today, he bought the story in The Gazette. I tell you, he's not the shooter."

So, Moorehouse was unconscious when Spratt was shot. Another dead end. But why was Liefson so insistent that Moorehouse was innocent. Again, he was back squirming. And how had he known there was a shooter? Then the penny dropped. Hadn't Gold been told the gun was in Spratt's hand? Or was that what

Gold surmised when he was told that the gun was in his hand?

"Mr. Lifson, when you arrived the gun was in Moorehouse's hand, wasn't it?"

Liefson went white as a ghost and it was minutes before he responded, I don't know how you figured it out but yes, the gun was in Reginald's right hand. But he's left-handed. I removed the gun, wiped it of all prints, and kicked it towards Spratt. I knew what Gold would do when he saw the gun in Moorehouse's hand. He had his favorites and Moorehouse was not one of them. I don't regret what I did. Are you going to book me?"

"No, I'm not booking you. Under the circumstances, I won't tell you what I would have done."

Chapter 39

Pacing back and forth, hands knotted behind his back, Nigel Gold felt like his skin was on fire, worse than when he'd stepped on a red ant hill. The lab had just called to tell him that they had retrieved the slug that had killed Lefty Lowland. It had been fired from a Colt and Dr. Neckroff was giving it to Carson. What if the Colt was the gun that he had sold to an anonymous buyer? Could he be charged with being an accessory to murder? Why, why had he sold it and why to an anonymous buyer? He couldn't stop stewing that he was in deep shit and felt so alone. Hung out to dry, as they say. How he hated that feeling.

He needed a cigarette, and this time, he didn't care if he was seen or not. The least of his worries. As he opened the window, it was freezing cold outside, the four Westcloxes chimed twelve o'clock and he heard a knocking at his door. Slamming down the window, he rushed back to his seat, pulled out a small hand mirror, plastered on a smiled, put away the mirror and shouted, "Come in, Miss Hussdon."

It had to be her. She didn't know enough to rap three times. What the hell was she doing there? How many times had he told her that it was taboo to interrupt him during his lunch break. In she walked and he could see that she was smiling, and was wearing a most becoming dress with a Pollock-like splattering of small red-and-blue petalled flowers. He snarled, "Husson, I told you to never interrupt me over lunch. Turn around and exit."

She looked startled but then continued to smile, "You joke. See, I brought lunch. I say I bring lunch. Okay you say."

Shit, he thought, how could he have forgotten that she offered to bring him lunch? He too continued to smile and said, "You right. Me joke. What did you bring me?"

She reached into a large satchel, fished out a Coke and handed it to him. It was ice-cold. How did she know it was his favorite? As he sipped on it, she pulled out a plastic plate with three cabbage rolls under cellophane and handed it to him. While the plate was hot, it was not piping hot. Quickly, he slipped off the cellophane, inhaled deeply, and took a bite. With surprize in his voice, he said, "M.m.m. They are good."

"You say you like cabbage. These, my favorite. Sarmale. No meat, special. You tell me if you like?"

After he inhaled all three, he drained the Coke. His skin had stopped itching, and he was feeling so much better. Looking at her, when had he really last looked at her, he had to admit that she wasn't bad looking. Then, he responded,

"Oh yes, I like Romanian cabbage rolls. I never had them, before, but I have to admit they are the best cabbage rolls I've ever had. Thank you Miss Hussdon. You really didn't have to do it, but I'm glad you did. I should not have joked when you came in."

She returned the plate and empty Coke can to her satchel and was about to leave, when she stopped and said, "Me happy. Me, never see you smile. My father never smile. He always yell. He cruel man. He say 'slut.' He laugh at me. I cry. He laugh more."

Suddenly he recalled when Abraham had caught him putting the dress on his mother's mannequin. He hadn't thought of it in years. When Abraham had screamed at him that he was a Namby-Pamby, he had cried, sobbed. But Abraham had laughed all the more and then ordered him to put on his mother's dress. And when he did, Abraham had almost died, laughing. How he wished he had died. Nigel had never felt so degraded, so humiliated. His father had then told him to burn the dress but Nigel hadn't. It was in his desk's lower drawer that he had moved from home when he was made chief. As far as he knew, it was still there. But what threw him for a tizzy was when his mouth opened, and he heard,

"My father too never smiled and when he made fun of me, he laughed and laughed."

"Mine sold me. I get even. I cheer when he die. I win. He lose. You get even? How you get even? Must get even."

Strange, he thought, a Romanian peasant of all people, was telling him that he must turn the tables on his father. Never, had he ever stood up to Abraham. But why not? How else to prove, once and for all, that he wasn't a Namby-Pamby? And just like that, without thinking, he opened his bottom drawer, took out the box, removed the silver-white dress and handed it to Hussdon. He had defied his father for the first time. The dress was going to be worn, not destroyed. But she refused to accept it and he had to insist,

"It's yours. You must take it. My father commanded me to destroy it. Don't you see? I'm getting even by giving it to you. I'm having the last laugh. You must take it."

She blushed, gazed at the gown with longing in her eyes, and said, "Me poor, dress too rich. Thank you. No one give me gift."

"Well, isn't that touching, Chief Gold. I never knew you to be so considerate or to have such good taste in women's dresses."

He swung around and faced Florence Coldwell. If Carson hadn't alerted him, he'd have thought for sure that he was seeing a ghost. Before he could say a word, Miss Hussdon rushed up to Coldwell, embraced her, and spilled out the words, "Miss Coldhell, you like dress, my dress? Me pretty?"

Chapter 40

No sooner had Tony sat down at his desk, he hadn't bothered to feed his fish, that his office door opened, and in strode Florence Coldwell. She was smiling, no, she looked like she'd won the lottery. And she was wearing a white shirt, jeans and boots, quite a change from this morning. "Florence, what are you doing here? You're supposed to be at Mulgrave's."

"Yes, yes, I promise to return. But I had to make sure my car was there, and when I saw it, well, I just had to get in and drive it. When I drove by the old place for one last look, the fire marshal spotted me. Was he overjoyed to see me alive. He gave me this slug to give to the police, and while I was going to give it to Chief Gold, I got distracted. Darn you for telling him I was in the land of the living. I wanted to surprise him. Instead, he surprized me. You won't believe this, but he bought Camelia a new dress. She's over the moon, a changed woman."

As she handed him the slug, he was amazed at how long her arms were, and was more amazed to be holding a Colt slug. She sat down, ramrod straight in the chair, and spoke, "The fire marshal found it where he estimated my bed was. Thank God I put all those pillows under the sheets. He agrees with you that it was a Molotov cocktail that sent my house into the clouds. I'm meaning to thank Betty and Judge Lispway for saving my life."

Shit, he thought. He had to tell her, the edited version. "You might hold off. Judge Lispway is dead. I found him at his desk, face down. Most likely a heart attack, but to be sure, I've asked the coroner to do an autopsy."

"Oh my… He was a gem. They don't make judges like him, anymore. He'll be missed. I'll see Betty at the funeral and thank her then. And Tony, I thank you for everything. You've gone way above the call of duty."

She turned and left, closing the door behind her, soundlessly. Tony got out Robins' trophy case and his magnifying glass. First, he examined Coldwell's slug and then, on a whim, compared it to the trophy and not the loose slug. He could not believe his eyes. But when he double-checked, the same. No way was he seeing things. They matched. But how could that be? Confused, to say the least. The trophy Colt was in the case. It had never left the case. And yet, a slug from it had almost nailed Coldwell. He then compared the loose and the trophy slug. They didn't match nor did the loose slug match Coldwell's slug. He sat back in his chair, closed his eyes to see if his thoughts fell into line.

What was he sure of? What did he know for certain? The loose slug had come from the Colt in Robins' trophy case. As the trophy slug was a match for Coldwell's, that had to mean that the Colt in Robin's case was not the trophy or Robins' Colt. And as there were only two Colts in town, the Colt in Robins' case had to be Gold's Colt. If Robins had ended up with Gold's Colt, then Gold had to have Robins' Colt. His eyes snapped open. Had Nigel Gold taken a shot at Coldwell? It sure looked like it as he had Robins' Colt, the almost murder weapon.

He was on a roll and got out the slug that had killed Spratt. It still matched the loose slug in the case. Then he knew that it had been fired from Gold's and not Robins' Colt. No way had Cain, the third man, wrestled free Robins' Colt from Spratt. He had Gold's Colt, all along. What must have happened was after he'd shot Spratt with Gold's Colt, he'd removed Robins' Colt from Spratt and planted it on Moorehouse. In turn, Liefson had removed it from Moorehouse and kicked it towards Spratt. Later, Abraham Gold had returned it to Robins, none the wiser that it was not his Colt that he was giving to Robins.

Again, he had a sinking feeling. Had Nigel Gold shot Spratt? Who else would have had Abraham's Colt? Abraham would never have shot him. It was not his style to dirty his own hands. Christ, Tony thought, what was he thinking? Nigel Gold, chief of police, had shot Spratt and had tried to gun down Coldwell. Was he a cold-blooded killer? Was he Cain? Or was there another explanation?

Chapter 41

Tony, who'd been deep in thought, heard someone clearing his throat and looked up and saw Ken Neckroff entering his office and walking right up to his desk. Without as much as a pleasantry, he handed Tony another Colt slug. Only this one was a dumdum whose metallic end had expanded into a mushroom cap.

"I personally dug it out of Lowland's bedroom wall, and let me tell you, it took me the better part of an hour. I knew it had to be a dumdum from the mess it made of Lowland's head. Can you have a look at it and tell me what you see before I send it to ballistics?"

Quickly, Tony, picked up the magnifier and examined it and then the trophy slug, the loose slug, and Coldwell's slug. It matched the trophy and Coldwell's slug. That meant it had been fired from Robins' Colt, the Colt that Nigel Gold had. He was flabbergasted. If Cain had tried to silence Coldwell, why had he killed Lefty?

"Tony, what's up? You look confused. Most unlike you?"

Should he tell him? Why not? Tony ranted, "The slug that took down the champ is a match for the slug the fire marshal found in Coldwell's bed. I'm stunned, yes I am, to think that the two are connected. And that's not all. Take my word for it, both slugs came from the Colt that Nigel Gold has. Before you came in, I'd concluded that it was Nigel who had shot at Coldwell. And then, you bring in the slug that killed Lefty and it's a match for the one that was meant for Coldwell. You see my dilemma."

Ken held up his hand, half-grimaced and said, "Hold your horses, Tony. Nigel told me some time ago that he'd sold his father's Colt to an anonymous buyer. Thank God, you didn't confront him. Your career would have gone south."

Tony was and wasn't relieved. As much as Nigel got on his nerves, he'd never in a million years figured him for a cold-blooded killer. Okay, he hadn't shot at Coldwell or shot Lefty. But had he shot Spratt?

Chapter 42

Tony drove under the stone arch of the Aberfoyle Highlands, Pinolta's enclave for the posh, and soon spotted Moorehouse's roadside '25' mailbox. Veering sharply onto a winding gravel lane, he passed through a small forest and parked in front of a mansion, complete with a three-car garage. All its doors were open and no car was inside. Didn't look like Moorehouse was home. Still, he walked up to the front door and peered through the frosted entry door glass at a crystal chandelier, mahogany staircase, and marble floor. Nothing but the best. But then, Moorehouse's mother was rumored to parade around in sequined evening gowns. Talk about flaunting her wealth. He rapped on the door and when he got no answer, he tried the knob. It was locked, but he recalled from Linda that there was a back door.

He followed the flagstones through a privet hedge and down an embankment. The side of the house was as massive as the front. He counted seven large windows and then, spotted an oversized French door at the far end. It was ajar. An open invitation. When he stepped inside, he was met by a wall of darkness. The seven windows were curtained. After he flicked on the switch and recovered from the flash of light, he saw that he was in a ballroom with teak-panelled walls and oak-plank flooring. Against the far wall was a teak desk and chair. His skin tingled. For a split second, he saw a body on top of the desk. Was he having a flashback to when he'd seen a body on the sandbar? Then he breathed a sigh of relief. It was a mannequin.

Up close, he realized it was a vandalized mannequin. Arms and legs were dislocated and hanging over the desk's edges. What must have been a jade-green gown, was torn shreds of colored cloth. In the middle of the left chest wall was a dinted safe's silver-and-black dial. He did a double take when he spotted under the mannequin, a folded, crimson rug. While he was no rug expert, it looked Persian. And if it was, then it was Maple's hallway rug? But what was it doing there? When he spotted a red-and-black jewelry box under the desk, he had a sinking feeling. Linda Stonemill had been there.

"SSS"

A black cat, with an arched back, walked toward him, ready to pounce, hissing all the way. A door, down the wall from the desk, opened and out stepped a white-haired woman in a beige apron that dropped from her neck to her knees. She was glaring at him and was shaking a duster at him. Her voice was deep, hoarse, firm and blunt.

"I've already called the police. They'll be here, any minute. They couldn't crack it and neither can you. It's a Chubb. Now git." The cat detoured and pressed up against her leg, but never stopped hissing at him.

Tony said, "I'm Detective Carson. I'm the police. If you want, I'll show you my badge."

She dropped her duster, bent down and petted the back of the cat that stopped hissing but continued to glare at him. "I'm Pearcum. I'm the maid. I've been coming her for 50 years. I don't drive now, and my son drops me off and picks me up. Well, you got here in record time."

Tony decided to go along with her and not tell her why he was there. "You said 'they.' Was there more than one?"

"Yes, two of them. Maybe more. I was upstairs. Heard a car and thought it was the Master. Thought nothing of it. But when I heard another car, I knew something was amiss. I got Magdalene and came down and saw they'd trashed the Missus's mannequin. They couldn't open the safe. Master is going to be fit-to-be-tied when he sees the Missus's mannequin."

Just then the cat, Magdalene, started again to hiss. She shook her duster at the cat and said,

"Magdalene, stop your hissing. He's the police, he's here to protect us."

"Is that your cat's name? I've never known a cat to be called Magdalene."

"She's a naughty one. She hisses at everyone. But I know she loves me. I'm the only one she doesn't hiss at."

At that moment, Tony heard the moving lyrics of "I Don't Know how to Love Him" from the musical, "Jesus Christ, Superstar." Wasn't it Mary Magdalene's giving voice to her conflicting feelings to Christ? Well, it could have been what was going through the mind of Fong Ching as she thought of Jonathan Spratt, her boyfriend. Christ, he swore. How could he have missed it? And then his blood curdled. Who had killed Spratt had tried to kill Fong Ching in Hamilton and finally snuffed Fanny Maple in Pinolta. All to get his hands on the evidence that would put him away for a long, long time and that was before murder was added to the charges.

"Detective, I can't help you. I never even saw a car let alone a licence plate."

That brought Tony out of the land of the dead and he responded, "Don't fret. I'm on my way to apprehend one of them."

Pearcum surveyed the crime scene, shook her head, and sighed, "They say no good comes from bad. Well, I never thought it wise for the Missus to keep her jewels in a mannequin that wasn't bolted to the floor. Maybe now, the Master will listen to me and get a proper wall safe and a security system. There's a fortune in that mannequin. I'll tell him when he gets back from the Park and Stonemill's cabin that this time, he has to listen to me."

Chapter 43

As Tony headed to Algonquin Park and Stonemill's cabin, he was greeted by a howling torrent of rain. Wipers and headlights gave him at most a car's length of visibility, while the heater was no match for the chill that knifed through his car. What he would have given for his hunter's wool jacket? The coat in the backseat was as useless for warmth as it was for dryness. No sooner had he passed the drowning spray of an eighteen-wheeler that almost washed him off the highway, than the storm's ferocity dropped to a whimper. The sky lightened to a seamless greyness. His tires sluiced through an invisible film of water on the asphalt, and he killed the wipers and felt a hint of warmth from the heater.

Turning on the radio, he heard from the Farmers' Almanac that it was going to be an early and severe winter. A vortex of American coal mine pollution in the east and an El Niño in the west. A fox darted across the road and disappeared into a lair of brambles and bushes. Most likely for the winter. Tony shut off the radio after the sixth ad for fat-busting vitamins.

Farmers' fields, silos and farmhouses morphed into craggy hills and canyons of wet stone, covered in a thin, silvery mist. He passed a Ford pickup with a cord of glistening birch, and then a flatbed truck brimming with a chained load of wet pine logs. While his eyes were glued to the road and every passing sign, he almost missed the signpost for "Loggers Trail." Swerving sharply onto the side of the road, he braked in an abrupt skid.

After he opened the gate, he found an old logging trail that wove its way through a forest of towering fir trees. Their branches dripped cold water like leaking faucets. Soon his boots and feet were soaked and chilled. Why hadn't he put on the rubber boots that were in his trunk? An eerie quiet muffled his footsteps, but not the sounds of scurrying mice and the fluttering of hawk wings. Without warning, the trail downgraded to a footpath that wove its way through a forest of stunted pine and cedar trees.

He climbed up and down mossy inclines, crossed elevated clearings, and circumvented fallen logs and moss-covered rocks. The path ended at a small pond whose surface was a dull, monochrome smudge. He trekked through a minefield of prickly weeds to its far side and halted when he heard voices on the other side of a screen of fir trees.

Crawling under their low-lying branches, Tony saw a two-storey log cabin; it was a good fifty yards away. Smoke trickled from a red brick chimney that sat atop a roof covered with resin and pine needles. Hopefully, it was Stonemill's cabin. Down from the cabin, was a pagoda of pine struts and a cedar shingle roof. It housed a shining, rose-colored, ceramic hot tub with clouds of steam and the blurred, bobbing heads of two blonde-haired men. They were sitting and talking at opposite ends of the tub.

When Tony heard, "Bruce" and "Mr. Moorehouse," he knew he was at Stonemill's cabin. The older of the two, had to be Moorehouse. Never having met Moorehouse, he as curious as to what he looked like. He appeared to be quite handsome, and as good-looking as the younger man who had to be Bruce Liefson. This must be the tail end of Bruce's inauguration into the Amigos. Then Tony heard a dog bark.

Below the pagoda, it was perched on a steep incline, was a white Siberian Husky with pinpoint blue eyes and a rather large, open mouth. It was sitting on a path that skirted a drop-off, on whose other side was grey sky. And it appeared to be barking at the pagoda. A woman emerging from the woods on the far side, walked up to the Siberian who stopped yelping and looked up at her.

Blond hair was matted down the sides of her face. Makeup was in free-fall. Blue eyes were glaring.

She wore a beltless, mud-splattered black Mackintosh. A cold uneasiness descended down his spine. Linda Stonemill, an angry Linda Stonemill, pulled out from under her Mackintosh a .30-30 Winchester Magnum, and aimed it in the direction of the pagoda. Then Linda screamed in a voice that could have been heard all the way to Pinolta,

"Reggie, you bastard. I found her hallway rug on your desk. You can't weasel out of it, this time. You killed her."

The older blonde-haired man stood up. Water lapped at his knees and steam swirled around his laser-white bathing suit. Even at a distance, Tony could see fear on the face of Moorehouse. When he spoke, he rushed his words, "Linda, I don't know what you're talking about. I don't know anything about a rug. Please, please, put down the gun."

Her index finger never left the Magnum's trigger. Linda wasn't buying a word he said. Raising his hands high in the air, Moorehouse stepped over the side of the tub and slowly started down the embankment. The younger blonde-haired man, Bruce Liefson, rose in a crouch, stepped over the tub's edge and crawled in slow motion toward the cabin. Tony inched out his Glock, started to crawl under the pine's spiky branches when he heard Moorehouse plead,

211

"Linda, Waverly's out back. Let's call him. We'll discuss this like adults. Linda, you're not yourself. You're upset. No, you're more than upset. You've been drinking. You told me you shouldn't touch a drop. Let's call Waverly."

"No way, it's between you and me, Reggie. You aren't going to sweet talk me out of it, this time, You bastard. You killed her. I know it. I want my picture. I know you have it."

Moorehouse inched his way down the embankment with his arms raised. It looked like he was headed toward a rifle that leaning against a tree. No, no, thought Tony, don't go for it. But Moorehouse when he was in line with the tree, slowly dropped his right hand to the rifle. The Siberian, it missed nothing, reared up and when it did, it collided with Linda who lurched backwards and pulled the trigger.

BANG

The roof of the pagoda exploded in flames; pine struts splintered and gave way with a loud cracking sound. Moorehouse, armed with the rifle, turned to Linda and pointed the rifle at her. Oh, no, Tony moaned. Just then shingles, timbers, floorboards and the hot tub thundered down the slope in a fireball of flame and black smoke. In the blink of an eye, it crossed over the path where Linda and Siberian were and disappeared over the edge. No Linda. No Siberian. Only a smoky haze remained on the path. Tony ran like hell toward it only to hear an ear-splitting explosion that shook the ground, worse that at Coldwell's.

KERBANG

Standing on the edge of a rocky cliff, Tony looked down a good hundred feet to a river that was as wide as the Osprey. A mushroom cloud of night-black smoke was rising over a slow-moving, smoldering float of burnt timbers and shingles. In its wake, was a pinkish-red blister on the river's surface. No sign of Linda. Not another body lost in Davey Jones' Locker. Waverly Stonemill, badly out of breath, flushed, and sweaty, rushed up to Tony's side. Craning his neck over the edge, he lamented,

"Linda, Linda, I don't see you."

Tony only too well, knew the feeling. First, when he'd stood on the edge of a frozen Lake Ontario, and more recently on the edge of High Falls. What he would have given for his father's partner, Ronny Mansfield, to have put his arm around him and said something, anything, when they stood on the shore of Lake Ontario. But when Tony went to put his arm around Stonemill, he pulled away and pointed down at the river.

"See her? See her?"

Fumbling in the pocket of his suit, he pulled out a small telescope, put it up to his eye, focussed it, and then mumbled with dejection in his voice, "It's her damn dog. It's got her Mackintosh in its mouth. Damn Reggie. He caused all of this. Here, you look."

Tony took the telescope and put it up to his eye. For a pocket version, it was deceptively powerful. Tony had no trouble seeing the Siberian swimming alongside the floating remains of the pagoda, with a teeth-hold on the Mackintosh.

"You're right Mr. Stonemill. She's not there. I see only her dog and her raincoat."

Stonemill's face turned ugly, and he spewed out the words, "I heard Linda screaming. I came running around the side of the house only to hear a gunshot and see the pagoda explode. I dropped my rifle. I could see that the pagoda had been knocked off its foundation and was firing down the hill. I heard another gunshot. I never saw Linda, again. I'm sure the goddamned bastard shot her. Where is he?"

Tony hadn't heard a second gunshot, but then the fireball had thundered down the slope. While he'd seen Moorehouse holding a rifle, he couldn't say if he had fired it. Nigel joined them, as sweaty and breathless as Waverly, but spoke with no difficulty, "I was upstairs when I heard an explosion. What happened? I saw the pagoda on fire, and it was going down the hill like it had been catapulted. There was so much smoke and flames. One minute I saw Linda and then I didn't see her. Did she make it?"

"No. My poor Linda went over the cliff into the river. I want the river dragged. And I want Reggie charged with murder. I'm sure he shot her."

Nigel said, "I saw Reggie and Bruce leaving. They were running, fast."

Nigel turned to who else, but Tony, and ordered in his official voice, "Carson, I'm calling Coast Guard and want you to assist them in dragging the river. When you're finished, I want you to question Reggie, and then book him on suspicion of attempted murder. I know he's an Amigo, but no one is above the law. When I saw him running, he didn't have a rifle with him. Do we know where it is?"

Stonemill said, "Nigel, I know exactly where the creep's rifle is. I'll get it for you, no problem. Glad to be of assistance."

Chapter 44

Cloud cover had rationed the light and discolored the ground mist into a dirty shadow. Carl Robins had arrived late and was still in the woods when he'd heard Linda screaming, although he hadn't heard what she was going on about. What was she doing there? She hadn't been invited. Was she having a row with Waverly? This, he had to see. He picked up the pace to get a ring-side seat. But when he stepped out of the woods, he spotted Reggie walking down toward Linda who had a .30-30 aimed at him. Christ, he thought, she looked drunk. When Reggie went for a rifle by a tree, Linda fired and took out the pagoda. When Reggie aimed the rifle at Linda, Carl pulled up his Remington and had Reggie in his crosshairs. This was his big chance. Gun down Reggie and for sure, Waverly would use his reefers. Closing his eyes, he always closed his eyes before he shot at anything, he tightened his index finger on the trigger and heard a gunshot.

Opening his eyes, he saw that Reggie was still standing. The flaming pagoda had passed over where Linda had been standing and vanished. Shit, he thought, had he hit Linda? Then he saw Carson and Waverly running to the cliff's edge. Double shit this time. They'd blame him; they always blamed him. Picking up his rifle, he threw it deep into the woods. No one had seen shoot. He'd say he'd never brought his rifle. No way were they going to pin a murder rap on him. Then he stepped back into the woods to plan his next move.

After smoking a pack of cigarettes, he figured he was in the clear. No one had come looking for him. But he was beginning to feel the cold. His mechanic's coveralls and windbreaker were not insulated. Leaving the woods, he saw smoke coming out of Stonemill's cabin's chimney and headed toward it. Opening the back door, it was never locked, he walked down the hallway and peered around the entrance to the living room.

Nigel was standing beside a large fireplace with a blazing fire in it. Its warmth felt so good. Waverly was standing on the other side of the room, a stand-off if ever there was one. Nigel got out a bottle of Tobermory single malt and placed it and two tumblers on the mantle. He must have brought it for Stonemill was a teetotaller. When he opened the Scotch, Carl, a single malt connoisseur, inhaled a whiff of fresh pear in oak and a mellow finish. While not his favorite, it would do. Carl watched as Nigel poured two hefty glasses, and then offered one to Waverly who shook his head.

"What are you doing, Nigel? You know I don't drink."

"You don't lose your wife every day, Waverly. I just thought you could do with a drop."

"I know what alcohol does and I don't want to talk. Not now, anyways. It's too painful. If I don't watch myself, I'll get into a rage and go after that crud, myself."

"Don't do that. I've impounded his rifle as evidence although you shouldn't have picked it up without wearing gloves. Okay, forget I offered you a drink."

Nigel shrugged his shoulders and placed Waverly's glass on the mantle. After a long swig, he sighed and said, "Waverly, we've been friends for a long time and while I wasn't going to tell you, I feel it's now or never. I know you don't want to talk about Linda, but hear me out. I've had my suspicions about her for some time. My mother was an alcoholic. I know one if I see one and I tell you, she's a closet alcoholic. There, I've said it."

Carl felt that his heart had stopped. Were they going to blame him for giving Linda the gin? Everyone knew he was a bootlegger. But she wasn't one of his regulars. Sure, she had dropped by once or twice, but that was all. Who'd believe him? Best to hit the road...

"Nigel, Linda was screaming that Reggie was a killer. And she was so right. I'm sure he shot her. As for drinking, she knows my rules."

"Waverly, was Linda accusing Reggie of murdering Fanny Maple, the missing whore?"

"Linda told me she picks her up her girlfriend every morning and they go to the gym. I'm sure it's no whore. Linda would never associate with that sort."

Nigel shrugged his shoulders. Carl thought wasn't this interesting and best of all, it had nothing to do with alcohol. It was time and Carl stepped into the room and spoke,

"Boys, where is the pagoda? I was going to hit the hot tub."

Nigel spun around while Waverly just stared at him, and then Nigel snapped, "Robins, why are you always showing up late?"

Waverly held up his hands, he often raised them when he wanted to speak; he was so official. "Robins, there's been a terrible accident. Lightning hit the pagoda and turned it into a raging fireball. Linda was in the wrong place at the wrong time. Detective Carson and the Coast Guard are looking for her in the river, as we speak."

"Oh my God, I'm so, so sorry Waverly, truly I am. I hope like hell that Carson finds her."

Just then, the phone rang. Waverly, picked it up only to hand it to Carl who was stunned to hear Pet screaming at him that she was married to a bootlegger and drug dealer. She was walking if he didn't reform. He hung up and left without another swig of scotch.

Chapter 45

All the way home, Reginald heard Bruce Liefson babbling on like a child that he'd never been more frightened in all his life. And that he'd be dead if Mr. Moorehouse hadn't told him to get out of the tub when he did. Bruce couldn't stop thanking him for facing down "a crazy woman." As to whether Linda was crazy, Reginald wasn't sure although she hadn't made much sense. The only rug in his home was in his mother's bedroom. When she had accused him of killing 'her,' she had to mean Miss Maple. If only, he could have talked more to her? Then, he regretted picking up the rifle. Had someone shot at her? Everything had gone so fast and so badly. Sure, he had warned her, for all the good that it had done. Despite Bruce's kind words, he couldn't shake the sinking feeling that he had caused her death.

He was giving himself a headache, and couldn't stop the thoughts that hammered away at him. Would they send the police? Weren't the police already calling about Spratt? What if the police found out the gun was in his hand? And what if the police found out he had been at Miss Maple's, the last person to see her alive? Dr. Ramsay couldn't help him, this time. Reginald felt a soul-piercing anguish and for a split-second saw Linda's blood dripping off his hands. Was he another Lady MacBeth?

When they arrived at the Liefson home on Dairy Street, Bruce ran faster than a jackrabbit up the patio stones and into his house. Herb's pickup wasn't on the street. If it had been, he would have asked Herb to accompany him home, but no such luck. As much as he knew he had to go home, he dreaded it. What if Linda had been there and seen a rug? He turned up the radio to full volume to drown out his thoughts, but they were too loud.

When his headlights found the single portico light in the foggy darkness, he parked on the driveway, and ever so slowly, walked up and opened his front door. But after one step inside the foyer, he stopped as if paralyzed. He felt so desolate, so miserable and so alone. Worse than when they'd lowered his mother's coffin into the grave and, he'd been tempted to join her. Should he call Dr. Ramsay? That would be the sensible thing to do, but everything was too much of an effort. He just stood there, in the darkness, hadn't even closed the door.

How long he'd stood frozen, he had no idea. Time felt like it had stopped. Then, a cool draft on his back broke the spell, he turned and shut the door. After he flipped on the light switch, he collapsed on the

223

bottom step of the sweeping staircase. Was he losing his mind? Was this what it was like to go stark raving mad? Why couldn't he cry? Had he lost all feelings? Rubbing his hands together as if they were flint, he felt a spark of warmth, and slowly got to his feet. He had to see what was downstairs before he did anything else, he had to do that.

He crossed the foyer, walked along the oak-paneled hallway and down the stairs to the door that led into the ballroom. Standing there, he felt his heart pounding and cold sweat dripping down the back of his neck. As much as he wanted to turn and run, he didn't. Opening the door, he closed his eyes and turned on the lights.

When he opened his eyes, he saw his mother's mannequin lying on top of the desk. Its dress was torn to shreds; its arms and legs were dislocated; its pearl necklace was missing, and its safe's dial was badly dinted. He opened his mouth to scream but nothing came out, and then he dropped to his knees. Why, why were the only thoughts in his head? It felt as if he had been torn apart on a torture rack. His hands clenched briefly and dropped, limp, to his sides.

Under the desk, on the floor, was the red-and-black jewelry box. He knew then, Linda had been there, had returned. Thoughts twisted in his head until he thought it would crack wide open. And then he saw under the mannequin, a folded-up red rug. That had to be the rug that Linda had seen. She had carried on like it was Miss Maple's rug. Sweat ran down the back of his neck, hot and burning sweat. The room began to spin. Thoughts that he was a Frankenstein filled his head. Herb was wrong. He had shot Spratt, his friend. Dr. Ramsay was wrong. He had killed Miss Maple. How else to explain how he had her rug and jewelry box. And he'd killed Linda as sure as if he'd shot her. He couldn't take it, anymore. He'd had enough. Why not shoot himself and end it?

He crawled under the desk, reached up and opened the drawer, retrieved his mother's handgun with his left hand, pointed it at his head, and pulled the trigger.

Chapter 46

For three hours, Tony had sat cross-legged and barefoot in the bow of a large, rubber dinghy with his eyes plumbing the depths of the river. Mahoney from Coast Guard, at the stern, had geared down the Johnson Outboard to a trolling speed. He was wearing a black baseball cap emblazoned with FLAMINGO in red letters, his lucky hat, but all they'd found was an empty, hot tub. On the bottom of the dinghy was Mahoney's bone-dry wet suit. The water was surprisingly clear, no excuse there. When Tony looked to the west, and saw that he had an hour of light, at the most, he raised his right hand in defeat.

Mahoney shouted, "Finally, what a waste of an afternoon. I tell you the bitch is in Lake Ontario. I had a hot date, and now I'll be sleeping, alone. Don't expect me back, tomorrow."

With a cynical curl on his lips, cynicism was in Mahoney's DNA, he cut the throttle, and they drifted onto a dirt beach near the smoldering, charred remains of the pagoda and the tail-wagging Siberian. Linda's Mackintosh was still in its mouth. Tony jumped into shallow water and pulled the dinghy onto the beach, while Mahoney waited to step onto dry land. He was wearing dress shoes. Tony fished out his shoes, bent

226

down to put them on when he did, he felt the warm, wet, Siberian's nose in his face.

"Git, git, you mutt." Mahoney growled, even though the Siberian was nowhere near him. Taking a cellular-mobile phone out of his windbreaker's inner pouch, he handed it to Tony, and gave instructions, "Dial 705 4560000. That's the number he gave me. I never forget a number. Make it quick, I'm feeling I can make my date, after all."

When Tony dialed the number, Stonemill answered on the first ring. Tony only got out a "sorry" before he heard an abrupt hang-up. While it irritated Tony to have a phone slammed down in his ear, not this time. No sooner had he handed it back to Mahoney, than he tossed it into the dinghy, gave the boat a mighty shove, and cleared its side without getting a drop of water on his shoes. With a mighty pull on the cord, he gunned it down the river.

The evening was cooling fast and losing light even faster. Tony, with the Siberian at his side, quickly crossed the beach, a minefield of mud puddles, and found a path that wove uphill through a forest of stunted pines. On the forest's other side, he was into an ankle-deep carpeting of whitish mist. Suddenly, the Siberian bounded ahead with the grace of an antelope, and Tony had to run full-out to keep the frolicking dog in sight.

After a good fifteen minutes, with no warning, the Siberian veered left and disappeared into mist that was up to Tony's knees. After that, Tony only caught infrequent snatches of the dog's white fur, and followed more the swishing sound of Linda's Mackintosh, his auditory compass. When they were back among stunted trees, he cursed that they'd gone full circle. Was the Siberian playing with him? No way could he catch up with the dog that had the energy of a racehorse. Suddenly, they were in pines that had the height of Douglas firs. He'd never seen them before. Where was the Siberian leading him?

Tony was gasping for breath from running up-hill, and was soaking wet and chilled from brushing against branches and their icy raindrops. How he hated the cold. The swishing sound of the Macintosh was getting fainter, and he couldn't recall when he'd last seen the dog. How much longer? More, where was the bloody dog headed? He was going to collapse, and if he fell down, he doubted he'd ever get back on his feet. Then he saw, in the distance, the back of the Siberian as it leaped high into the air and landed with a 'THUD' in an explosion of mist.

He faced head-on the dog that was sitting on its haunches. When Tony doubled over, breathless, cold sweat dripping down the sides of his face, he saw wooden slats and then heard a gurgling sound.

Unbelievable. He was standing on a wooden bridge that spanned a fast-moving stream. No way had he crossed a bridge on his way down. Was he hopelessly lost? Never again would he leave home without a compass.

When he glared at the dog's pleased-as-punch puss, it barked, dropped Linda's Mackintosh, and bolted into waist-high mist, on the other side of the bridge. Tony cursed, ran across the bridge, grabbed the Mackintosh and sprinted after it, although he couldn't hear or see the dog. Somehow, he side-stepped trees and boulders in the darkness as he ran uphill. Within minutes, his heart was pounding, and his lungs were gasping for air. His Police training hadn't included scaling cliffs or mountain climbing.

When he heard an ear-piercing howl, followed by a string of barks, he knew it was coming from just ahead of him. His auditory compass was back in business, and he was on course. Miraculously, he gained a runner's second wind, rarely had it ever happened before, and kept up with the woofing sounds. Just as he was closing in, he tripped over a tree root and fell on the cold, hard ground. His heart was not so much beating as fluttering. He was finished, spent, and lay motionless, except for his beating heart. He'd hit the wall.

When he found the strength to raise his head, he was incredulous. He closed and re-opened his eyes to

229

make sure he wasn't hallucinating. He wasn't. Straight ahead, the Siberian's two neon-blue pinpoint eyes, motionless in the mist as if they were painted there, were suspended high above the ground. How could that be?

Slowly getting to his feet, he felt like Lazarus must have felt when he left the grave, he advanced at a turtle's pace. But the Siberian's eyes were fixed on him, unmoving. No bolting this time. Tony's right foot and leg brushed up against something hard and cold. Swishing at the mist with the Mackintosh, he discovered an open convertible with the tail-wagging dog sitting up in the back seat. In the ignition was a key on a chain with a silver disc, emblazoned with the initials 'L.S.' What luck. It was Linda Stonemill's BMW.

Tossing the Mackintosh into the passenger seat, he reached back to grab the Siberian when up went its ears and, it jack-knifed out of the car and disappeared into the mist. What was it with that dog? With nothing to lose, he had Linda's car, he chased after the white blur as it zigzagged around shadowy clumps and leaped over dark rocks. Thankfully, the dog had whiter fur than the mist. This time he didn't lose sight of it, either it was slowing down, or he was into his third wind. Suddenly, it went airborne and landed in a pool of grey mist, soundlessly, except for a woman's excited voice,

"Doggie... Oh Ami, it's you. Thank God, I thought you were a goner."

In the darkness, Tony saw two outstretched, bare, blackened arms that were holding the Siberian that was in a licking frenzy. Whoever she was, the dog sure knew her and then, Tony screamed, "Linda Stonemill, is that you?"

A dog-slathered face smiled at him. "Yes, it's me, Detective Carson. Am I glad to see you, and of course, Ami. My two knights in shining armor. I was so worried I'd have to spend the night here. My head aches from where I landed on a rock. I must have been out for hours. I never wear a watch. Do you know what time it is?"

He looked at his watch and said, "It's 8 o'clock. Any thing broken? Can you move all four limbs?"

"I'm all right, nothing is broken, bruised, yes. So, it's still Wednesday. I wouldn't have been surprised if it was Thursday."

Incredible, Linda Stonemill hadn't gone over the cliff. Didn't sound like she had been shot, either. She was sprawled out on the ground with Ami in her arms. There was a nasty cut and bruise with dried blood on her left temple. A string of large pearls were around her neck. As her knit dress barely covered her, he handed her the Mackintosh and she slipped it on.

He asked, "Where did you get the rifle and were you drinking?"

"No, I wasn't drinking, and don't try to pin that one on me. At Moorehouse's, when I saw Fanny's rug, I lost it. I stormed out and went home, picked up Ami and a rifle, and drove like mad to get to the cabin. I wasn't planning to shoot poor Reginald, only scare him into confessing and giving me my picture. But when I saw him go for the rifle, Ami jumped up and bumped me, and I pulled the trigger. Thank God, I missed."

As good a time as any to ask her, "Did Moorehouse shoot at you?"

She sat up straight and looking intently at him, said, "Why, would you think that? No, he didn't. Reginald shouted at me to jump. I had no idea the pagoda was moving as fast as it was down the hill. And just as I jumped, I felt a bullet whiz past the side of my head. Reginald saved my life, twice."

He could see that she wasn't the same woman who had stood on the path with a loaded rifle. "If Moorehouse saved your life, do you still think that he killed Maple?"

She grimaced, blushed, and spoke in a contrite voice, "You would ask me, that. I had it coming. If there's one thing I know about Reginald, it's that's he intelligent. No way would he be so dumb to incriminate himself. And another thing I know, he's too sensitive and caring to be a cold-blooded killer."

Tony could see that hitting her head on the rock had knocked her back into sanity. Linda shuddered and continued speaking, "If you're going to pay him a visit, can I come with you? I need to apologize, and also show him that I'm alive. He may be thinking I'm dead and blaming, himself. I never met a more guilty man."

He nodded and they walked, arm in arm, to her car. She was wobbly, at first. Ami jumped into the back seat, his territory. She got into the passenger seat and he got his wish for he was dying to get behind the wheel of a BMW.

Chapter 47

When Tony arrived at Aberfoyle Highlands, the Beamer's headlights, so much brighter than his Malibu's, located Moorehouse's numbered mailbox as though it was the middle of the day. The gravel lane seemed shorter this time. When he parked behind a Porsche, in front of the mansion, he knew Moorehouse was home this time. Linda ran ahead of him up to the porch, rapped and then plastered her face against the entry door glass.

"I don't see him. He must be downstairs. He can't hear us when he's down there. I have a flashlight in the glove compartment."

He found the flashlight and handed it to her. She followed the flagstones through the gap in the hedge to the embankment where there was plenty of light coming through the windows on the side of the mansion. She pocketed the flashlight. The French door that was open. In the ballroom, he immediately noticed that there was no mannequin on the desk against the far wall. The rug was there. Linda's right arm jerked up and she screamed,

"Look, lying under the desk, isn't that Reginald?"

Moorehouse was lying, motionless and prostate, on the floor, just where she had pointed. He was wearing a dirty sports jacket and an even dirtier pair of slacks. When he saw a gun in Moorehouse's left hand, he turned to Linda and said, "You wait here. I'll check on him."

She started to cry but never moved as he walked up to Moorehouse. Tony smelled gun smoke. Had Moorehouse shot himself? He didn't see any blood. He felt warm skin and a strong carotid pulse on his neck, and saw that his chest was moving. There was a thin reddish-blue line along his left temple. Tony traced an imaginary path in the air from the blemish on his temple to a small, round black spot, high up on the teak wall. Moorehouse's hand must have been shaking when he shot himself. One for the records. Turning, he almost shouted,

"Linda, he's alive."

She mumbled in disbelief, "Are you on the level?"

"Yes, I am. His heart is beating and he's breathing. The bullet grazed him, nothing else. I'm going to try and rouse him, but if I can't, you call 9-1-1."

She jumped to her feet, brushed her eyes with the Mackintosh's sleeves, raced over, and while he was gently slapping Moorehouse's cheeks, she bent down and whispered in Moorehouse's ear, "Reginald, wake up. I'm alive. It's me, Linda. You saved my life. I know now you didn't harm Fanny. How could I have accused you? I'm such a fool. Wake up, Reginald. Please."

Tony saw Moorehouse's eyelids flutter, and then heard a hoarse, soft moan. "My head hurts... Linda... Linda, am I dreaming? Did I hear your voice?" Moorehouse sounded groggy but wasn't slurring his words, a good sign. Then Tony saw that the gun in his left hand was a Colt, removed it and placed it on the crimson, folded-up hallway rug on the desk.

"Reginald, you're not dead. It's me, Linda. I'm not dead. It's no dream. You saved my life. You warned me and I jumped. Missed the pagoda and a bullet with my name on it."

He opened wide his eyes, and his voice was strong. "Linda, you're not dead. I see you. I'm not dreaming. But I shot myself. I couldn't take it anymore. I should be dead."

"Mr. Moorehouse, we never met. I'm Detective Carson. Yes, you shot yourself. But the bullet barely grazed your head. You are a lucky man, Mr.

236

Moorehouse. If you don't mind me asking. Where did you get the gun?"

"Mother kept a Smith and Wesson in the desk drawer." Moorehouse sat up, grimaced in pain but did not hold his head.

Linda interjected, "Reginald, you shot yourself because of me, right? I'm so sorry, so very sorry. You didn't deserve it, any of it. What a mess I've made of everything. Thank God you're alive. I don't think I could live with myself if you were dead."

She had started to cry again, but nothing like before. Moorehouse gently touched her on the cheek, Tony was impressed. Then Moorehouse got to his feet, held on to the edge of the desk and faced Tony. "Detective Carson, when I shot myself, I was sure I had murdered Mr. Spratt and Miss Maple and caused Linda's death. I was on the worst guilt trip of my life. I was out of my mind with guilt. But now I see that Linda is alive. Herb said I didn't shoot my friend, Mr. Spratt, and Dr. Ramsay said I didn't harm Miss Maple. Have you come to arrest me?"

Tony heard his earworm playing Bronislau Kaper's score to the 1944 version of the movie, "Gaslight." His earworm and he were on the same wavelength.

"Mr. Moorehouse, I've talked to Herb Liefson and I believe him. You did not shoot Mr. Spratt but someone set you up to take the rap by planting the gun in your right hand. As for Miss Maple, it sure looks to me that evidence was planted on you, and you were gaslighted. What I'd like to know Mr. Moorehouse, were you at Miss Maple's on Monday?"

He blushed, looking sheepish, but spoke without hesitation,

"Yes, I was there on Monday, I'm not denying it. She was helping me to overcome a phobia for looking at naked women. Dr. Ramsay sent me. To help me relax, she went so far as to remove her wig to appear less feminine. That's when the lights went out. I woke up with a splitting headache and she wasn't there. Dr. Ramsay says that someone knocked me out."

Christ, thought Tony, when she removed her wig, that's when her killer knew she was Fong Ching. But where could he have been to have seen her?

"Mr. Moorehouse, were the drapes open in Maple's bedroom, when you were there?"

"Yes they were. I asked her to close them but she wouldn't. I felt I was on Main Street. When I came to, they were closed and it was pitch-dark."

Linda blushed and said,

"I once looked out Fanny's window and looked right at Bruce's bedroom window. I'm sure, if I had Waverly's telescope, I could have seen right into his bedroom."

Tony's heart leaped, it was a sign he was headed in the right direction, and he asked,

"Mr. Moorehouse, do you know in what room was Bruce's inauguration held on Monday?"

"It was in Bruce's bedroom. That was Nigel's idea."

That meant that Cain had been at Bruce Liefson's inauguration on Monday. Who had been there? Carl Robins, Waverly Stonemill and Nigel Gold had been there. Discounting Carl and Waverly's joint alibi, all three had been at Thackeray's when Spratt was shot. And he was sure that all three had been at Joe's Gym for the East End Kid's gala. What about Moorehouse and he asked,

"Mr. Moorehouse, were you at the East End Kid's gala?"

Moorehouse looked momentarily befuddled, hesitated, and then answered,

239

"I don't know if it's a trick question or not but no, I wasn't at any gala and to be honest, I never heard of any East End Kid. Why do you ask?"

"My hunch is that Miss Maple's killer was there. Another question, Mr. Moorehouse. When Linda jumped out of the way of the pagoda, someone shot at her. Any idea who it could be?"

"No, no I don't. But I do appreciate you not blaming me. Until I shot myself, I 've never pulled the trigger on any gun. There were woods there. Could have been a hunter. Besides Nigel and Waverly, you might ask Carl Robins. When I was leaving, I saw him in the woods. I doubt he saw me, but if he did, he didn't wave although he's not that friendly, to me, anyway."

Tony was back to the same three suspects he had for Spratt, Maple and Lefty. But why shoot Linda? He didn't see what Cain had to gain from her death. Just then, Linda took off the pearl necklace, turned to the desk, and screamed again,

"Reginald, where's the mannequin? Because of me, you haven't thrown her away, have you?"

Moorehouse spun around and was speechless, in shock. Interesting, thought Tony. Someone had made off with the mannequin and from Moorehouse's reaction, after he had shot himself. Whoever it was, hadn't closed the door behind him.

"Mr. Moorehouse, I was talking to your housekeeper, and she told me that it contained priceless jewels. Who knew the jewels were there, Mr. Moorehouse?"

"Beside mother and me, only Pearcum. Oh, I should add Abraham Gold. Mother told him everything. As for Pearcum, I trust her implicitly."

Linda, still with the pearl necklace in her hand, opened the desk drawer to put it there, only to drop the pearls and exclaim,

"Reggie, there's an explicit photo of your mother and Abraham Gold in here. It was taken in your mother's bedroom; I recognize the ruby-red wallpaper. Where did it come from?"

That gave him another start and this time, he muttered,

"It was in the safe with the necklace. I removed it without looking at it and was going to show it to Dr. Ramsay. I thought maybe he could use it in therapy for my phobia. You say it was taken in mother's bedroom. Strange, I'd forgotten she had red wallpaper."

241

Just a minute, thought Tony and said,

"Linda, if it's a photo, what's the name of the photographic paper on the back of it?"

"It's Fujifilm paper."

Chapter 48

A 'thudding' sound awoke Tony. Opening his eyes, he heard it again. Strange, it sounded as if it was coming from outside his bedroom window and not from his front door. Getting out of bed, he walked over to the window, opened the blinds to a glimmer of yellow light leaking under the cloud cover in the east and a red-breasted robin. It was sitting on his windowsill and shivering in the cold. Poor, misguided bird, he knew exactly how it felt. Checking his watch, it was 8 o'clock, he thanked the robin for rousing him but couldn't redirect it to Mexico.

In the bathroom, he threw freezing cold water on his face, no time to shave, and sprinted to his closet across the cold oak floor. There, he threw on his uniform, and then grabbed a bulky sweater, an old pair of jeans, and two heavy woolen socks. When he rapped on the guest room door, he got no response and had to pound and wait, before he heard Linda's voice,

"Tony, what time is it?"

"It's 8 o'clock; time you were up. I'm putting a change of clothing on the floor outside the door and going downstairs to make a coffee. No time for breakfast. We got to get a move on to be there before your husband leaves for work."

Downstairs, Tony stepped over a snoring Ami. In the kitchen, he filled the percolator with ground coffee beans, added water, placed it on the front burner, and turned on the gas. If he was in town, he could have read the morning paper, but there was no delivery in the country. Instead, he sat down, closed his eyes and thought.

Cain had set up Moorehouse to take the rap for Spratt's death and gaslighted him for Maple's death. While Tony was sending the Colt from Moorehouse's to the lab, he was sure that it too had been planted. Three times unlucky or lucky, depending on whether the killer or the patsy, when he included Lefty's murder. It had spanned more than 20 years. Whoever Cain was, he had to have known that the jewels were there. That meant Cain was who had snapped the photo in his desk that had been in the safe with the jewels. Tony cursed out loud. He hated it when crime paid as much as he hated a crooked cop.

Hearing footsteps, he opened his eyes. Linda, wearing his hand-me-downs with the black Mackintosh over her arm, walked into the kitchen with a tail-wagging Ami at her side. Its nose was in the air; did dogs drink coffee? Tony got up, poured them a coffee, not Ami, turned off the stove, and sat down across from her. After she'd taken a healthy swig, Linda placed down her cup and spoke in a calm and measured voice,

"Tony, I feel I can call you Tony, in private of course. I want to thank you for allowing me to spend the night here. I was scared that whoever had shot at me was out there, and knowing that Waverly was in the house, was of no help. I slept well last night, hard to believe, and waking up this morning, feel that I'm ready to face the world. Again, thank you for being so understanding. Tony, could it have been a hunter? Reginald mention that possibility."

While he hadn't included a hunter as a suspect, he had to admit that it was a possibility.

"You know Linda, he may be right. It is deer and moose hunting season."

"Okay, I feel even better. Now take me home."

From the hallway closet, he extracted his shoulder holster, Glock and jacket. Outside, it was cold and windy, but inside the Beamer and its climate control, he felt almost too hot. When he dialed to his favorite FM station and heard a full orchestra in the back seat, he knew he had to get a Beamer. In the rear-view mirror, he saw her squirm and look on edge. She wasn't hearing the music. Suddenly, she pointed and shouted,

"Tony, there's my house."

It was a brown brick, two storey that ran deeper than any other house on the block. And it was the only house with an extra-wide driveway and a three-car garage. He parked alongside a red Cadillac that had recently been washed and polished. Linda got out, walked slowly with a feigned limp to the front door, all the time, glancing over her shoulder to make sure he was still there. At the front door, Tony stepped up to her, and whispered.

"Linda, let's review what we went over last night. Ami knocked you out of the way of the pagoda fireball. You went flying and landed on a rock. You were out cold all night and only regained consciousness early this morning, just before I found you. I picked up some clothes, and dropped Ami off before I drove you home. Don't mention that you heard and felt a shot."

"Tony, what would I do without you?"

As Linda rapped on the door, she grimaced in pain, a born actor. After a long minute, Waverly Stonemill, dressed in what else but a three-piece suit, opened the door. He was eating an apple, that is until he saw Linda and dropped it. Teetering backwards, he opened his mouth but was speechless. Tony thought for sure that he was going to stroke-out when his face went a ruddy- red and he quickly spoke,

"Mr. Stonemill, I should have called ahead and prepared you. I found your wife in the woods by the cabin this morning. Her dog had knocked her out of the way of the fireball only she hit her head on a rock and was out cold until early this morning. I found her, more good luck than anything, and she insisted I drive her car. I dropped her dog off at my home and loaned her a change of clothes. I was going to drive to the hospital but she insisted that I drive her home."

Linda teared but didn't sob. Stonemill lurched forward and grabbed her with outstretched arms.

"Linda, you're alive. I prayed that you were. It's a miracle."

Chapter 49

Linda was in disbelief when Waverly reached out and held her, okay, at arm's length but still a first in a long, long time. While she couldn't stand men who smothered her, she had no worry of that with Waverly. But just as quickly as he had almost hugged her, he let go and turned to Tony.

"Thank you, Detective Carson, I can't thank you enough. Nigel says you are the best. She hit her head; I should call our doctor."

"No, no I don't want any doctor, Waverly. I'm fine, really, I am. I know my name, where I live and that you are my loving husband. What more do I need?"

Linda noticed a twitch in Waverly's left nostril and cringed. He had a hound dog's sniffer for alcohol but dammit, she hadn't been drinking. But if he thought she had been, there was no changing his mind. Then she spotted a rifle leaning against their hallway wall, and felt faint.

"Waverly, why is there a rifle in our house?"

He looked at her with one of his signature blank looks.

"Oh, I dropped it yesterday and Nigel found it and returned it, early this morning."

Then he turned to Tony and she could see a twitch in his right nostril. He was angry and she feared, she was in for it. Why hadn't she stayed away, longer? He almost shouted but at Tony,

"Detective Carson, is Reggie behind bars where he belongs."

"Mr. Stonemill, I didn't charge Mr. Moorehouse. He denied shooting at Linda. I'll discuss it further with Nigel."

"You discuss it with Nigel, the sooner the better. He has Reggie's rifle and it's been fired. I won't rest until he's behind bars where he belongs. And now, goodbye Detective Carson."

Linda felt a wave of unease as she watched Tony drove away in her car. How she wished she could have been in the car with him. As soon as he was out of sight, Waverly picked up the apple core, tossed it on to the side table, and nudged her left elbow. Nothing had changed. That was his way of telling her to move, and she stepped inside. He closed the door behind her, stepped around her, careful not to touch her, and faced her with the expression of a cigar store wooden Indian. He'd made no attempt to remove the rifle even though it was unnerving her. After he cleared his throat, he spoke as though addressing a child,

"Linda, I know you were drinking."

Christ, she thought, the same old rigmarole. Nothing had changed, if it was not worse. What had the lawyer told her? Document everything and then return and see him. And nothing in the meantime when she needed help the most. Where was the man who had courted her and she made one more attempt to elicit the man she knew was there but where?

"Oh Waverly, you don't know how glad I'm to be home. Last night I had a dream when I was out cold that you had found me, and had whispered in my ear, 'come home baby, I miss you.'"

"It was a dream. I would never say that. I've never call you baby but come to think of it, why not. You know that I forbid you to drink and you've deliberately disobeyed me, baby."

"No Waverly, I was not drinking. Upset, yes, and who wouldn't be. I had just lost my best friend. What would you be like if someone murdered Nigel?"

"He's the police chief. They don't get murdered. Baby, up to your room. You're grounded."

Chapter 50

At the police front desk, Tony saw a changed Camelia Hussdon whom he'd never seen before. She'd combed and brushed her mousy blonde hair, had applied lipstick, and had on a bright, white dress. Was it the one that Nigel had given her? Coldwell was right, Camelia was a Pygmalion. Who says that clothes don't make the woman? And to top off the transformation, Camelia spoke in a clear voice that again, he'd never heard before.

"Chief Gold want see you,"

Tony knew that Gold would be champing at the bit to know why Moorehouse wasn't in jail. He walked slowly up the stairs and down the hallway, rapped three times on Nigel's door and entered his corner office. Gold was seated and, never moved out of the shadows that poured in from the King and Victoria Avenue windows. Before he got to the chair in front of his desk, Gold snapped,

"Well Carson, don't tell me that you forgot to pay Reggie a visit? Waverly wants his hide and who can blame him. The poor man is beside himself with grief."

Tony took great delight in correcting Gold, and said,

"Moorehouse never shot Linda Stonemill..."

"Carson, Waverly saw him pick up his rifle, aim it at Linda, and heard a gunshot. What more do you need to charge Reggie?'

"Nigel, Linda Stonemill told me that Moorehouse was not the shooter."

Nigel looked at him as though he had two heads and sneered,

"And when did you start communicating with the dead, Carson? Have you lost it?"

"Nigel, good news, Linda is not dead. I found her in the woods early this morning. She was dazed and groggy from hitting her head on a rock when she jumped out of the way of the fireball and a bullet. I just dropped her off at home."

As Nigel's jaw dropped, he jerked backwards and almost did a backflip. After he collected himself, he flicked at his epaulets, cleared his throat, and spoke in a softened voice,

"Linda is alive. I was wrong. I was sure she was dead. Unbelievable is all I can say. Okay, you said she jumped out of the way of a bullet. Well, why wasn't Reggie the shooter?"

252

"She told me that Moorehouse yelled for her to jump. Linda credits him with saving her life. She's sure he wasn't the shooter. She told me the bullet was fired behind Moorehouse and he told me that he'd never fired his rifle."

Gold jumped up as if jolted by lightning. With smugness written all over his face, he announced,

"Well, he's lying. I have his rifle and it's been fired. I found Waverly's rifle by the cabin, it hadn't been fired, and I returned it this morning. As for Linda, she had a head injury and is not credible. Well, how does my number one detective explain that?"

Tony was perplexed. Yes, Gold had a point, but there had to be another explanation. No way had Moorehouse hoodwinked him and Linda. First chance and he was paying the Stonemills' a visit, and having a closer look at the rifle in the hallway.

"Nigel, all I know is what Linda and Moorehouse told me. I'll investigate, and get back to you."

"You do that, Carson, and now if you don't have anything else to report, I have to get back to work. Oh, you might inform Grant at The Gazette that Linda is alive. He dropped by after Carl had left and we had to tell him that Linda was dead, although he told us that he wouldn't print it until we gave him confirmation. He was visibly shaken."

Okay, Tony thought, time to drop the bombshell. No excuse for procrastinating. Slowly, thinking out every word, he said,

"Nigel, I'm not finished, and what I have to say, you are not going to like. Dr. Neckroff retrieved the slug that nailed Lefty Lowland and it came from the Colt that you sold."

Whatever coloring that Gold had, disappeared into the shadows. He mumbled, worse than Camelia ever had,

"I know I should never have sold it to an anonymous buyer. And I regret it, yes, I do. I don't often apologize. But Carson, I take no responsibility for what the buyer did with it, none. And now if there's nothing else, I'm busy."

What cop in his right mind sells a gun to an anonymous buyer? Nigel could whitewash anything. But he was not finished and, could only hope that he was not signing his death warrant as a cop. After a deep breath, he proceeded,

"I have more to tell you, Nigel. The Colt that you sold at auction was not Abraham's, it was Benjamin

254

Robins' Colt. Whoever shot Spratt, used Abraham's and not Robins' Colt. After he planted Abraham's Colt at the scene, he must have returned Robins's Colt to you. Nigel, who gave you what you thought was your father's Colt on the day that Spratt was shot?"

Gold held up both hands for a time-out, and then closed his eyes. It was a good minute before he re-opened them and looking at Tony, replied in a barely audible voice,

"I just knew that someday I was going to have to face the music. You don't know how much I've dreaded this moment. I need a cigarette to get through it."

And with that, he got to his feet and walked over to the window, shoulders hunched as if under a weight. After he pulled a pack of Victoria Slims out from the flower box, he lit one but not on the first try, his hands were shaking. Puffing on it for all he was worth, he shocked Tony when he sat down next to him and looked at him as he whispered,

"Tony, what I am about to tell you is between you and me. I'd prefer it never leave this office but I can't insist."

Taking the Victoria Slim out of his mouth and holding it in his trembling hand, Gold talked with the speed of a metronome in slow motion.

"The morning after Abraham sacked Spratt, he came into my bedroom, and almost threw his Colt at me. He ordered me to take it to school and to shoot the pervert Spratt, if he ever showed up. I took it but I had no intentions of shooting Spratt. I was going to give it to Reggie, if anyone needed protection from the pervert, it was him. I looked all over for him, even went down to the showers, and when I didn't see him, I dropped off the Colt in my room and went to class. At the end of classes, I returned to my room, picked up the Colt and it was only when I gave it to Abraham that I learned that Spratt had shot himself and to keep it under wraps. Carson, you have to believe me."

Nigel was in anguish, stood up, walked over to the window, opened it, and tossed the butt into the flower box. After he closed the window, he sat back down beside Tony, sighed deeply, and looked at Tony with tears in his eyes. Tony was touched but had to ask,

"When you went into the showers, was there anyone else there?"

"I had taken out the Colt to give to Reggie but he, no one, was there. Why do you ask?"

It had to be. There was no other explanation.

"Nigel, there's a closet with a peephole back of those showers. I'm sure that the killer shot Spratt from

256

that closet. Well, he must have been there and seen you with the Colt, followed you up to your room and after you left, took off with it. He then switched guns with a dead Mr. Spratt who had brought Robins' Colt to school, and then returned it to your room."

Nigel shook his head as if to shake off the cobwebs of disbelief and then stunned Tony when he reached over and put his arm around his shoulders. With tears on his cheeks, he spoke,

"Tony, you are one hell of a detective. Anyone else would have pinned Spratt's murder on me. I owe you, more than I can ever repay you. And if there's anything I can do for you, just ask?"

Music to his ears. Nigel had had a human moment. Tony took advantage of it and asked,

"Nigel, did you keep your father's black book or books? And if you did, I'd like to see the one that is dated for the year that Spratt was shot."

"I have all of Abraham's black books in my bottom drawer. I'll have a quick look."

Nigel bent over, rummaged in his bottom drawer, and then extended an over-sized black notepad to Tony. With no trouble Tony found the day on which Spratt had been shot, and read out loud,

"Source called to say Spratt had been shot in the showers, and the gun was in his hand."

So, the Source had called Abraham after he'd shot Spratt with Abraham's Colt, planted it in Moorehouse's hand, and removed the Colt and photo from Spratt's hand. Thanks to Liefson, Abraham thought that the Source had referred to Spratt's hand. The Source hadn't specified in whose hand that he had planted the gun. Then Tony leafed back a day to another entry and read,

"Source called in a tip to search Spratt's locker for contraband."

"Oh my God, Tony, the Source could have been setting up Spratt. Just a minute. The source could be the killer. Damn it, I have no idea who the Source is. Abraham never told me. I knew he had snitches but he was never open about who they were. And I can't reach him, now."

What else was new, nothing in this case was easy. But then he had a most interesting thought. As the Source planted the photos, he must have taken them just as he had taken the photo in Moorehouse's safe. Tony asked,

"Nigel, the porn photos were printed on Fujifilm paper. I heard that Thackeray's had a photographic club, do you know if they had a dark room?"

"I don't honestly know. Carl and Waverly headed up the photography club. I'll call Waverly."

Nigel opened another drawer and pulled out a phone, dialed, and got a pick-up on the first ring; he and Waverly must have had a hot line.

"Waverly, need to know if Thackeray's had a dark room... Yes, they did... and the door to their dark room was always open... Thank you Waverly, you've been a big help as always. And good news about Linda, Carson just told me."

Tony was down to two suspects: carl Robins and Waverly Stonemill. Believe it or not but he was making headway. Then he found an entry for the day after Spratt was shot and his gut knotted.

"Source called to say that a homeless woman was breaking into shops on King Street. She was crazy delusional that she had a daughter. She needed to be admitted as she was violent."

Chapter 51

No sooner had Tony returned to his office and sat down, than he heard a soft rapping at his door. None too pleased, he yelled,

"Who is it?"

He barely heard a voice that could have been a timid mouse's.

"It's me, Mr. Carl Honeywell."

Christ, he thought, what did he want? As tempted as he was to send Honeywell packing, Tony couldn't rein in his curiosity, and said,

"Come in."

He shuffled in at a tortoise's pace. Dressed as he had been on the other day, nothing appeared to have changed with Honeywell except Tony was sure he spotted frustration in his eyes, behind the oversized, black rimmed glasses. Without asking for permission, he mumbled,

"Detective Carson, I give up. Every night I've hidden in the bushes. No one has left the Glendale Building with suitcases, two or one."

Suddenly, Tony was interested. Best to get rid of Honeywell and see for himself.

"Mr. Honeywell, thank you for your surveillance, an invaluable service."

"No, no, I give up. I quit."

"Mr. Honeywell, you've been a big help, really, you have. I'm putting your name forward to get a citizen citation award."

That caught Mr. Honeywell off-guard, and his eyes brightened as it they were light bulbs. As soon as he had departed, Tony ran down the hall and out of the building, jumped into Linda's Beamer, and sped over to the Glendale Building. There, he raced through the foyer and up the stairs, no smell of cabbage, a blessing. Opening Maple's door, he walked down to her bedroom and just inside the doorway, were two opened suitcases and a spill of clothes, two dumb bells, a pair of shoes, and at least twenty large envelopes, all empty.

Dammit, Lefty's killer had made a clean getaway with Maple's life savings. What bugged the hell out of Tony was knowing that the killer had been upstairs all the time that he'd been in Lefty's apartment. He must have left after Tony and before the lab boys had arrived. Cain was getting richer by the day, he now had

Moorehouse's mother's necklace, while Tony had nothing to show for all his hard work.

Chapter 52

Tony was lucky to park behind Grant's Ambassador in front of The Gazette as parking spaces were at a premium on King. Hungry customers were lined up to get into Mabel's. After Tony retrieved the graphic novel from the back seat where he had tossed it, he headed to The Gazette. Inside, Judy was not behind the linoleum counter and he was about to rap on Grant's door when she stepped out of the pressroom with a pistol in her right hand. Puffing away on a cigarette, her visor had slipped down on her forehead, she must have been deep in thought for she hadn't seen him. When he saw the black arm band on the left arm of her mechanic's coveralls, they were navy blue except for the grease stains, he knew it was now or never. When he cleared his throat, she started and the visor almost bounced off her head. Spotting him, she exclaimed,

"Carson, you gave me a fright. I didn't expect to see you, here. If you're here to see Grant, he's out, and I have no idea when he'll be back. And if you're here to tell him that Linda Stonemill is alive, he knows. Her husband called to tell him. He'd already told me that he was at Stonemill's yesterday and heard that she'd fallen off a cliff. When Grant told me that he held out no hope for her, I cried. You see I'd met her at Mabel's and we girls, had a morning group. But when Grant told me she was alive, I cheered. Finally good news."

"Judy, I didn't mean to startle you. Yes, I came to tell Grant that I'd found Linda Stonemill, and also I have something to show you. But I have to ask, why the gun?"

"Oh it's Grant's air pistol. He's had it since he was a kid. He was a naughty boy with it in those days, from the stories he tells. I use it to nail rats. They like to chew on our wires and the bloody vermin, they never get electrocuted."

Getting up his nerve, he pointed at the arm band and said,

"Yes, it sure was good news that Linda was alive. I see the arm band and wonder if you ever heard from your sister or your niece?"

Instantly her face dropped and any sign or joy, vanished.

"No, nothing. It's been over 20 years. When you brought in that article on Spratt, I didn't tell you, but it was around the same time as they left for Winnipeg. Abraham Gold checked for me and as far as he could tell, they never arrived. But he told me there were a lot of stops between here and Winnipeg, and he hadn't the manpower to look, further."

He had one more question to clinch it although when he heard Winnipeg, he was almost certain.

"Judy, what was your niece's name?"

With that she started to cry, put down the pistol, and brushed roughly at her eyes with her sleeves to tell her eyes to stop.

"Her name was Belinda. I find it so hard to talk of her. We were so close. I never had a child, and she was like my daughter. She was beautiful and so bright. She spoke English like there was no tomorrow, while my sister could only speak French. Her name was Belle."

Shit, he thought, knowing who Belinda was did not make it any easier, if not worse. In a hushed tone, he spoke,

"Judy, I have something upsetting, very upsetting, to tell you. Please sit down."

Suspicion returned to her watery eyes, but she sat down, and he continued,

"We found the body of a woman, yesterday, in the whirlpool below High Falls. She'd been strangled. She was a mental patient at the Osprey, had been there most of her adult life. Her name was Arabelle Sirene. But when the chief psychiatrist checked her room, he found this."

Slowly he pulled the graphic novel, "Arabelle: Le Dernière Sirene," from his inside pocket, and handed it to her, cover side up. She took one look at it and gasped, but did not let go of it. After she flipped open the cover, she read the inscription, and clutched the novel to her chest like a lost child. Looking up at him, she mumbled in a broken stream of words with tears streaming down her cheeks,

"She was Arabelle Sirene. She was a mental patient at the Osprey. She was strangled. She's my sister. She's Belle Fontaine. She's been there all this time. I will never see her alive, never. The police never looked there. Who would have thought?"

Then she wailed,

"Where is Belinda?"

"Judy, the police were misled that she was a crazy woman going on about a missing daughter when she was childless. She wasn't fluent in English and couldn't set them straight. After the treatments, she was

266

so confused she thought her name was on the cover of the book. The chief psychiatrist, he found the book in her room and gave it to me, apologizes profusely to you but realizes it's too little, too late. I assure you we're looking for who killed her. She was in the wrong place at the wrong time. As for Belinda, we have no idea where she is, and doubt we will ever know. But you never know."

She put the book to one side, folded her arms on the counter, laid her head on them and sobbed. It was heart-wrenching to stand there, helpless, and feel her pain as she poured out her grieving soul. Then, he had an idea.

"Judy, I'm going to get Petula Robins to come and stay with you. Why don't you take the rest of the day off, I'm sure Grant will understand? And whenever you're ready, take your time, there's no rush, we need you to identify her body. She's in the morgue under Jane Doe. Whatever you do, I don't want you going alone or being alone for the next few days."

Tony quickly exited, rushed down the street to Robins Hardware, opened the door, and sprinted to the back where thankfully Petula Robins was sitting behind the counter. She was wearing the same white shirt and black skirt as the last time. When she saw who it was, concern in spades jumped into her face. Before he could speak, she shouted,

"It's Carl, isn't it? What's happened? Oh, I feel so responsible after what I said to him. Is he... alright. Oh, please tell me."

"No, it's not Carl. I just told Judy that her sister is in the morgue and was murdered. Understandably, she's a mess. Could you be with her? Grant isn't there."

"Yes, of course. I'll close shop, this minute. Poor Judy, she never lost hope she'd find her sister. When you have a moment, could you check on Carl? He doesn't answer his phone, most unlike him, and I'm so worried. I was just about to leave and see if he was at the trucking yard."

Chapter 53

On his way to Stonemill's brownstone, Tony slowed down and parked at the corner of Victoria and Bethune. There was no one on the sidewalk and next to no traffic, ideal for what he wanted. Slowly, he walked up and down the corner, scanning sidewalk and the gutter; he was so thankful they hadn't cleaned the street. There was the usual throw-away garbage in the gutter, nothing of note on the sidewalk. As he was about to call it a day, he spotted a half-smoked cigarette but in the gutter, and when he picked it up, he saw that it was an Export 'A,' unfiltered. The black thought crossed his mind that it was also known as the "Green Death" cigarette. How appropriate for the Grim Reaper. Did he know of anyone who smoked them? No.

At Stonemill's, he pulled into an empty driveway. When he rapped on the door and got no answer, he tried the doorknob and, to his surprise, opened the door. His heart thumped. What was he doing if not breaking and entering without a warrant? On the right hallway wall, was a large, numbered print of Franz Johnston's, "Fire swept Algoma." He hadn't noticed it before. On the side table was a half-eaten apple core, and leaning against it was the rifle, butt end on the floor. Then he decided it was best to check and he half-shouted,

"Linda, it's Detective Carson."

THUD

It sounded that something heavy had fallen on the floor above where he was. this time, he yelled,

"Linda, are you alright?"

No response. What to do? Without giving it a second thought, he walked upstairs and came to a hallway with the same, pink-veined marble flooring as downstairs. It had four closed doors. The first door opened into a den with a few scatter mats on the floor and nothing else. The next one opened into a spacious bedroom with pink wallpaper, plush white carpeting and a four-poster, king-sized bed with a white-tufted canopy. Had to be Linda's bedroom. Then he spotted around the bed's far corner, on the white carpet, ten pink toenails. Rushing up to them, he saw Linda Stonemill in yellow pajamas, sprawled out on the floor. She was motionless except for a frothing and bubbling slime on her lips; it had a fruity smell.

He couldn't see her chest moving. Was she dead? Her neck was cool to his touch but she had a weak sputtering pulse. Pupils were pinpoint. When he pinched her right calf muscle, he got no response. She was comatose and barely alive; she must have fallen out of bed just as he had yelled out her name. Her head was inches away from a solid wood, end table. If she'd hit it, she'd be dead.

On the end table was a pill vial: Chloral Hydrate 500 mg. From the date, it had been filled 2 days ago for 30 pills; it was empty. Beside it was an open Poison perfume bottle that smelled of gin. Not seeing a phone, Tony raced to the study, dialed 9-1-1, reported a chloral hydrate overdose, and gave the address. Then he noticed a large legal sized envelop on the desk; what caught his attention was that there was no postmark and Waverly's name was in cut-out block letters from a magazine. Lifting it, he saw in the same lettering, a note that read: CUCKOLD.

After he opened the front door, downstairs, he quickly returned upstairs. In that short time, Linda's coloring had faded, her pulse was almost flat-lining, and the bubbles in the slime were in slow-motion. He put his hands on Linda's chest to begin CPR the moment that the slime stopped bubbling.

It was obvious that Linda had overdosed. But why? No way was she depressed when he last saw her. Anxious yes, but not depressed. Something must have happened after he'd left? Had Waverly threatened divorce and Linda panicked? But why not a token overdose? Why go all the way? Just then, two paramedics in service blue, long-sleeved jumpsuits rushed in with a stretcher on wheels. They were twins in height and build, distinguishable only by their hair coloring: one had black and the other had red hair. He was never so glad to see them in all his life; he'd only performed CPR in class and that was years ago.

The black-haired paramedic slapped a stethoscope on Linda's chest and a cuff on her right arm, while Red attached an IV bottle to a pole on the side of the stretcher and inserted a line into the back of Linda's left hand. The black-haired one spoke in a clipped voice,

"Ted, pulse is 160 and erratic. Pressure is 80 over 40. She's on the way out. No time to get her on the stretcher. Is she in Torsades?"

Ted, the red-haired paramedic, reached under the stretcher and produced a beaten-up black suitcase, flipped open the lid, and in one motion attached electrodes to Linda's chest. Tony heard first an electronic hum and then Ted's flat voice.

"Reynolds, she's in Torsades. QTc is off the scale. She's flatlining."

Reynolds sniffed at the slime on Linda's lips, turned to Tony and questioned him,

"Officer, I smell chloral hydrate. Am I right?"

"The Chlorate Hydrate vial is empty, and she may have been drinking."

Spinning around to face Ted, Reynolds almost screamed,

"Shit, Ted, get the syringe and fast."

Ted took out a pre-loaded syringe from the black suitcase, and expertly injected it in record time into the IV line. Then, he gave a thumbs up sign to Reynolds, who turned back to Tony and spoke in his staccato, Joe Friday voice.

"Officer, what's your name and what's her name? I'm Reynolds and Red over there, is Ted."

"I'm Detective Tony Carson and she's Mrs. Linda Stonemill, wife of Waverly Stonemill, the brick man."

The ECG machine hummed as if it had found new life. Ted tore off a strip of paper, and without looking at it, handed it to Reynolds, who spoke as if reading from a boring book,

"Ted, she's in sinus. The propranolol worked. Let's get her on the stretcher and then off to the ICU. Let's hope they have beds, and don't keep us waiting."

Together they lifted Linda and placed her on the stretcher without disturbing the IV line. Then Reynolds looked around the room, and whistled,

"Detective Carson, the poor-little rich girl will live to shop another day. Tell her husband she's in the ICU but not to visit until the morning. Chloral hydrate is one hell of a sleeping pill. And warn him that she will require a psychiatric consultation."

After they left, Tony closed the front door and went into the kitchen for a glass of water although if he'd been at home, he'd have headed straight to the liquor cabinet. The kitchen was a showcase of stainless-steel appliances and white cupboards; much like Mabel's. While pouring a glass of water, he noticed the number '2' was flashing on the dishwasher. Didn't that mean 2 minutes to wash? Had Linda put something in the dishwasher?

Curiosity got the better of him, and opening it, he found inside, a single glass tumbler with a white powdery residue on its bottom. After he put on gloves, he picked it up by the rim, and smelled lemonade. Looking closer, he wondered if the powder was crushed-up chloral hydrate and if it was, then someone had crushed up 28 chloral hydrate pills and mixed them in a lemonade Mickey Finn. Was the someone, Linda? Doubtful she would have put the glass in the

274

dishwasher. Damnit, he thought, knowing a little about Chloral hydrate, he knew enough that Linda when she awoke, would have no memory of ever taking the pills.

Holding the glass up to the fluorescents, he noticed a large thumb print. Too big to be a woman's thumb print? He found a plastic bag, wrapped the glass in a paper towel, and placed it in the bag, his new evidence pouch.

Walking back down the hallway, still with gloves on, he picked up the rifle, and noticed a wad of dirt was embedded in the end of the barrel. Removing it, he saw that the rim of the barrel was an untarnished silver. The rifle had never been fired. It had to be Moorehouse's. Whoever had shot at Linda, had used Stonemill's rifle, and after he had switched it for Moorehouse's rifle, had tossed Moorehouse's in the air to land near where Stonemill's rifle had been. Its barrel end had hit the ground, first.

Chapter 54

Tony drove under the prestigious, multi-colored metal sign for W. S. Stonemill Bricks, and then between two towering aisles of red bricks to an over-sized lot. He parked beside a beat-up Volkswagen Beetle and Stonemill's Cadillac, still sparkling clean although the Beetle was covered in dust from a country road. At the two-storey, red brick office building's front door, Tony bypassed the knocker and pressed the intercom's buzzer. Immediately, he heard.

"Who are you? You have some nerve driving Mrs. Stonemill's Beamer?"

It was a loud woman's voice with the bark of a bulldog. Had to be Stonemill's secretary.

"My name is Detective Tony Carson. I have something important to tell Mr. Stonemill regarding his wife, and you ask him if I'm not allowed to drive his wife's car."

After a long pause, the door swung open, and a short, fleshy woman glared at him. He felt that he was under a microscope and on a hot griddle, at the same time. Rarely had he seen a woman with shorter hair or bigger eyes, both were brown. In looks, she was as plain as her houndstooth-patterned dress that dropped below her knees. While she looked up at him, he could tell that she only knew how to talk down to people and that included police officers.

"Mr. Stonemill will see you. He's a busy man, so say what you have to say and leave. Follow me, and don't dally."

She marched past her desk with two diminutive piles of paper on it. After a short and a long rap, she opened the inner door, ushered him in without a word, and closed the door, firmly, behind him. Stonemill's office outdid Gold's, a first for Tony. On the sidewall, was the biggest tv screen that Tony had ever seen and his desk was massive; a lone Coke can looked lost on it. Like Gold, Stonemill remained seated when Tony entered; they both must have attended the same finishing school. Stonemill barely looked at him and with an emotionally challenged face, dismissed him.

"Are you returning Linda's car? You'll need a ride back. Gertrude can drive you."

"Actually, Mr. Stonemill, I have some unsettling news. I found your wife unconscious on her bedroom floor. It looks like she overdosed on chloral hydrate; the vial was empty. I called the medics and in the nick-of-time, they revived her. She's being admitted to the ICU

277

as we speak. They told me that you can visit in the morning, but not before. She's stable."

Stonemill's bushy eyebrows raised a millimeter, but nothing else; for sure, he'd test the needles of a polygraph. When he spoke, his voice remained pancake flat.

"Linda overdosed. Not like her. She's taken chloral hydrate for years. I should have taken her to the hospital. Good news that she's alive. Two close calls. Tomorrow morning suits me fine. Did you discuss Reggie with Nigel? Well, did you?"

Tony was amazed at how quickly Stonemill jumped from his wife's near-death suicide attempt to Moorehouse. It was so obvious that he wanted Moorehouse's blood, and wasn't about to let up. Tony took delight in proving him wrong, but was so careful not to show his true feelings.

"I checked, Mr. Stonemill, and the rifle in your hallway belongs to Mr. Moorehouse. I could tell from the rim of the barrel, after I took out a plug of earth, that it had never been fired. Someone fired at your wife and then switched rifles. I'm sure that Nigel has your rifle, thinking it's Moorehouse's. I will confirm it with Nigel."

278

Stonemill's eyebrows dropped back to neutral, and Tony wouldn't be surprised if that meant that Stonemill was perpetually seething. He could suck the life out of any party.

"When I heard Linda scream, I dropped my rifle and started to run. I never run with a loaded gun. If Reggie wasn't the shooter, tell me if it was Carl. He said he came late, but you can never trust what he says. Well detective?"

Nothing like telling Tony what he should be doing as a police officer. How Tony hated it when anyone other than Nigel gave him his marching orders. From the first time that they'd met, Tony had felt his back was up in the presence of Stonemill. To say the least, they had not hit it off. How he'd love to have cuffed the stone-faced prig, but he was only whistling in the wind.

"I'll pay Carl a visit and see what he has to say."

"You do that and like I said, he's as dishonest as the day is long."

Just as Tony was about to leave, the Coke can on his desk jumped out at him. Well, not exactly. A most comforting thought involving the Coke can popped into mind. No music to back it up but so what.

"Mr. Stonemill, you wouldn't have an extra can of pop, would you?"

"Why yes I do, and I can do one better. I'll bag it for you."

Chapter 55

When Tony turned on to Raymond's Road, he was in disbelief as an elongated Dali-like cloud of black smoke was where Robins' mugshot sign should have been. Stepping on the gas, he veered into Robins' lot and saw flames and black smoke spewing out of the back of a Volvo reefer in the middle of the pack. Braking, no sense in getting closer, he jumped out and felt a gale-force wind and hot smoke. His eyes smarted, his throat tightened and choked on the stench of nuked turkeys and fried metal. Gasping for air, he covered his mouth and nose with his right hand, for all the good that it did as there was no escaping the burning smoke and the red-hot cinders that were raining down. The noise was deafening. Walking toward the burning truck, he yelled,

"Carl, where the hell are you?"

A waste of breath. His scream had gone nowhere. Carl had to be there, but where? And what if the truck on fire ever exploded? Wasn't there gasoline in it? Christ, a chain reaction would wipe the earth clean for a country mile. He had to get to the truck on fire, and get it out of there.

Tony sprinted to the truck's cab, a black coffin of soot with a glowing red-hot door handle. Jumping up on the runner, it felt like he had stepped on hot coals, he whipped off his overcoat, almost lost it in the wind, but managed to wrap it around his right hand. Grabbing the door handle with his mummified right hand, he flung it open.

A thick, warm, grey smoke had pooled around a man in the driver's seat; he was slumped over the steering wheel and was not moving. Reaching in, Tony cleared the smoke from the side of the man's face; it was Carl Robins. Eyes were closed, mouth was open, and his chest was moving in slow motion. Tony gave him a sharp jab to the ribs. No response. There was an open gin bottle and a pack of cigarettes on the seat beside him. Tony swore. Had the drunken fool set the truck on fire?

No time to lose. He heaved Carl out of the truck and the gin bottle went flying with him. While the bottled bounced, Carl lay still on the gravel. Holding his breath, the stench inside the cab was worse than the heat, Tony shifted the wooden knob gear stick into drive, and rammed down both feet on the gas pedal. The truck lurched forward. Craning his neck and head out the open door, smoke had obliterated the windshield, he held steady the steering wheel with his coat-wrapped right hand that felt as hot as the running board had on his feet.

When he rounded the corner of Carl's office, he turned the steering wheel sharply to the left, drove straight into a cloud of smoke to the count of '5,' and jumped. The gravel was unforgivingly hard and searingly hot as he rolled over and over before coming to an abrupt stop; how he wished he had left on his overcoat.

BOOM

The loudest explosion he'd ever heard sent his eardrums into a ringing frenzy. The ground shook like he was in an earthquake. In front of where he lay, a spiral of flames shot up into a mushroom cloud of hellish-black smoke. Was this Armageddon? But with the wind in his back, in no time, Tony was breathing in country air. What a relief. Sure, his throat burned and his eyes smarted and his body ached, but no more stench of burnt turkeys. Stretching out his arms and legs, he felt no sharp, jabbing pain and knew that nothing was broken. He'd never felt so good to be alive and in so much discomfort at the same time.

Sitting up, he combed his hair with his fingers for any errant, live embers. After he got to his feet, he brushed soot and ashes off his shirt and pants. Looking around, he spotted his overcoat on the gravel, it was burnt beyond recognition. Slowly, he had to make sure the ground was not about to crumble, he advanced to the edge of a large saucer-shaped crater. On its bottom was the smoldering, unrecognizable remains of the Volvo that was giving off a strident sizzling sound. Nothing was left of Robins' sign as if it had evaporated. He wondered if the birds and crickets had packed up and left for good as he heard not a peep from them.

Turning around, he surveyed Linda's BMW, the corrugated office shack, Robins' pick-up, nine idling Volvos and Carl Robins, still in a heap on the ground nearby where the missing Volvo had been. As he walked over to where Carl lay, motionless, he was re-assured when he saw the rising and falling of Carl's chest. Tony bent down and felt a strong carotid pulse. Carl's mouth was open, and Tony got a whiff of gin. After gently brushing the ashes and soot off of him, he didn't see any blood. Gently, he moved Carl's four limbs and didn't see or feel a fracture. Then Tony heard the screeching of tires, turned, and saw a purple school bus careening into the lot. It missed the crater by a hair's breathe, and in a grinding of brakes, stopped beside Linda's Beamer.

A purple-faced Reverend Mulgrave raced toward Tony only to stop dead in his tracks when he spotted Carl on the ground. He whispered in a soft drawl,

"Is he dead?"

"No, he isn't. As far as I can make-out, Carl's dead drunk but alive. Do you have a phone in your bus? We need to call an ambulance and get him admitted."

"You say he's dead drunk and alive. Thank God, he's alive. No way would that heathen get past the pearly gates with alcohol on his breath. Yes, I have a phone in Betsy. I'll call 9-1-1."

Mulgrave raced back to his bus, while Tony positioned Carl on his side and extended his chin to prevent him swallowing his tongue. Slightly out of breath, Mulgrave returned, and said,

"They'll be here in minutes. They were at Fat Frank's on a break. Carl sure is a lucky cat. I saw smoke and heard what I thought was an A-bomb going off. I thought for sure The Jehovah Witnesses had finally got it right. What happened?"

"I found a comatose Carl in one of his trucks on fire. I threw him out, drove the truck out of harm's way, and jumped just in time. What you heard was it blowing in one hell of an earth-shattering blast. Over there is a crater; all that's left of the Volvo and Carl's sign. By the way, I smelled nuked turkeys, I don't now. Would you know if there were turkeys in the Volvo?"

Mulgrave puffed out his chest, and spoke in a stentorian voice,

"Carl, thanks to me, got a Hail Mary pass from a turkey farmer. Yes, the Volvos are filled with frozen birds. The farmer needed refrigeration for his turkeys until Thanksgiving. He's not going to be none too happy with the loss of a truckload."

Strange, thought Tony, how does one set a truck full of frozen turkeys on fire with a cigarette? Putting on gloves, he picked up the gin bottle, found the remains of his coat, and wrapped it in it. More evidence to give the lab.

Chapter 56

The wind had dropped to a cool breeze and the smoke cleared but a heavy cloud cover left it murky looking. An ambulance pulled into the lot, missed the crater and parked alongside Mulgrave's school bus. Black-haired Reynolds and red-haired Ted jumped out and wheeled a stretcher up to the prostate Carl. Reynolds slapped a stethoscope on Carl's chest and a cuff on his left arm, while Ted attached an IV bottle to a pole on the stretcher and inserted a line into Carl's right hand. Reynolds gave a reading of Carl's vitals in a calm voice.

"Pulse is 70 and steady, pressure is low at 60 over 40. I smell gin. Ted, is he in sinus?"

Ted had already opened the black suitcase, attached electrodes to Carl's chest, and flipped a switch. Tony heard the familiar electronic hum, and then Ted's unhurried voice.

"Reynolds, he's in Sinus. QTc is okay."

Reynolds looked at Carl, and then at Tony.

"Detective Carson, this is becoming a bad habit. We'd just ordered lunch at Fat Frank's when an explosion unseated Frank. Wish I'd had a camera. Frank on his ass on the floor was quite a sight. I need skid row's name; do you know it?"

"He's Carl Robins, the owner of the truck yard. I found him comatose in one of his trucks that was on fire, threw him out, and drove it away from the pack before it blew."

Reynolds and Ted walked over to the crater, shook their heads in disbelief, returned, and loaded Carl onto the stretcher. Then Reynolds with a wry smile on his face spoke,

"Detective Carson, you've saved another one. If I'm ever in trouble, I'm calling you before I call 9-1-1. Well, we're off to the ICU. Booze boy will need cardiac monitoring. Hopefully, the hospital is not on break. We don't want to spend the rest of the shift in the parking lot."

As the ambulance pulled on to Raymond's Road, on went the siren and the flashing lights even though they had the road to themselves. Mulgrave turned to Tony, and scratched his head.

"The heathen sure messed up this time. He has no one to blame although knowing Carl, he will find an excuse. He called me last night, crying the blues. His wife had threatened divorce. He hadn't made up his mind to get down on his knees and beg for forgiveness.

He told me his lucky plant was going to see him through it, the heathen."

Tony had forgotten all about the jade plant, and was curious if it was still there. Walking over to the office building, he opened the door, but there was no plant and barely any furniture in the office. Knowing that Carl had a shed out back, he headed over to it, with a breathless Mulgrave in tow. Its door was wide open, and on the dirt floor, a make-shift ash tray and trash can, was an empty gin bottle, a sprinkling of cigarette butts but no plant. Against the back wall were two cases of gin. In the middle of the wall on the right, was an old, rusted steel drum. The locking bar on the padlock was in the open position. Mulgrave came up to Tony and wheezed,

"I don't see it. Carl would never have trashed it."

Then Mulgrave pointed at the drum, and spoke, with excitement in his voice,

"I've never seen the lock open. Always wanted to see what was inside. Carl would never even let me peek. Do you think he'd mind if I looked?"

"Tell you what, Mulgrave, I'll look and tell you, that way, Carl won't come after you."

Tony slid the lid off onto the floor with a thud. It was dark inside the ramshackle shed and peering into the drum, he couldn't see a thing. He was about to reach in when he caught himself. Suppose there was evidence inside the drum? After he put on gloves, he gingerly felt inside, and only when he got to the bottom did he feel what felt like paper. He pulled out an his hand, he realized he had a Polaroid in it.

Two women were standing, facing the camera. They were both blonde and both naked. They had their arms around each other, and were smiling, warmly. It had to be Linda's missing picture. The one that she claimed was in Maple's jewelry box. No wonder she was so desperate to retrieve it. Anyone who didn't know, would think they were lovers. Immediately, he pocketed it. While he could tell that Mulgrave was disappointed not to see it, Tony had no intentions of showing it to him.

It was sure looking bad for Carl. What was Linda's photo from Maple's jewelry box doing in his drum? Had he known of the other peephole into Thackeray's showers? Had he developed porn pictures in Thackeray's dark room with Fujifilm paper? Had he borrowed Stonemill's telescope in Bruce's bedroom and seen a wigless Maple? Had he shot Lefty, and then returned to the gym? Had he taken a shot at Linda at the cabin? But no way had he accidentally set a truck of frozen turkeys on fire with a cigarette? The missing jade plant and almost incinerating himself did not fit. Suppose Cain had come, seen the jade plant, set the fire with a drunk Carl in the cab, and planted the photo. Tony was at a crossroad, saw a cigarette butt, bent down, picked it up and saw that it was a Marlboro.

"I can tell you that Carl smoked only Marlboros, if that's what you want to know?"

Dammit, thought Tony, why couldn't it have been an Export-A? But what was he thinking? Carl was not his man as much as he wanted him to be. Why was that so hard to digest? Carl was looking to be another patsy but no way was Tony going to shed tears over him.

Chapter 57

When Reginald opened Dr. Ramsay's office door on the main floor, he was dismayed not to see the secretaries, but then he'd never been there at twelve o'clock. He worried that he had gotten the wrong time, or that there had been an emergency and that no one was there. Nevertheless, he walked through the empty office and stood in front of the inner door, his heart was pounding and his right hand, holding the envelope, was shaking. It had not trembled at school, and for that he was grateful. He still fretted that he'd be mistaken for an alcoholic. He rapped on the door.

"Come in Mr. Moorehouse."

Obsessing again for nothing, when was he going to stop it? Slowly he opened the door, and was surprised to see Dr. Ramsay taking one look at him and jumping to his feet. He didn't know what to do and then Dr. Ramsay grabbed him by the shoulders, peered hard at his head, and said,

"Thanks for the heads-up phone call. So, you shot yourself in a pit of despair, and you weren't drinking, right?"

"Yes, that's true. But I don't feel suicidal anymore. I told you I thought I'd caused the death of

Linda Stonemill only to find out that she's alive. And Detective Carson assured me that I hadn't shot Spratt or harmed Miss Maple. I can't tell you what a relief that was. I almost feel like a new man. Linda is not mad at me and promised to still visit."

Dr. Ramsay smiled, let go of him, and pointed to his favorite chair, under the doctor's diplomas and not under Queen Elizabeth. But before took a step, he handed the envelope to Dr. Ramsay, and when he did, he felt a wave of relief. Dr. Ramsay returned and sat down, opened the envelope, took out the photo, looked at it and then placed it in front of him. Reginald then remembered and said,

"Dr. Ramsay, I have good news. I told you that someone had stolen the mannequin and mother's priceless necklace was in it. Well, Pearcum, my housekeeper, handed it to me, this morning. After yesterday's break-in, she had removed the necklace from the mannequin and taken it home with her. I told her that I'd go to the bank today and get a safety deposit box. I gave her a hefty raise."

"And well, she deserves it. What do they say, all's well that ends well. But we're not there yet, Mr. Moorehouse. I've never seen you wear a leather jacket or a blue dress shirt. Significant?"

"I bought them years ago, but mother never liked them and to please her, I never wore them. This morning, when I saw them in the closet, I felt it was about time, and put them on."

"Good for you, Mr. Moorehouse. I always say, when we're spontaneous, we're in the driver's seat. And now for the business of the photo that causes your eyes to close. It's time you got the monkey off your back, the one that puts its hands around your eyes. When you're ready, close your eyes, and I'll begin. At any time if you want me to stop, raise your left hand."

He sat back in the chair and for once, his heart wasn't pounding, and he wasn't dizzy. He picked a spot high up on the wall in front of him, and stared at it. Soon, his eyelids felt heavy, and he closed them.

"You are at the top of ten steps, walk down slowly and breathe slowly. You told me they are moss-covered. 1-2-3-4-5-6-7-8-9-10. At the bottom, you will feel tranquil and rested. Open the door in front of you, and start to walk down the hallway that leads into your past. When you find the door that leads into your mother's bedroom, the one with the ruby-red wallpaper, open it. Trust your judgement as to what door it is. And when you enter it, let me know and we will begin to chimney sweep. If at any time, you feel terrified, raise your left arm."

At the bottom of the steps, he opened the door into a hallway with a high ceiling that had holes in it and through which, leaked enough light for him to see what was in front of him. He walked slowly on the earthen floor along a serpentine course, glancing into the rooms but as soon as he didn't see red wallpaper, he kept going.

In anticipation, his heart was racing, his breathing was all over the place, and a cold sweat dripped down his face. Worried that he would either miss the room or worse, would enter the room only to have his eyes close? What then? He stopped and dithered as to how he was going to open his eyes if they closed? Then he told himself that worrying was getting him nowhere, it never had, and best to soldier on.

After another few steps, he spotted the ruby-red wallpaper, in the very next room. Suddenly, his body started to move on its own. What was happening? He had no control over it. Just like when his eyes closed only this time, his body got down on all fours and crawled into his mother's bedroom. Then he remembered and his lips moved,

"I was small. Nights were tough. I'd lay awake for hours, counting sheep until I ran out of numbers. My older brother, Adam, had drowned. I knew my mother wished it had been me and not Adam who had drowned.

295

I never got to be with her. She was spending more and more time with the police chief. He never liked me and had favored Adam who was rough-and-tumble. When he wasn't there, I'd crawl into her bedroom, late at night, listen to her breathing, fall asleep, wake up before she did, and go back to bed. I felt so close to her then and dreamed that she was holding me. After Adam drowned, she never touched me."

Tears came to his eyes. How he missed her. She was all he had and he'd felt so alone, so insignificant. Slipping into her bedroom when she was asleep had been so rewarding. Then he had the warm feeling that he not only had a mother but she loved him. His lips moved,

"One night, I was sure he was not there but when I crawled into her bedroom and was well into it before I heard his voice. They were talking. Before I could turn and get out, I heard my mother scream like I'd never heard before."

He felt terrified and raised his left hand and arm. His heart felt like it would explode. He wanted to end the session. He was gasping for air. So much for chimney sweeping, whatever that meant. And he opened his eyes.

"Mr. Moorehouse. There's a man and a woman in the picture that you gave me. If I'm not mistaken, Linda Stonemill told you that the man was the police chief and the woman was your mother. The picture wasn't taken on the night that you recall; they are smiling for the camera but most likely were smiling before they spotted you. I know this is not easy but don't forget you've faced death; you can do this. Trust in yourself. I want you to continue the session and when you're finished, open your eyes and tell me what to do with the photo."

He was too afraid, no, terrified. Sweat was pouring off his head as if there was a fountain inside it. Was he ready to continue? No, he was not ready. He wanted to give up, call it a day. So what if he went through life with blinkers. But then he recalled that Mr. Spratt had also told him to trust in himself. Yes, he had to, had to trust in himself. Taking a deep breath, he closed his eyes and immediately was back in his mother's bedroom, her scream was ringing in his ears.

"She had screamed, 'What are you doing here. You have no business being here. Get out, you bad, bad boy.' I was frightened, I'd never seen her that angry. I wanted to run far, far away but I couldn't move and couldn't look up. I always look down when she was angry with me. I was ashamed. I was a bad, bad boy. I cried and cried. Why was she always angry at me? What had I done? I didn't know he was there.

And then I heard the police chief yelling, 'Didn't I tell you Vicky that Namby-Pamby was a peeper, a pervert. Well, bad boy, your peeping days are over. If I catch you so much as looking at another naked woman, I'll blow out your brains, so help me God.'"

Reginald opened his eyes and knew exactly where he was. He was amazed that he could change gears that fast. One minute, he'd been terrified out of his mind and the next he was angry, no, incensed. How could he talk to a child like that? He was worse than a bully, he was a sadist. And why hadn't his mother defended him? That's what good mothers did.

"Show me the photo, Dr. Ramsay."

As he held it up in front of him, Reginald yelled,

"Abraham Gold, you had no right to talk to me like that. You should be ashamed of yourself. And mother, why couldn't you have been a mother for once and defended me."

He glared at Abraham Gold and his mother. They were naked. And his eyes did not close.

Chapter 58

Tony parked in front of Robins' hardware where there was plenty of parking as Mabel's breakfast crowd had cleared out and were at work. Briefly, he felt the warm glow of nostalgia as he walked down the aisle with the screw drivers and hammers to the back, but lost it when he spotted Petula Robins with concern written all over her face, behind the counter. How was he going to tell her that her Carl was a cold-blooded killer? There was fear in her voice.

"Did you see Carl? Is he all right? I'm so worried."

"Mrs. Robins, did you not hear an explosion, or see a cloud of black smoke in the sky?"

"No, but I was in the back room going over the books. I never hear a thing in there. Why do you ask? Tell me, has something happened to Carl?"

Her face turned an unhealthy crimson and her voice hit the panic button. Tony picked his words carefully with lots of edited omissions as he spoke,

"I found Carl comatose in the cab of one of his trucks; it was on fire. I threw him out, drove the truck out of harm's way, and jumped before it exploded. All that's left of the Volvo and Carl's sign is a giant hole in the ground. Carl was breathing and had a strong carotid pulse. The medics have taken him to the hospital to be admitted for observation but they told me that he's stable and in no danger."

Tears came to her eyes but she never lost her coloring. There was anger in her voice.

"Okay, he's alive but he's not going to worm out of it, this time. I told him to clean up his act and what does he do? Get drunk and set one of his trucks on fire. I married a drunken fool. I've had it. I put up with his father but I have a limit. I'm walking, yes, I'm walking."

"Well Mrs. Robins, you're right. He was dead drunk when I found him. As for setting a truckload of frozen turkeys on fire with a cigarette, I'd still like to know how he did it?"

"Well, he did it. The truck was on fire. If you hadn't gotten that truck out of there, God knows what would have happened. Thank you Detective Carson for saving his life. We can never repay you and will always be in your debt. You'll never have to pay for anything you buy from us. Do you think that Nigel will charge him? I know that Nigel is none too happy with Carl. When Carl was at Bruce's inauguration on Monday, he was bugging Waverly for his telescope, and Nigel told him to stop being a child."

Tony was stunned. If Carl hadn't seen a wigless Maple, the case against him was nothing more than a house of cards in the wind. He was turning out to be another Moorehouse, a patsy. The photo been planted. The only consolation was that Cain had walked away with Lefty's jade plant which below the surface was nothing more than dirt and roots.

"Mrs. Robins, I think you should give Carl another chance. Things may not be as they appear. I can't say more until the police investigation is completed."

She looked quizzically at him, shook her head and then said,

"If you say so but I'll be calling you, sooner than later, to hear what you have to say. Oh, and by the way, I almost forgot as I never thought I'd run into you, but I just came from the gym and Joe asked me if I saw you, to tell you he found what you wanted."

Chapter 59

When Tony hit the Dog-Patch end of King Street, he was surprized to see that both sides of the street were jammed with cars and people were lined-up on the sidewalk in front of Tim Hortons' bright new sign. At that hour, it was usually a ghost town except for Joe's. Parking around the block, he by-passed the congestion and walked down the stone steps to the gym.

Inside, the gym's murky lighting, he saw that both sides were jammed with men in white shorts, pounding away at heavy bags. In the center ring, two boxers in red shorts were slugging it out while Joe was pacing back and forth in front, shouting out orders like he was still in the Italian army. His T-shirt had the colors of the Italian flag.

"Mark, keep your eyes open. Don't shut them and then throw a punch. You're giving it away."

When he saw Tony, Joe strode over to him, grabbed him by the shoulders, steered him into his office and closed the door. Facing Tony, he said,

"You won't believe this, but Grant was in here. The Gazette is putting up a $5,000 reward for the capture of Lefty's killer. Paisano, you could be a rich man."

Knowing how cheap Grant had been at Mabel's, Tony was impressed.

"Joe, I found Lefty's suitcases in the Glendale building minus the money. All I have to go on is the slug that killed him."

"Well, as they say, get to it. I'm depending on you to book the killer, and then we'll see if Grant pays up. He's a cheap son-of-a-bitch. By the way, I found what you asked me to look for, and just like I remembered, it's damn ugly."

Joe stepped over to the filing cabinet, rummaged in the bottom drawer, and came up with a black ornament. When he held it up in the room's grimy light, Tony took one look at it and asked,

"Is it a toad?"

"Yes and you've never seen an uglier toad until you've seen it. I talked to an antique dealer on Barton Street in Hamilton, and he told me it's a Chinese good-luck piece. It has three legs, and three is Chinese lucky. The string of three coins on its back forecasts a windfall. He pointed out its in sad shape as the coins are loose and the lucky coin that is supposed to be in its mouth is missing. Well, Paisano, Lefty unloaded it on me and now, it's yours."

Tony's heart was pounding as he took it, held it up to his ear and shook it. When he heard a soft muffled sound, his heart jumped.

"Joe, you wouldn't happen to have a table knife, would you?"

Joe dug deep into the pile of papers on his desk and came up with a white plastic knife. Tony inserted the tip of its blade as far as it would go into the toad's mouth, and slowly pulled down and back on the knife. Out came a sleeve of negatives.

Tony extracted the negatives from the sleeve, and held up all five frames to an excuse of a light. O'Brien was riding Brenda in all of them. What a bloody let-down. There was nothing in them that he didn't already know. There was nothing to implicate Cain who was still as big a mystery as ever.

Chapter 60

Tony gave Camelia Hussdon the tumbler from Stonemill's dishwasher and his Coke can, and Carl's gin bottle to be sent to the lab for fingerprinting and in the case of the tumbler, for analysis. He couldn't help but notice that she was looking straight at him with a smile on her lips. She was a changed woman, no doubt of that. He hadn't sent off the photo of Linda and Maple to be finger-printed; he was returning it on the q.t. to Linda.

Tony walked up the stairs and down the hall to Nigel's door, rapped three times, and entered. This time, Nigel actually stood up and his voice sounded upbeat, a first,

"Tony, this is unexpected. What can I do for you?"

While Tony should have rehearsed what he was about to say, he hadn't. He began,

"I found Linda Stonemill comatose on her bedroom floor. She'd overdosed on chloral hydrate with a gin chaser. I called 9-1-1, and the medics saved her life with seconds to spare. She's now in the ICU. I've already informed Mr. Stonemill."

Nigel didn't speak for a half-minute, most unlike him, and then he almost yelled,

"She's crazy. I always knew it. Gorgeous but a lunatic. Poor Waverly, to be stuck with the likes of her, I feel for him."

While Nigel was looking out for his best friend, Tony wondered if Stonemill would do the same? No way was he bringing up a Mickey Finn until he knew for certain. Instead, he said,

"I examined the rifle that you returned to Stonemill. There was dirt in the barrel end and when I removed it, I realized it had never been fired. It's Moorehouse's."

Nigel didn't blink an eye and muttered,

"Well then, Reggie was telling the truth. I hate to admit it, never been wrong before but maybe, just maybe, I have him sized up all wrong. Carl said he came late, but who knows how long he was there? Interrogate him and find out if he's telling the truth. Also, check to see if he was supplying Linda with alcohol. There's a nasty rumor going around that he's a bootlegger."

"Carl's in the ICU. After I left Stonemill's, I saw smoke and flames coming out of the back of one of Carl's reefers. I managed to open the door and found

306

Carl inside, comatose, beside an empty gin bottle. I threw him out, stepped on the gas and bailed just before the Volvo exploded. The medics say he's stable; they've taken him to the hospital."

Nigel sat down behind his desk, rested his chin on his outstretched hands, and spoke,

"Shit, Tony, if that truck blew, I'd hate to think of what it would have taken out. How did Carl manage to set an empty truck on fire?"

"They were full of frozen turkeys."

"Really, but no difference. How does one set a truckload of frozen turkeys on fire with a cigarette? Talk of a cigarette, I need one."

He jumped back to his feet, headed straight to the Victoria window, opened it, and fished out a pack of Virginia Slims from the window box. Pulling out a Slim, he lit it, returned to his chair, leaned forward on his desk, took a couple of puffs and said,

"Tony, Carl is a crook, a pain-in-the-ass, a blow-hard, but he's no arsonist. And I'm not taking his side because he's an Amigo? Did someone try to kill him? Wipe him clean off of planet earth? What do you think?"

Wow, thought Tony, Nigel really was a policeman.

"The thought crossed my mind. I found a photo that belonged to Maple in Carl's steel drum and I was sure he'd killed Maple. But after talking to his wife, I realize that he couldn't have killed her. Just take my word as I don't have the time to explain. That means it was planted and being in a steel drum, would have withstood the explosion."

Nigel butted out the cigarette on his desktop, another first.

"So, whoever killed Maple framed Carl to make it look like he was Maple's killer? That's my take on what you're telling me."

"Brilliant."

"Unbelievable. Talk about a cold-blooded killer loose in Pinolta. Do we have any prime suspects, anyone?"

"Not so far. But I have a question for you Nigel. When you were at Bruce's inauguration on Monday, did you see Stonemill take out his telescope?"

"No, but I wasn't there all the time. Back to who shot at Linda. Waverly and I were talking, actually he called me. Now that you've ruled out Reggie, Carl is the prime suspect. I could tell that Waverly was heating up and let me tell you, he has a hell of a temper. But after all Carl's been through, I'm sure his memory is blotto, it was never good at the best of times. No sense in asking him anything about Linda. I hope you don't mind, but I'm telling Waverly that you're sure it was a hunter in the woods who fired the shot. I don't want Waverly heading Carl's way."

"Nigel, by all means tell Waverly I said it was a hunter in the woods. I didn't tell you but I sent off evidence to the lab that will tell us if Linda overdosed or was poisoned."

"Did I hear you say that Linda could have been poisoned?"

"Yes, you did. Why the surprise? Whoever shot at her and missed, returned and would have succeeded if not for me and the medics."

Chapter 61

Back in his office, Tony turned on the overhead fluorescents, bypassed his fish tank, sat down and rummaged through the papers on his desk until he found the copy of The Gazette from Lispway's office and the photo of Spratt's crime scene. He placed the front page of The Gazette with its three circles alongside the photo. Looking at the circles in the judge's shaky hand, he just knew that Lispway was spelling out for dyslexic Tony who Cain was. Okay, Cain had been at Liefson's inauguration, at Maple's apartment, and at the East End Kid's gala. Was that what Lispway was telling him? But he already knew that. Just a minute. How could Lispway have known about Maple removing her wig or Lefty throwing around 50s and going on about the lucky jade plant that a Chinaman had given him? Why the hell had he drawn those three circles?

When he heard his door open, he looked up and was astonished to see Herb Liefson, in his mechanic's coveralls, standing in the doorway.

"Can I come in? I know I don't have an appointment. The girl on the desk said to go right up. I'd really like to talk to you."

"Come in, Mr. Liefson, have a seat and, tell me what's on your mind?"

As soon as he was seated, Liefson leaned forward and with concern etched in his face, said,

"I heard the explosion at Carl's trucking lot, saw the hole in the ground, and met a minister who was loading boxes from the bay into a purple school bus. He told me that you'd saved Carl's life and that Carl was in the hospital, drying out, after accidentally starting the fire. He said he couldn't make sense of it. Carl had called him last night to remove his stash and his cases of gin. He had one more customer to serve early this morning, and then he was closing up shop, for good. I asked Mulgrave if he'd told you what he told me, and he said that he hadn't. I thought you should know although I hope you won't charge him. He was only dealing in weed."

"Well thank you, Mr. Liefson. And I won't tell Nigel what you told me."

But Tony's cop mind was headed in another direction. He then knew for certain that Cain had the jade plant. Cain had to have been Carl's last customer. After he'd got his hands on what he was sure was Spratt's incriminating evidence, he had then set-up Carl for Maple's murder. He was one hell of a chess player, always two or three moves ahead of his opponent. As for Mulgrave removing his stash, he made a note of it. But Liefson was not finished and said,

311

"That's not only why I came here. Reginald dropped in and told me that he'd been gaslighted. When I told my wife about Reginald and Carl, she insisted that I see you and find out if my life too was in danger. She thinks that someone has it in for the Amigos…"

Liefson was tall, and even though seated, could easily see what was on Tony's desk. In mid-sentence, he pointed at the crime-scene photo and with surprise in his voice, said,

"Carson, that photo has been doctored. I know you told me there was a marking on the floor, well, it wasn't there when I was there. Nor were there any blood stains on Spratt's fingers. Is that marking that looks like an 'A' why you zeroed in on the Amigos?"

Tony was stunned. No way was Liefson mistaken from the sound of his voice or the look on his face. And no way had the photo been doctored. What the hell was going on?

"Okay, Mr. Liefson, besides the blood stains on Spratt's fingers and the marking on the floor, do you see anything else in the photo that was not there when you were there?"

Liefson stood up, he was taller than Ken, almost put his face on the photo, turned to Tony and spoke with a cynical curl on his lips,

312

"The gun was not lying next to his right hand. I used my shirt tail to remove the gun from Reginald's hand, carefully wiped it clean of prints, and then placed it down on the floor. Clumsy me, when I picked up Reginald, my foot accidentally kicked the gun. But it went nowhere near Spratt's right hand."

Just then Tony's earworm re-played the zither music from "The Third Man" movie. What the hell was it telling him? That Cain had doctored the photo? Impossible. Just a minute. What if it was telling him that Cain had doctored the crime scene after Liefson had left with Moorehouse? Cain, in the peep-hole closet, had seen Liefson take away his patsy, and being ever so resourceful, had then framed the Amigos. Spratt was dead when the marking was made in his blood. But when Cain had moved the gun close to Spratt's right hand, Abraham Gold had jumped on suicide and iced the case.

"The picture was not doctored, Mr. Lifson. Actually, I'm going to call you Herb from here on in. My name is tony. Whoever shot Spratt, wrote the 'A' in a dead man's blood with the dead man's hand. Besides being a cold-blooded killer, he's a master at setting up others to take the wrap."

"Am I safe, Tony? My wife needs to know."

"Tell her, yes, you are safe. I hope soon to have the killer behind bars."

"Reassuring. By the way, Spratt never called us the Amigos. He called us the Five Horsemen. Oh, I almost forgot. Reginald told me to tell you that his maid had removed the jewels for safe keeping. They were not in the mannequin."

Chapter 62

After Herb Liefson left, Tony locked his door as he didn't want any other interruptions. Sitting down, he leaned back in his chair, and closed his eyes. After what Herb Liefson had just pointed out to him, it was time to think out of the Amigo box. No easy task after all the time he had spent in it. Clearing his mind of anything to do with the Amigos, he imaged the three circles on the front page of The Gazette. Who had been there who was not an Amigo? That was the path he needed to take. At first, his mind tried to slip back into the Amigo gear but each time it did, he moved on. Over and over, he kept letting go of thoughts that had to do with the Amigos and then, just like that, a name jumped out at him. The three circles morphed into the face of Cain. What a dolt he was not to have seen it, sooner? Sure, it had been there all the time, but how could he have seen it through the smokescreen of the Amigos. He had to give himself some credit and not be so hard on himself.

Suddenly, he heard a loud rapping, opened his eyes, got up and opened the door. Camelia Hussdon almost knocked him over as she stormed in; flushed, breathless and wide-eyed.

"Boss not here. Stoney know who killed wife. He has gun."

A word salad. Talk about being blindsided. He replayed what she had just said in slow-time and came up with Nigel was out, Stonemill knew who'd shot at his wife and he had a gun. Most likely Moorehouse's rifle.

"Who called you? Did Mr. Stonemill call you?"

"No, no. Stoney's girl called. He left."

Had to be Stonemill's secretary. Then he asked,

"Where did he go? Did she say?"

"No. he left."

Shit, he thought. Had Nigel told Stonemill about the hunter in the woods? If he had, no way would he know where to go. But he had left with a gun. Hadn't Nigel warned him that Stonemill could be explosive? It was a toss-up where he went. Flip a coin. No. Go to where Tony had been headed but he'd better hightail it over there, before there was another murder.

Chapter 63

When Tony saw Stonemill's red Caddie parked behind Grant's green Ambassador in front of The Gazette, he cursed. There was no heading Stonemill off at the pass. Parking behind Stonemill's car, he got out and looked around. No one was about; the sidewalk might as well have been rolled up for the night. The only place that was open was The Gazette. Peering through its grimy window, he saw in the dull fluorescent lighting that the reception area was empty. Stonemill must be in Grant's office.

Was he too late? No sign of Judy. She'd probably clocked-off for the day after visiting the morgue. His heart was racing. No time to call for back-up and who to call? Nigel wasn't there. Brock Cook, as far as he was concerned, was a liability. And where to call? Linda's car didn't have a police radio in it, and to call from The Gazette was too risky that he'd be over-heard. He had no choice and opened The Gazette's front door.

As he walked up to the front-counter, he noted that Grant's door was closed, stopped and listened. The presses out back were silent. He heard what could have been a chair being pulled along the floor in Grant's office but heard no voices. The cars out front told him that Stonemill and Grant had to be in the editor's office. If Stonemill had arrived and Grant was not there, he would have exited. Slowly, Tony unbuttoned his coat and when he did, he felt the Chinese toad in the outer pocket press in against his hip. Was it trying to tell him to clear out of there? He unsheathed the Glock from its shoulder holster and held it firmly, in his right hand.

A black-and-white photo in a frame on the counter caught his attention. It was new. He'd never seen it, before. Two women, arm-in-arm, were standing, posing, in front of The Gazette. Both were smiling, warmly. The way they were dressed and the age of the photo, it must have been taken over twenty years ago. The younger of the two, he was sure was Judy. The older had to be Belle, her sister. Why else would it be there, at this time? With his left hand, he turned around the photo and a cold chill snaked down his back. It was printed on Fujifilm paper. That clinched it. Whatever doubt there was in his mind, evaporated. Grant was Cain.

As he stepped up to the side of Grant's office door, he raised high his Glock in his right hand and shouted,

"Mr. Stonemill, it's Detective Carson. I'm alone. I thank you for making a citizen's arrest. I'll take over and escort the prisoner to the jail. I can assure you that he won't be granted bail. Can I come in? Don't be rash."

He heard the clearing of a throat and a muffled voice,

"Come in. I have him tied to a chair. I didn't shoot him, not yet."

Tony felt relief. It sounded that Stonemill must have gotten the drop on Grant, wonders never ceased. For sure he'd put Stonemill's name forward for a citizen's citation award. He turned the doorknob with his free hand, nudged the door open with his boot and stepped inside only to feel the barrel end of a gun pressed hard against the back of his head.

"Both hands up, Detective, and then, don't move or I'll shoot."

Out of the corner of his eye, he saw a large, muscled hand snatch the Glock out of his hand. And then he saw Stonemill, duck-taped and gagged on a chair in front of Grant's standing desk. Red-face, sweat-drenched, he struggled in the chair but wasn't going anywhere. Leaning against the desk was a rifle, most likely Moorehouse's although he couldn't see the rim of the barrel. A fist-punch between the shoulder blades sent Tony lurching toward the black board, and Grant walked past him with a 'gotcha' smile on his lips. In his right hand was a Smith and Wesson aimed at Tony's heart, most likely Moorehouse's mother's gun. Shit, he thought, why hadn't he asked Brock Cook to accompany him? He was a sitting duck in a lion's den. So much for the lucky Chinese toad.

Grant's Harris Tweed still had the button missing on the right sleeve. Strange, thought Tony, what he noticed as he faced the final curtain. Beside the Narcissus on top of the desk was an uprooted jade plant atop a mound of dirt. While Grant placed down Tony's Glock on the desk, the Smith and Wesson never lost sight on Tony's heart. Turning to Stonemill, he sneered,

"Fat man, I always knew you were a fool. You thought you could take me down. Me. You have no idea who you're dealing with. Fat man, you're no better than me, and I didn't shoot at Linda. Why should I? I shot at Reggie. Been trying to nail him for years. But in the end, he handed me on a platter what I wanted. He's the biggest fool of all."

Tony suppressed a smile; no way was he going to tell Grant that the mannequin's safe was empty. Turning to Tony, Grant smiled ever so sweetly, a crocodile smile if he'd ever seen one, and said,

"Detective, I'll tell you how this is going to play out. Stonemill came raging in here; held me prisoner at gunpoint, in my own office. You arrived. Stonemill was out for my blood and nothing you said changed his mind. As he went to shoot me, you tried to disarm him only to be shot, dead. I jumped on him, we struggled, and his rifle went off for the second time only this time, Stonemill was dead. You've been a pain in my ass one time too many, Detective."

Looking over at Stonemill, his head had sunk onto his chest and his body was stone-still, Tony wondered if he'd given up the ghost. Christ, Tony thought, this was looking black. All he could do was keep Grant talking, and hope and pray for a miracle.

"I must hand it to you Grant. After Liefson removed Moorehouse from the showers, it was pure genius on your part to dip Spratt's fingers in his own blood, and trace out a mark on the floor to implicate the Amigos."

"Yeah, I pulled that off, didn't I? I sure fooled Gold, the smug bastard."

"Grant, a close call when I spotted you on the corner of Bethune. Never knew you smoked Export As."

"Hah, bet you never knew I could run that fast. Yeah, I smoke Export As. You must have found my butt. Like I said Detective, you are a pain in the ass."

"I hope you don't mind me asking but how did you know that Coldwell was Spratt's sister?"

"I was visiting pop when I overheard the do-gooder spilling out her genealogy to Reggie. I got quite a kick out of seeing her house going up in flames. Just like at Carl's. Used to set fires when I was a kid and never got caught. Okay, Detective, enough questions."

But Tony had one more and riding on it, was the hope that it rattled Grant and the Smith and Wesson lost sight of his heart, if for only a split second.

"Grant, it's not a question. When you were dumping off Maple's body, how did it feel when Belle, Judy's sister, whom you had locked away for life in the asylum, recognized you?"

He scoffed,

"She never knew I'd admitted, the dumb bitch. But you're right, she recognized me. She thought I was dumping Belinda, and she was going to save her precious daughter, the stupid cunt. She was shrieking like a banshee. I couldn't let a wacko call me all those names. I thought, why not? Let's have some fun..."

Tony heard a step behind him and Judy yelling,

"You raped and killed my sister? You cried when you saw her on the slab. You told me that you'd move heaven and earth to catch her killer. You snake."

Judy stood in the doorway; she was holding Grant's airgun. Tony had never seen her that angry, the veins on her neck were popping. Grant smiled, nothing rattled him, but then he had a Smith and Wesson to her airgun. Slowly, he moved toward her. Dammit, thought Tony, the Smith and Wesson was still fixed on his heart.

"What did you do with Belinda, my niece, you monster?"

"Judy, I tried my best to keep her safe but she would have none of it. I was too tame for her. She was a wild one, how was I to know. She took off, never saw her again."

"Liar."

"Would I lie to you, Judy, never? Now give me the gun?"

By then, he was close to her but as he reached out, Judy pulled the trigger.

BANG

Grant winced and his right hand with the Smith and Wesson jerked up. Tony's hand slipped into his coat's pocket, grasped the three-legged toad, and swung it hard at Grant. It landed with a 'thud' on his mouth.

Grant staggered backwards and slammed into the blackboard; the toad went flying, Tony leaped and grabbed Grant's right hand, trying to wrestle away the Smith and Wesson. They both hit the floor. Tony couldn't pry loose the gun; Grant was too strong. Then Grant grabbed Tony by the throat with his left hand, and crushed down on his windpipe. Tony felt the room spin and a wave of vomit rise in his chest. Suddenly, Grant let go of Tony's throat and the Smith and Wesson, rolled, over and over, his hands pounding at his throat. He was gasping for air and turning purple. Hands and arms dropped lifelessly to his sides, eyeballs rolled up into his head and he stopped breathing. Caine was dead.

Tony heard sirens in the distance, and was shocked to see Mabel, in her apron, rushing into the room, wielding a cleaver. She put her arm around Judy who was sobbing.

Chapter 64

Tony awoke with a start in his pitch-black bedroom. Checking his watch, it was only 7 a.m. He had planned to sleep to at least 9 a.m. After Grant's body had left for the morgue, Mabel had invited Judy and himself over for a late dinner that had gone on to midnight. As he was too awake to ever get back to sleep, he got out of bed, crossed the cold floor, and cursed when he turned on the hot water. It was ice-cold water; the hot water heater had not been serviced.

Downstairs, he hadn't shaved but had brushed his teeth and was fully dressed, he stepped over a snoring Ami who was having the sleep that he should have had. On the hallway phone, he called Dr. Neckroff answering service, and asked for the coroner to meet him with a stretcher on the banks of the Osprey, just down from the hospital, in an hour's time. Then he called the Osprey and arranged for a kayak to be ready for him. After he put on a hunter's jacket, the insulated and windproof one, and a pair of leather gloves, he left.

By the time he arrived at the Osprey, there was a faint yellow glow on the eastern sky and no sign of the cloud cover that had been there for days. While it was cool, it was not as cold as yesterday, but then, there was only a breeze in the air. The hospital's parking lot was empty, and he parked close to the Osprey River. Walking briskly down to the riverbank, he spotted a badly dinged, yellow, one-person hard-plastic kayak. After he took off his shoes and socks and rolled up his pant legs, he pushed the kayak into frigid water, the same temperature as his bathroom's hot water, and jumped in.

Paddling hard against the current, he headed upriver, hugging the opposite shoreline, the same side as the boat ramp. In the early morning light, he had no trouble seeing to the bottom of the river that was Gulf Stream clear. He was certain that Maple's body was in the river. All he had to do was find it. While he was obsessively careful as he paddled, in not splashing water on himself, soon, he was chilled to the bone. Telling himself that ice water was a great natural preservative for Maple, didn't cut it.

Too soon, he heard the sound of rapids, and around a sharp bend in the river, was into them. His arms dug in his paddle to the left, and then to the right, over and over, as the kayak lurched and pitched through the swirling, frothing turbulence. Waves crashing and splashing against rocks sent an ear-piercing sound off the scale. Heart was pounding, breath was short, skin was numb, hands and arms were dead tired, and his stomach was in his throat. Thankfully, he hadn't had any coffee that morning. Somehow, he avoided jagged rocks and wicked eddies, but couldn't shake the depressing thought that Maple was there and he'd never find her. Coast Guard would never risk plumbing the rapids. He was drenched and approaching hypothermia but he kept paddling for all he was worth until...

"BANG."

A jolt almost snapped the kayak in two, but bless its hard plastic, it remained in one-piece and above water. On the upside, most of the free water in the kayak had swooshed overboard but his skin was too numb to notice. Narrowly missing another over-sized boulder, he gave it everything he had and shot forward into frothing water but no more rocks. Around another corner and he could hardly believe it, he was into quiet and nonturbulent waters. He'd made it.

Heart slowed, breath lengthened, and skin warmed. What he would have given for a change into dry clothes. He eased up on the paddle as the current had weakened. With a golden glow in the east, he had more visibility, and craning his neck, he again scanned the river's bottom but there was no sign of Maple. While a wind had picked-up, the temperature hadn't dropped and he'd stopped shivering, but his skin was still numb. Would it ever regain feeling?

Half-paddling, half-floating he rounded another bend in the river and noticed in the sunlight, the reddish glow of the clay flats on the shoreline. Ahead, was the boat ramp and further along the pedestrian bridge. He cursed, loud and louder. Maple's body had to be in the bloody rapids. She like his parents was doomed to an unknown, watery grave. What a depressing thought. Below the boat ramp, a fir tree leaned out a good fifteen feet over the river. Its lower branches that brushed the river's surface were a dam for gum wrappers, plastic bags, a lone Coke can, and a ghost-white birch limb whose leafless branches bristled in the air. As he neared the fir tree to turn around, a discolored birch branch caught his attention.

Paddling closer, he gasped. It was no birch branch. It was five outstretched, dark purple-bluish fingers. Closing and re-opening his eyes, he validated they were no mirage. Adjacent to the fingers, was what looked like a white bump on the birch branches except it was a human fist with a protruding thumb. It was a woman's fist. Looking down into the water below where the fingers and fist were, he spotted an elongated whitish blur. His heart leaped with joy. He could have sworn he'd heard an 'Alleluia'. He'd found Maple.

With the tip of his paddle, he gingerly poked at the birch limb above where the hands were wedged to see if he could dislodge them. They never moved. They might as well have been welded into the branches. What to do? Go back and get a chain saw? The thought of leaving Maple was not appealing. What if the fir branch snapped and she truly ended up in the rapids? Why not go for it?

With heart racing, he turned, lined-up the bow of the kayak to a spot on the fir tree branch above where the birch branch and its two ghoulish hands were; took short, swift digs with his paddle, and hit the kayak's bow, smack on target.

BANG

The sound was as loud as any gunshot he'd ever heard. The kayak whiplashed and he flattened against the bow else he would have been jettisoned before the kayak righted itself. Looking around, he smiled as the birch limb with its hands was impaled on the kayak's bow and the whitish blur extended underwater on either side of the bow. Behind, was the fir tree's splintered branch and in its wake were plastic bags, wrappers, and the lone, bobbing Coke can. He had pulled it off. What a feeling. He was off to the races on a winner. The current was going his way, and he barely had to paddle. He was on easy street and then he heard the rapids. Damn hubris. Why had he let himself feel he was in clover? Too late to portage and who was he kidding, he couldn't lug a kayak and a corpse two feet, let alone fifty feet.

Around a sharp corner and he was back into the ear-deafening, freezing white-water turbulence. Paddling furiously and blindly, he gulped in air in between wave after wave that splashed over him and his kayak. His skin again, was feeling so cold and numb. His arms were lead-heavy weights that took more and more effort to raise and lower. In a cruel game of pinball, his kayak was tossed this way and that way. Worries jumbled around in his mind. Would the kayak capsize? Would he drown? Would he lose Maple? Would Maple make it and he not?

BOOM

The kayak tilted dangerously low and water slapped his face. He held his breath or he would have drowned. His arms kept digging and digging on the opposite side, and with a resounding bump, the kayak righted and he was gulping in air. Wiping off his face with a soggy sleeve, he saw that he was out of the rapids, but had no memory of navigating the final bend in the river. Quickly he checked and breathed a sigh of relief when he saw two hands, one open and one closed, on the bow. How had they made it in one-piece? A miracle? But this time, he wasn't going to celebrate or rejoice. He'd learned to respect hubris.

Ahead, there was barely a ripple on the surface of the quiet, the ever so quiet river. Weeds had replaced the red clay on the shoreline. Heart and breath slowed, and while his skin regained feeling, his fingers and toes were still numb. Soon after he'd spotted the roof of the Osprey, he spotted Ken in a white lab coat, standing on the shoreline, beside a stretcher on wheels. On cue, the sun's rays showered down a golden-yellow glow on the river. And in the sun's warmth, finally his fingers and toes warmed.

Ken waded in as Tony neared the bank, expertly disentangled her hands and arms from the birch branch, lifted the branch off the bow and sent it floating down river. After Tony beached the kayak, he jumped out and with Ken, they gently delivered a naked female corpse out of the water and, laid her out with reverence on the stretcher. Tony saw black stubble on her head, a reddish-black choker around the middle of her swollen neck, and black-and-blue long toes. Not a pretty sight but a lot better off than the eel-tattooed Fontaine.

"Well Tony, is she the missing Maple woman?"

"Yes, she's Fanny Maple, no doubt."

As Ken grabbed her fist to bring it in closer to her side, her fingers released a button onto the ground. When Tony picked it up, he saw that it was the missing button on Grant's Harris Tweed; he dropped it into his evidence pocket. It could have convicted Grant and no lawyer could have overturned it. Ken, who hadn't noticed the fisted button, draped a white sheet over Maple, turned to Tony and spoke,

"As soon as I get her to the morgue, I'll cross and type her. If she's not a match for the two stains on the Eaton's T-shirt, I'll call you. Early this morning, I matched Grant's thumbprint in size and contours to the gloved thumbprint on Saul Lispway's neck. Your suspicions were on the money. The evidence is that Grant applied pressure to the judge's neck and stopped his heart. I wrote murder on the death certificate."

Tony felt sad to know what he had always suspected was true. Sure, Grant was dead and Cain would never kill again but that didn't help poor Lispway. Ken continued,

"I also matched Grant's thumbprint, again in size and contours, to a print on the Bombay Gin bottle. He sure got around. He was worse than a virus."

"Judy told me that it was Grant who had gone to Carl's on the day of the fire to buy his marijuana. That made him Carl's last customer before he reformed and closed up shop. Grant saw Lefty's lucky jade plant there and he took the opportunity to frame Carl for Maple's murder. Earlier, he'd planted the Colt he bought from Nigel and shot Lowland with on Moorehouse."

"What I don't get was why had Grant bought Gold's Colt in the first place?"

"Grant intended to switch Gold's Colt for the one in Robins' trophy case. That would ensure that he was never implicated in Spratt's murder. But as I had the trophy case, he couldn't."

Ken broke out into a smile as he produced the three-legged toad figurine from a black bag on the shelf under the stretcher.

"I examined the Chinese three-legged toad from the crime scene and found two compartments inside its mouth. Look what I found in one of the compartments."

Like a magician pulling a rabbit out of a hat, Ken produced a sleeve of negatives that he handed to Tony. With shaking fingers, Tony slipped the negatives out of the sleeve and held them up to the sunlight. There, in glorious black-and-white was a naked Cornelius Grant riding the ass of a naked and drugged Belinda Fontaine. No wonder Grant had been so desperate to get his hands on the negatives. And to think, he had them all the time.

"Thank you, thank you so much for finding them, Ken. The tarnished name of Mr. Jonathan Spratt can now officially be cleared. I'll leave it up to Judy but I wouldn't be surprised if she prints on the front page that Spratt was an unsung whistle-blower. I can't wait to tell Judge Lispway that thanks to him that Spratt finally got his day in court, and his name was cleared. Justice prevailed."

Ken still smiling, said,

"I'm not one to blow my horn, but I'm sure going to blow it now. I'm going to tell you how Mr. Cornelius Grant died, and it had nothing to do with you, Tony."

Suddenly, Tony felt Grant's hand choking off his windpipe. He couldn't breathe, felt dizzy and would have sat down if there was a chair near-by, and felt so cold as if there was ice in his veins.

"Tony are you alright? You don't look so good."

Tony focussed on Ken's moving lips, and repeated what he had just said to him and when he did, he snapped him back into the present. Back breathing, he managed to say,

"Give me a minute. I've just had the most unsettling flashback I've ever had. After my parents' deaths, I get them with regularity but never as bad as the one that I just had."

"Tony, you've never almost been killed before, no wonder it was a bad one. I've often wondered how you cops cope with all you go through. Feeling better?"

"Yes, I am. As bad as it was, thankfully it was a passing flash."

Ken's smile returned as he dug into his black bag and came up this time with a single tarnished silver coin. It was one of the coins on the back of the toad. With triumph. Ken announced,

"I found it lodged in Grant's throat. When you hit Grant in the mouth with the toad, the coin was jettisoned into his throat. He choked on it and tried to dislodge it by whacking at his neck, only to turn the coin into a guillotine. It sliced through his trachea. He killed himself and, thank God for your sake, he did. I'm giving you back the three-legged toad and if I were you, I'd never let it out of my sight."

Chapter 65

Stepping off the elevator on the second floor of Pinolta's Memorial Hospital, he saw and heard Waverly Stonemill in yesterday's three-piece suit that was not fit for a casket yelling at a six-foot tall, uniformed policewoman with flaming red hair. She was standing with her arms crossed in front of a closed patient's room's door. His voice easily carried to the other side of Pinolta.

"What do you mean I can't see my wife? I'm Waverly Stonemill. I'm her husband. If you don't get out of my way, I'll have you sacked. Now move."

The policewoman's freckled face neither blanched nor flushed; it was as impassive as her crossed arms and her matter-of-fact tone of voice.

"I have my orders. No visitors."

Stonemill, who wasn't used to a woman or for that matter, anyone, standing up to him, stamped his feet like a child in a tantrum. Tony made a mental note of the policewoman's name tag, Constable Gertie Pride. Coming up to Stonemill from behind, he tapped him none too gently on the right shoulder. Spinning around, a purple-faced Stonemill recognized Tony and with fury in his voice, ordered,

"Carson, talk sense into her. I'm a busy man and time is money. I demand I see my wife, now, and not a minute later. I've already waited too long."

"Mr. Stonemill, Constable Pride is following orders. I have to make sure your wife overdosed, before she's allowed any visitors."

"I see, well let me tell you, if she was poisoned then Grant is your man. I never believed him when he said that he'd aimed at Reggie. I should have shot him when I had the chance."

Tony stepped around Stonemill who while still damn mad, never moved. As he passed Gertie Pride, he whispered,

"Pride, you're doing a great job. I'm putting in a good word for you."

Inside, Linda was sitting up in bed, as washed-out as her hospital gown, with tears running down the sides of her face. If she had applied make-up that morning, it was not to be seen. She jumped but seeing that it was Tony, she reached out and spoke in a hoarse voice,

"Tony, a nurse told me I'd overdosed and you saved my life. Is that true? I don't recall a thing. It's worse than when I hit my head."

337

"Well, the entire bottle of chloral hydrate was gone. I'm not a doctor but I know chloral hydrate can give you a blackout worse than alcohol."

Suddenly, she looked terrified, grabbed the bedsheet, and pulled it up to her chin as though it was a shield. In a tremulous voice, she said,

"Tony, I don't recall taking one let alone the whole bottle. Why should I have? I was resting in bed, that's all. Am I losing my mind? Have I gone off the deep end?"

She was deeply troubled, more than when she had found the rug on Moorehouse's desk. Then, she had been in a rage but this time she was in a panic that she'd lost what she had taken for granted all her life, her sanity.

"Linda, I'm investigating whether you took an overdose or someone slipped you a Mickey Finn. As for who shot at you, that was Grant shooting at Reginald. Your husband thought it was Grant who'd shot at you and when he went after him, he ended up tied to a chair. I got into a fight with Grant and he's dead. By the way, Grant killed Maple. He tried to frame Reginald and when that didn't work, he framed Carl Robins by planting a copy of the picture of you and Maple. The original was a Polaroid, wasn't it?"

"Yes, it was. I remember that much. So it was Grant who was gaslighting poor Reginald. And Waverly stormed up after him when he thought he'd shot at me? And it sounds like you saved Waverly's bacon and the day when you took Grant out. Do you think it was Grant who tried to kill me? I've only met the man a few times. Why would he want to kill me?"

She half-dropped the sheet. Who could blame her for not dropping it all the way? To think that she had almost been murdered, had to be unsettling. Suddenly, Tony heard Stonemill screaming, "You snake, You traitor. When this is over, I'm suing the pants off you."

Linda must have heard it too, for she covered her head with the sheet. As Tony stepped toward the door, it opened and in walked a grim-faced Nigel, in full uniform. While his epaulets were gleaming, nothing else was. He held out a Polaroid to Linda who as soon as she saw it, she grabbed it and clasped it to her bosom, tighter than she had ever held Maple's jewelry box. It had to be their picture but where had Nigel found it? Turning to Linda, Nigel said,

"I just booked your husband on a charge of attempted murder. I assume his lawyer will have him out within an hour but I've left orders that he not return home and that a restraining order be issued. I'd advise you to get a lawyer, Mrs. Stonemill. Thanks to Carson, we have circumstantial evidence, a thumb print on a tumbled containing chloral hydrate powder, that it was Waverly who poisoned you. I obtained a warrant and when I searched your house, I found that Polaroid and an anonymous letter sent to him with it, inside it. I figure it was Grant stirring the pot but that's no excuse for what he did. You heard him when Constable Pride led him away. Not an ounce of guilt or remorse. When he threatened me, I knew I'd done the right thing in charging him, without a second thought. It was not easy. I thought he was a good friend but I have no use for anyone who mistreats women, let alone tries to murder women."

Linda was shocked and gazed at the photo before she spoke,

"Fanny always told me that Waverly didn't love me. She said she often saw men like him who loved to control, to throw around their weight, and who didn't have an ounce of love in them. I knew she was right but I hoped that one day he'd change. It will be a relief not to be yelled at anymore or to be told I was a bad girl. Thank you Chief Gold for what you did. I know it was not easy going against Waverly. By the way, I do have a lawyer who told me when I was ready to leave him to call him. Well, I'm calling him today and I have heard he's a barracuda."

Nigel flicked his epaulets and puffed out his chest.

"Well, thank you Linda. I appreciate that. It was the hardest thing I've ever done when I charged Waverly but he had it coming to him. No man is above the law.''

Chapter 66

When Tony opened his office door, there was a Metro-uniformed policemen who was standing in front of his fish tank, with his back to him. His heart leaped and then skidded. He was too tall, had to be upwards of six and a half feet, to be Mansfield. Whoever he was, he must have seen the reflection of Tony entering in the fishtank's glass for he spun around. He had wavy black hair with a touch of grey in the temples, and running down the middle of coarse facial features was an aquiline nose that was as straight as his back. While he had piercing, cold brown eyes, he had a warm smile on his lips and spoke in a friendly tone,

"Detective Tony Carson, I hope you don't mind the intrusion but your front desk gal told me to walk in and wait. She's Romanian if I'm not mistaken, I have Serbian roots. I'm Superintendent David Markovic, knew your father although I never worked with him. Why don't we both sit down as I have some disquieting news."

Tony didn't like the sounds of 'disquieting news,' and sat down behind his desk while Markovic sat down in front, bolt upright. At his height, he was looking down at Tony. Not one to waste time, Markovic continued,

"Before I get to the news, congratulations on nailing Grant. If you ever think of moving into Toronto, give me a call. Okay, enough distractions. You won't be seeing Ronny Mansfield anymore. He's disappeared with five million, street value, of our impounded cocaine. We figure he's been siphoning off cocaine for years. We also figure your father was onto his partner. Did he ever mention any suspicions he had of Ronny?"

To be honest, Tony had never taken to Ronny whom he found to be a cold fish. He'd never forgotten that Mansfield, he'd never called him Ronny, had showed him no support when he first pointed out the black hole in the ice of a frozen Lake Ontario. But he'd never thought that Mansfield was a dirty cop. His father had an even greater distaste for them.

"Dad was a by-the-book cop. He always complained about Mansfield's high-handed methods in getting a confession. Said as a team they were chalk and cheese. Never socialized with him. And no, never talked about anything to do with cocaine."

Markovic grimaced and when he spoke, after a deep sigh, his voice had softened,

"From what I can piece together, your father was collecting evidence to nail Ronny when your parents had their so-called accident."

343

Tony gasped and felt an ice-flow coursing down his back. Markovic squirmed in the chair. His eyes had lost their cutting edge and were pools of sympathy. Tony blurted out,

"Are you questioning if it was an accident?"

"You're sharp. I found the Coast Guard's original report. The one Ronny filed, had been doctored. All they found beneath the hole in the ice was a large boulder. Your parents' car never went through the ice. We're looking for it but it's like trying to find a needle in a haystack."

Tony felt ice-cold tears in his eyes. His parents had been murdered. His hands clenched. How he hated Mansfield and at that moment, would have pummeled him to death. Never had he felt in his entire life the murderous rage that he then felt. It terrified him. Markovic must have sensed what was whirling around in Tony's mind, for he said,

"Tony, I hope you don't mind a first-name basis, we'll find your parents and we'll find Mansfield. The word on the street is that he's yet to unload the cocaine. I don't want you to go looking for him, Tony. That's not an order, but it's a strong plea. I can guess how you must feel. If there was ever a snake in a uniform, it was Ronny. But we'll get him and you can be assured, he'll never see the light of day. And you will be the first to know, promise and I never squelch on a promise. Oh by the way, I noticed that Brock Cook is on staff, here. He was in Toronto. Tell your boss to keep a close eye on him, he's a stair climber, and they don't care who they step on to get to the top. Does he still go by Hot Dog, he loved that name?"

The End

Manufactured by Amazon.ca
Bolton, ON